PRINCESS OF FRANCE

THE QUEEN'S PAWN BOOK 2

CHRISTY ENGLISH

For Alais

PART I
PRINCESS OF FRANCE

PROLOGUE

Henry

HENRY'S LIPS WERE WARM ON MINE. HE TASTED as he always had, of cloves, of almost forgotten spices, of danger and of longing, of all the things I wanted but could not have.

"Still sweet," he said as he pulled away.

We were naked under the covers of the great bed of state. We had never slept together in his room at Windsor in all the months that I had been his mistress. I knew that this was a dream.

I lay beneath him, the canopy high above my head. The curtains blocked out all sound and light, save one candle that burned beside the bed.

Yet I could still see him, not as he was now, old and feeble, sick from a long winter of coughing. I saw Henry as he had been when I loved him, still vital, his strength and warmth cocooning me, making me long to forget the world that lay beyond his bed. But even in the dream, I could not forget.

"You are still beautiful, Alais, and taste as sweet as the day I first had you. Tell me why that is."

I caressed his face. I pushed his long hair back from his cheek, fingering the gray where it shone amidst the red in the light of our one candle.

"Henry," I said. "I am as beautiful as you want me to be. This is only a dream."

He kissed me again, his tongue stroking mine until a fire began to burn in me, the old fire that I had never forgotten, though it had been almost twenty years since he had touched me. Henry's hand moved beneath our coverlet, lightly skimming over my body, all his hard-won skill as a lover brought to bear on me.

Henry made love to me in that dream, and it came back to me all at once, how I had hungered for him in the end as much as he had ever hungered for me. Our bodies joined, we spoke words of love, as we never had in the waking world. We lay together afterwards, spent but blessed, safe still from the world beyond the light of that one candle.

"I have always loved you, Alais," Henry said. "From the moment I saw you holding that dog in my horse stable." He kissed me so that I did not have to answer. "Richard is a fool," he said. "I would have had you, no matter what came before or after, had I been free. The rest of them be damned."

Henry's mouth came down on mine once more, and I knew it was for the last time. The waking world began to draw me back. The light of our candle could not hold it at bay any longer.

"I love you, Henry," I said.

I do not know if he heard me. I woke on my slender cot, beneath the narrow window of my cell. Mother Bernard's hand was on my arm.

"My lady, I bring sad news. You must prepare yourself."

She watched as I woke, drawing my mind back from my dream. But I felt as if Henry stood beside me, his hand on mine. I could still taste him on my tongue.

"The king is dead."

Henry's touch dissolved. I lay alone, looking into the brown eyes of Mother Bernard, the kind woman I had known almost all my life. I did not weep but swallowed my tears. I was a woman grown, with more than thirty years behind me. I would mourn Henry in private.

"Thank you for telling me."

Matins that day would include a mass sung for the king's soul. The first of many such masses that I would pay for with the gold he had given me when I went away.

For I did love him. And never more so than in the moment when I first heard of his death, the taste of his lips still on mine.

I was not surprised. Henry had brought the news himself, before his soul flew away.

1

ELEANOR

THE ABBEY OF ST. AGNES, 1189

"THE QUEEN IS HERE." MOTHER BERNARD'S hand was gentle on mine, her voice soft in my ear.

I sat in the sunshine of the simples garden, painting the lavender which grew there onto the page of the psalter I was illuminating. I lay my brush down, the clean linen beneath it catching the purple paint as it fell.

They had come for me. It had been two months since Henry's death and I had known that someone would. I felt Mother Bernard's lips on my hair, warm where the sun hit my curls. I had grown older and used to my own ways, and I no longer wore a veil.

"So, little princess. You have not lost the common touch, I see."

Eleanor stood in the sunlight of our garden, as if she had appeared there by magic. Her face was shadowed by her veil, but I saw her beauty, still radiant, undimmed by time and pain. Her beauty was in her bones and the magnificence of her soul shone through them. Though the skin of her face was crumpled, like a piece of vellum that could no longer be smoothed out, her eyes burned like beacons of green light. Like all men, I stood in her sight and felt her power. I knelt without thinking and Mother Bernard knelt beside me.

"Rise, little princess. You do me too much honor."

"My lady queen, that is not possible."

She stared down at me, her face unreadable, as it always was. I rose, and Mother Bernard left us silently after I touched her once, then let her go.

Without my having to ask, lay sisters came into the garden, bringing the nunnery's best chair, a small table, and wine. They set these things on the grass in the full light of the sun. Though it was spring, a wind still came from the north to chill us.

Eleanor did not sit in that fine carved chair with its cushions worked in cloth of gold. She stood instead in the full light of the afternoon sun and took in the sight of my face.

"I have missed you, daughter. Though I did not know it until now."

I crossed our garden to stand before her and took her hand in mine. Eleanor still wore the great ruby that Henry had given her when they wed on the middle finger of her right hand. I bent down and kissed that ring.

We stood together, my lips on her hand, birdsong the only sound. Before long, Eleanor pulled away from me, and sat in the abbey's best chair.

I sat across from her, for the lay sisters had brought my chair forward into the center of the garden. Neither of us spoke. As I watched, Eleanor cast her mind back over the years we had been apart, all the years of her imprisonment, when Henry had locked her away from the living and the dead, as if she were one of the dead herself.

Eleanor took in the sun under the open sky. She leaned back and breathed in the perfume of the lavender. She had been released immediately after Henry's death two months before. It was the first thing Richard had done. Even before burying the king and holding his funeral rights, Richard had sent word to set his mother free.

Eleanor looked at me past the folds of her veil and smiled. The wind caressed my hair and moved Eleanor's veil against her cheek.

I turned my face to the light so that she could see me clearly. I still bathed my face in goats' milk every day. I had a few lines around my eyes, but little else marred my skin. The passage of time had been kind to me. My skin was as soft and fair as it had always been. No silver marred the dark chestnut of my hair. The auburn highlights perhaps were clearer, for I often sat in the sun when it was warm enough. The sun brought out the light in my dark curls.

"You are as beautiful as when last we met. How can this be so?"

I did not smile or look away but met her gaze so that she could see I was not afraid of her. I had not grown timid during my years locked away in this nunnery.

"I thank you, your grace. Perhaps my mother had good looks and passed them on to me."

"No doubt."

I watched Eleanor as she gathered her forces. I did not speak again but poured her a glass of wine. It was the light sweet wine that I had brought up from Anjou, my one indulgence. I had loved that wine since Richard first gave it to me, and I drank it still. Every year at Christ's Mass, a large cask would arrive from Richard's vineyards. His steward never sent a note, but I knew it came from him.

I did not speak of this to Eleanor as she took the bronze goblet from my hand. She sipped the wine and sighed. I saw that her back pained her, for she shifted against the cushions. She was nearly seventy now. Her journey had been long, and she was tired, though she would never admit it.

"I am going to meet Richard in Poitiers," she said.

The name of my old love was a sharp pain. I listened to it and remembered the time when I had thought he would be mine, when I was certain that our union had been blessed by God.

Sitting with Eleanor in our cloister garden, I remembered a different garden on a different summer day, when Richard knelt before me and swore that he would love me all his life. I wondered if he remembered that moment, as I did. I wondered if he loved me still.

Eleanor drew a letter from her sleeve, its vellum crisp and new, its seal untouched.

"He sends word to you by me, if you will take it from my hand."

I felt the first taste of hope since I had laid my daughter in the ground twenty years before. I had lived so long without it, subsisting only on pain and loss, that I almost did not recognize the taste of it. Hope burst on my tongue like a ripe fruit. I savored it – Richard's letter in my hand.

We had been betrothed before his father touched me. We were betrothed still, though I had not seen his face in years. He had never married. Perhaps this letter was the first sign of him relenting, Richard calling me to his side at last.

I wanted to rise, to turn my back on the queen, so that I might read the words my love had written. He had been unrelenting in his youth. I had thought never to hear from him again.

I did not turn away, and I felt her eyes on me like hands. I broke the seal, and read his words, and knew that she had read those words already.

"Alais, Countess of the Vexin, Countess of Berry, Princess of France. Greetings. We send you word by way of the Queen, our mother, that you will no longer be kept in the Abbey of St. Agnes under our care. You will take ship to France, where your brother, King Phillipe, waits for you. Go with God and live in peace. Richard, by God's Will, King of England, Duke of Normandy, Duke of Aquitaine."

I wondered if he had even seen the letter. I

wondered if he had simply ordered it written, one more task in a list of many, bits of old business to be discarded upon the death of his father, drawn up by a clerk and sealed by his chamberlain.

Then I looked down to the end of the page and saw his name, scrawled in his familiar hand. Richard had never written to me before, but I had seen his writing often when I was a girl at his mother's court. He composed many songs for the minstrels and wrote them out, that the bards might learn them by heart. Always, under each song and poem, he had scrawled the same word, "Richard," as if no other man bore that name on earth. And for me, no other man ever would.

Tears rose in my throat to burn my eyes. A sob began in my stomach and made its way to my chest where it lodged and stuck, old pain, a bird that would not take flight. I covered my mouth, his letter clutched in my hand. I gripped it hard as if it were his hand in mine, as if it might give me comfort, as if I might look up and once more see his face.

"Alais. I am sorry."

Eleanor's pity was the hardest thing to bear in that long moment of pain. Her pity was like acid on my skin. She had prompted him to write to me, so that I would know there was no hope of going back.

Richard would not forgive me, even now, for all that I had done. For all that Henry had done. He would not forgive, but would send me from his realm, without honoring our betrothal, without seeing me.

I wanted to comfort myself, to believe that he did this out of policy, that he sent me away because he had no choice. That he had to stand strong before his lords, both in England and in France. Though nothing had ever been proved of my relationship with Henry, the whole of Christendom knew me to have been his father's whore. Though my child lay dead in the cold ground at Winchester, Richard still would send me from him. His pride would allow nothing else. His pride had always been stronger than his love.

"Alais. Forgive me."

I met Eleanor's eyes, two tears coursing down my cheeks. Only two, for I had remembered myself. I had remembered that I had sworn never to weep in front of her again. I breathed once, drawing my sorrow back into my heart, where I locked it away.

I met her eyes. I watched as her pity changed to admiration.

"You love him still," she said.

"Yes."

"Even death will not change it."

"No," I said. "Nor whatever comes after."

Eleanor did not speak again but took my hand in hers. Her rings were cold against my skin. The north wind came to chill us, moving through my uncovered hair.

Her message delivered, Eleanor still did not leave me, so Mother Bernard gave up her rooms to the queen. Though I offered mine, I knew it was not grand enough. Even the Abbess' rooms were not suited to the queen of England, but Eleanor accepted them graciously, as if they were very fine. I suppose anything was better than the prison she was coming from. The door to Mother Bernard's room locked, but only from the inside.

We took a late supper in my room for I knew that Eleanor would not be able to bear the silence of the convent table. I had no musicians to play for her, no troubadours to sing of her beauty. So, as we finished our wine, I sang a song for her, one Richard had written long ago about beauty that never fades and love that lasts forever.

I was no troubadour, but my voice was clear and sweet. Eleanor wept when I was done.

She wiped her eyes with a linen kerchief. We sat in silence then, and I thought perhaps we would part, she to her bed, and I to mine, that we might not hurt each other anymore that day. But then she spoke.

"I put flowers on her grave, before I came away."

I sat very still, my goblet in my hand. I knew that if I moved, I would drop it and spill Richard's precious wine down the front of my homespun gown. I had only two bottles left.

I set my goblet down carefully, as if it were made of glass. I set my hands on the arms of my chair. They lay like wounded birds, my rings catching the light from the candles.

"There is a mass sung for her soul each morning and each night. I left enough money with the bishop to see to it that this practice will continue, long after I am dead."

I found my voice, and it sounded to my ears as if it rose from the depths of a tomb. The pain of my daughter's death never left me. I knew that it never would. "And the priest is sworn to this? He will sing for her soul, every day?"

"He is sworn. I made him swear."

I lost my battle with my own pain then and knelt at her feet, my arms wrapped around her knees, a suppliant for all that could not be given back to me. Eleanor caught me as I fell against her, and she held me, though her back was paining her.

I wept for my daughter as if she had died just that night, and not twenty years before. I wept for the loss of her, for the loss of her father. And for the loss of Richard, who should have been her father, and now would never father a child of mine.

I wept until I had no tears left in me. Eleanor raised me up and drew my kerchief from my sleeve. It was the kerchief that bore her crest, one that she had given me years before. It was never far from me. She wiped my tears away and kissed me.

"There is more for you to hear, before there is less. Can you bear it?"

"I can bear anything."

I saw the light of pride in her face, as I folded my kerchief and tucked it away.

"You will leave for Paris within the month."

As distant as its memory was from me, I still dreamt of Paris. The soft spring rains in the garden of my father's palace. The flavor of fine watered wine. The taste of pastry that melted as it touched my tongue. I had longed for all these things the whole of my exile. I had thought never to have them again.

Eleanor smiled in the firelight, lifting her bronze goblet to her lips. "I would like to tell you that your brother calls you to him because he wishes you near him."

"But that is not why," I said.

"No."

I thought of Richard's letter, still tucked away in my sleeve. After I had read it, Eleanor did not ask for it back. I drew it out. It lay in my palm like an accusation, like a knife I could not wield.

I rose from my chair, my face blank, as I had been trained to school my expression as a child. My old lessons came back to me as I stood alone in that room with Eleanor. I would need to remember them all, before I returned to my brother and his court.

I held Richard's letter in my hand, my last link to him in the waking world. The vellum was smooth against my skin. He had used a new piece, a fresh bit of calfskin. I did not know if this was to honor me, or simply that, as king, he used nothing less.

I cast his letter into the fire and watched the expensive vellum burn. Smoke rose to choke me, but I did not move away. I watched the flames consume that letter until it was nothing but ash.

I met Eleanor's eyes.

"You have changed, Alais."

"And not for the better."

Eleanor raised one elegant brow and extended her hand, reaching up to touch my cheek. "That I could not say. But you are not my little princess anymore."

"Phillipe brings me home to marry a man of his choosing," I said, finishing the tale she had begun. "He calls on me to strengthen his position as king. To keep the peace in his realm. To shore up the throne of France."

Eleanor smiled, the old wry smile I loved, free of bitterness and pain. "Your brother the king does not confide in me, and my spies are not as good as they once were."

"I am not to marry Richard," I said.

"No," she answered. "I have seen to that."

I felt the pain of my loss for the last time. My heart burned with it, flaring once more with that inner fire, before the flame guttered out.

I sat down in my cushioned chair, taking Eleanor's jeweled hand in mine as I kissed her cheek. "Once I am gone, we will not meet again."

"Very likely, we will not."

I spoke the words aloud then, as for the last time. "I love you, Eleanor."

"You always will, my dear." She smiled her wicked smile.

I remembered my childhood and how I had feared her like a demon in the night. I thought of how powerful she was, and of how much harm she had done to me, more harm than I ever could have conceived of as I lay in my childhood bed. And still the power of my love bound me to her, even now, after all those years, after all the pain she had caused me. I knew that I would love her for the rest of my life.

I did not ask if she loved me. Though she tried to hide it, Eleanor's love shone in the green of her eyes. Her love for me was a beacon of light that would never go out.

She would leave on the morrow to go to Richard in Poitiers. Our paths were parting once more, perhaps forever.

So, we stayed together that night and neither of us slept. We sat at my table, Richard's wine between us, holding each other's hands.

2

THE COUNT OF VALOIS

I WAS RESTLESS WHEN ELEANOR LEFT ME. SHE had brought with her the scent of the world beyond the walls of my convent. I was drawn in by temptations I had not thought of in years: roasted meat on the bone, fresh baked bread torn for trenchers, the scent of Henry's skin when he lay beside me.

As I worked in the garden three weeks later, up to my elbows in loam, Jean Pierre came to me.

It was an ordinary day until he stepped into my garden. I was wearing one of my oldest dresses made of linen and flax. The sleeves dragged in the dirt as they always had, for I used that gown for gardening only. It had once been a soft blue but had faded to a light gray.

As was my habit now, I wore my hair long down my back, unbound but for a strand of silver cord that kept it out of my eyes.

I was directing a lay sister in the planting of the newest cuttings of lavender and thyme, when

Jean Pierre, Count of Valois, entered the garden as if he owned it and bowed to me.

I saw at once that he was no ordinary man. The count wore bright blue, which brought out the sharp blue of his eyes. His eyes appraised me, taking all of me in at once, not only what I wanted seen, a pious woman working for the good of God, but all that I did not, my hidden self, the part of my soul that no man had ever seen, save Henry.

Though Jean Pierre was fair, he had been often in the sun. His face was craggy and his eyes intelligent. He looked at me as if he knew me, though I had never seen him before that day.

The sight of him was like a bolt of fire that struck me, taking my breath.

Jean Pierre looked as though he could see behind my eyes. He smiled a small half smile, as if we shared a secret. I pushed my lust aside, to be brought before the priest at my time of confession. I hesitated only a moment before I smiled back.

"If you are looking for the buttery," I said, "You have taken a wrong turn."

He laughed as I had hoped he might, bowing again to me. I saw that, in spite of his fine hose and his gown shot through with silk, he was a man who did not take himself too seriously.

"I assume that I address Her Royal Highness, Alais, Princess of France."

"Indeed, you do, sir, if you can find her behind all this dirt."

"I am Jean Pierre, Count of Valois."

He bowed a third time. I thought for a moment that he might kneel, but the dirt was dark and his silk hose were very light.

I saw the thought of kneeling cross his eyes, and I smiled when he changed his mind.

"My lady, I would not have known you."

"The dirt is thick here, sir, but it does not cover my face."

"It is not the dirt that would have deceived me. I have heard it said that Princess Alais has been within these walls for almost 20 years. Perhaps you are her daughter?"

I pushed my lust aside once more, back into the box where I kept it. From the first, I saw that he was a man of honor. I need not fear for myself with him, in spite of the flirtation between us. I had never before flirted with a man, not even with Henry.

"You are impertinent," I said. "But it is such a lovely day, that I will let your impudence pass."

I was charmed. It had been many years since I had seen a man as well dressed as he, as self-possessed and as confident. Priests of the church, I found, were none of these things.

I gestured to the bench in the garden, and Jean Pierre sat down while I knelt once more to plant my lavender.

"So, my lady, are you not the least bit curious why I am here?"

"You are the messenger from my brother, come to tell me my fate."

"God forbid. I am no fortune teller." Jean Pierre leaned down to me, his long blond hair

21

falling in a curtain across his cheek. He pushed his thick hair back, but it had been cut in the latest style and would not obey him. His hand was still gloved from his ride. I wondered what his skin was like beneath the leather, and what it would feel like on mine.

As I looked into his eyes, my hands covered in loam, I saw that his blue eyes were clear, like the summer sky. I knew that he would not lie to me, then or ever.

"You are here to tell me when my brother wants me to come to France," I said.

"Indeed, my lady. I have come to take you there."

At the sound of his words, my heart lifted with a hope that I had tasted only once before in my life. I savored that hope as I knelt in the dirt of that convent garden. I thanked God there in silence, even as I did His work. I had left Paris when I was nine years old. I longed to go home.

I stood and wiped my hands on the kerchief laying close by. "When do we leave?"

The Count of Valois smiled at the sudden joy he saw in my face. A shadow crossed his eyes; he seemed to know what my decades behind convent walls had cost me. How he knew, as a man who lived in the world among men, I never understood. But he knew me, even from the first, better than most.

He rose when I did. "As soon as you are able, Your Highness."

"Tomorrow."

"Oh, lady, let my horse rest a day at least."

The thought of delay left me cold, even in

the warmth of the garden. My freedom was so close, I wanted to reach out for it even then and take it in my hand. In truth, if he had been willing, I would have fled on horseback that very hour, without even changing my gown. I longed to see the sky once more without walls around it, and to feel the sun on my face, and the wind in my hair.

"The day after," I agreed.

His smile faded. Jean Pierre raised his hand, and for one electric moment, I thought he might touch my face. But he knew his place as my brother's vassal, and he did not step out of it. "As you say, my lady. We will be ready."

Jean Pierre had brought a retinue of men-at-arms to guard us on our way to Paris. They were ranged in the guest house, playing cards and swearing. I heard this from the lay sisters as I bathed in my room before supper.

I laughed when they told me, but the sisters looked scandalized. Truly, I was not suited to a religious life, for men and their antics no longer shocked me.

I took my dinner with the count, a bevy of lay sisters standing by to guard my virtue. I did not point out to them that the tatters of my honor had long since been buried.

I received him formally, dressed in my best gown, which was made only of spun cotton and flax. I had dried my hair by the fire, and it hung long down my back, covered by a thin veil of linen; the linen was very fine and did little to hide my curls, but I felt it better to extend the count the courtesy of my modesty, though I had long since left such trappings behind me.

Jean Pierre stepped into the room and bowed to me, disconcerted at first by the sight of my narrow bed, visible in the room beyond. I saw his discomfort and gestured to a lay sister, who drew the door to my bedroom closed.

Once that was done, Jean Pierre smiled and was his easy self again, bent on charming me and setting me at ease, as if he was the host, and I his guest.

We ate by the light of many lamps, as if the candle wax and oil alone could guard me. Lay sisters stood along one wall, not serving us, but watching every morsel of food that went into my guest's mouth. They did not begrudge him any of it, only me.

I watched the count to see if this close scrutiny disturbed him, but after the first few moments he seemed not to notice them. He spent the evening telling me of all that had gone on in Paris in the last fortnight. He kept his gossip quiet, the kind of stories of home that one might tell an elderly maiden aunt: who had married whom, and how many children were expected before the harvest, how my brother fared in his search for a wife, and how the court spoke of little else.

It grew late, and the lay sisters left off their vigilance, nodding by the wall. The tapestries strained on their hangings as the sisters leaned against them. As they dozed, the count talked on.

I found myself watching his mouth as he

spoke, watching his hands when he picked up his dinner dagger or when he held his bronze goblet of wine. I kept my own desire guarded in its chest, but the scent of it rose to me, even though I kept the lid of that chest closed.

I watched him closely, but I could see no evidence of his fascination for me, the answering desire I had seen in his eyes in the cloister garden. I began to believe that he did not see me as a woman at all, that he had spoken of my beauty that afternoon as a matter of courtesy.

But as the evening wore on and my protectors began to doze, the light of desire came back into his eyes. I knew he would never speak of it. His honor bound him, as mine bound me, but I found myself basking in the knowledge of his desire, and in my own. It had been many years since I had felt such warmth.

Before, with Henry, I had been little more than a child. As much as Henry taught me, I had hardly begun to know myself at the tender age of fourteen. Now, I was a woman, and I felt rising heat in my face and in my belly. I tasted once more the hunger that Henry first woke in me, so long ago.

I raised my eyes to Jean Pierre, hoping that my face was blank, that he could not see the desire behind my eyes. My hope was in vain. But Jean Pierre seemed to see beyond my lust, to the fact that I wanted to hide it. He desired me, but he also felt something more. It seemed that he wanted to protect me, not only my honor, but my heart.

"I have heard songs of you," he said. "Of

how your beauty caught the eye of a king, and your love took his soul prisoner."

I did not speak. I sat very still, my bronze goblet close by my hand. My fingertips were numb, and I could not move them.

"I have heard no such songs."

Jean Pierre sang for me, his tenor low and sweet, like honey in old wine. At first, I could not hear the words, because his voice held me in thrall. And then I could not hear the words because they were in the *langue d'oc*, which all my life had meant nothing but Richard. But finally, in the last verse, I heard his voice and his words together, how I had compelled a king, of how I could have held the kingdom in my sway, but I had turned back at the last and given myself to God.

Tears ran down my nose and into the lap of my gown as I bent my head, for the song was true. Henry had loved me, even at the last. And I had turned away, out of piety, and grief, in the hope that my absence would bring peace between Richard and Henry once more. I had locked myself away in a nunnery for the rest of my life in this vain hope. There had been no peace between them. In the end, my sacrifice had been for nothing.

I was lost in this sorrow when Jean Pierre drew me back, touching my hand.

"I do not mean to pain you. I am sorry. The song was badly sung."

"No," I said. "It was beautiful."

I forgot Eleanor's handkerchief, which was always in my sleeve. I simply reached up, as a peasant might, and wiped my tears away with one hand.

Jean Pierre saw me do this, and without letting go of the hand that still lay on the table between us, he offered a cloth from the table beside him. I accepted his kindness and dried the last of my tears. I had no more use for tears.

"Thank you," I said. "For the song, and for everything else."

As silence fell between us, I saw for the first time how beautiful he was, and how this beauty lay not just in the planes of his face, but in the kindness of his countenance. I found myself taking in the blue of his eyes and the curve of his cheek.

I pressed myself back against the cushions of my chair, so that I would not lean closer and take in his scent. I did not trust myself to speak. I kept my eyes on his so that I would not lower my gaze to the beauty of his calves in their silk hose.

His eyes held mine. He did not look away.

Between us rose something that I had never before considered in my life, something I had not known existed. I loved Richard deeply, but we had been very young when we met, and he had never honored me as I had hoped he might. Now, between Jean Pierre and myself, rose a longing and a mutual consent. In all of the time I had spent at the courts of France and England, I had never seen its' like. I would not have thought it possible.

I had not known that a man and a woman could face each other as equals. I had not known that lust and equality could exist side by side. Jean Pierre's blatant respect for me only made me want him more.

It was a temptation I could not live with. I rose to my feet, and Jean Pierre stood when I did. The warmth in his blue eyes told me that I was a beautiful woman still, despite my black gown, despite all the years that had passed since my youth was spent.

He might have offered some flowery compliment to break the tension between us, as men had offered me empty words at Henry's court, long ago. But he said nothing and our silence lingered, speaking for us.

Jean Pierre did nothing to deny the knowledge of what lay between us. He only took my hand and kissed it, cradling it as if it were the Holy Grail.

My self-control drained away with his hand on mine and the heat under my skin flared. My mouth went dry, and my tongue stayed silent, though I had meant to wish him a good night before he left me.

The lay sisters still nodded by the south wall. Jean Pierre only looked at me, the light in his eyes hot enough to scorch me where I stood.

"Good night," I said at last, hoping to break the spell that had fallen between us.

Jean Pierre left me without another word. I felt the press of his hand on mine long after he had gone. The sisters woke finally to douse the many lamps and find their own beds.

I spent a sleepless night on my cloistered cot, until the sun began to lighten the sky to gray.

Only then did I sleep, to wake again when the sun shone in warm, the sound of the bell rising on the wind, calling me to prayer.

After mass, I stayed on my knees. When I stood, my prayer finished, I found the Count of Valois watching me.

He regarded me without smiling. Lust rose in me like sap in a tree, and I moved to escape it.

Jean Pierre stepped forward and blocked my path to the chapel's only door. "Your Highness."

His voice was deep and low, almost subservient, as if he had not willfully stepped between me and the warmth of the day beyond. My knees were cold from kneeling on stone. I focused on that chill in an effort to keep my mind on the things of God, but the pain was fleeting, for I had been kneeling on a cushion.

I did not speak but moved again toward the door. This time, Jean Pierre stopped me by taking hold of my arm, as if I were some servant girl he would dally with behind the laundry. The taste of anger on my tongue only made me more aware of my desire.

I cast my gaze down to my arm where his hand lay, but he did not let me go. No one had ever touched me without my permission. No one but the king. "Release me." My voice was calm and betrayed none of the desire I felt.

But Jean Pierre seemed to know the desire buried deep within me, as Henry once had. His eyes never left my face. Once again, I was struck by the thought that he knew me, as no other man ever had, save one.

"My lady, there is unfinished business between us."

I kept my voice even, my tone severe. "That is so, my lord. You will bear me to my brother the king in one day's time. You will lead me to his court and leave me in his care. That will conclude the business we have between us."

Jean Pierre heard the lies I spoke, but he ignored them. He stepped so close that I could smell the scent of sandalwood on his skin.

Henry had worn that scent, but it was forever changed for me after that day. When I took in the sandalwood on Jean Pierre's skin, it made me feel like a wanton woman, as if to be wanton was a blessed thing. The scent made my limbs heavy, and my joints liquid. That scent made me think of a dark bed with silk hangings, where we might lose ourselves.

I tried to draw back from him even as the fire in me rose to meet his. But he would not let me go.

"My lady, I would bear you other places than to your brother."

Jean Pierre drew me away from the door, back into the shadows of the church, where the sun had not yet come. He pressed me against a wall, and I let him. "I know you, my lady. I know that you would go with me."

"I will not," I said, though my breath came short. I knew that if I tried to pull away again, he would let me go. Something in the way he stood told me that, as he looked down at me, his blue eyes filling the world.

It was I who took the last step toward him. I raised my lips to his, though it had been almost twenty years since a man had kissed me.

I found that a kiss does not leave you once you have learned the way of it. The method of it lingered and came to me again as I stood in that church and let him taste me. His lips were soft and cool, but soon warmed over mine.

I tasted his tongue, the bread he had eaten at breakfast, the wine he had taken in the mass. I knew then that he had knelt behind me. He had watched me all that while and had stayed with me even as I prayed.

The thought that his eyes had been on me during the mass as his hands were on me now made my desire for him crest and threaten to overwhelm me. I pressed myself against him, and his arms tightened around me, the last of his hesitation vanishing like so much smoke.

For all his bold words, Jean Pierre had waited for a sign from me. Now that I had given my permission, the last of his reserve was swept away.

He pressed me against the stone of the church wall. I could feel the uneven places digging into my back, though to the eye, the stone looked smooth under its coats of whitewash. His thighs pressed against my own as his hands slid up my arms, down my neck, and over my breasts.

It was his touch on my breasts that was my

undoing. I remembered myself, who I was, and where. I fought him as a cat might fight a dog.

Jean Pierre let me go. I stumbled as I moved away from him into the watery sunlight coming in the stained-glass windows. We stood together in that church and stared at each other, both of us panting for breath, both of us at a loss for words. It had been so long since I had been touched, but it seemed my body and my soul both remembered the way of it.

The desire in his eyes was as strong as a siren's song and I almost went back to him, whatever the sin. But my mind was beginning to come unclouded, and I thought of my brother.

King Phillipe Auguste meant another alliance for me or he would never have sent this man to fetch me. I had to keep what was left of my honor for that unknown man, whoever he was. As always, I belonged not to myself but to the kingdom of France.

"We will not touch each other again," I said.

"We are not finished with each other."

I felt my lust cooling, the fire in my belly beginning to go out. I could not control what I felt for him. But I could control my actions. I was bound to my honor, what little was left of it. I was a woman now, no green, defenseless girl. I would choose for myself.

"There is much that will remain unfinished. I am for France, to do my brother's bidding. You are for the holy war in the Levant, to win glory for God. What we feel must stay here and end now."

"What I feel for you will never end."

Jean Pierre met my eyes, and I saw that he thought he was telling the truth. I did not doubt his intention, only the strength of it. For I knew enough of men to know that while their pretty words were sincere when they spoke them, those words faded as cut flowers fade after a day when they are set upon a table.

He had been half in love with me before he came to fetch me. I feared that he had written the tale of some phantom woman on the vellum of his mind, and now called her by my name.

Even as I denied him, I wanted to offer comfort, to show him that, if I had been free to choose for myself, he would have been my choice. I touched his hand once. Jean Pierre did not clutch at me, or pull me to him, as a lesser man might have done.

Instead, he took my hand in his and kissed it, as if my palm were made of old parchment that might split under the lightest touch. I was sure in that moment that Jean Pierre loved me in truth, for after he kissed my hand, he bowed to me and let me go.

3

THE JOURNEY

"IT IS GOOD THAT YOU ARE LEAVING, MY LADY."

Mother Bernard spoke gravely after she had heard my confession of all that had passed between myself and Jean Pierre. "Perhaps you should call for another man to lead you home."

I smiled, for she spoke as if I were some girl coming home from a fair after being gone for only one day.

I kissed her, despite the years of hard training in my father's court, and in Eleanor's. Love's expression flowed from me ever since my daughter had been born and died. Rose had given me much in that one day, and easy affection with those I loved was one of those gifts.

My brother would send no other man to fetch me. And I had no desire to delay.

Even then, my litter waited outside in the sunshine. Already, I could hear the horses gathering and the men at arms. My things were packed, paltry though they were, and loaded on a mule. My brother would have to give me new dresses when I came to him. For now, I wore the dark dyed linen of the nunnery.

Mother Bernard must have seen the resolution in my eyes, and she kissed me once, clutching me hard, for I had been in her keeping for many years. In the end, she remembered herself and let me go. I stepped onto the stones of the courtyard and saw that the women had gathered to see me off, as they had done for me once before, long ago.

A little girl offered me a clutch of flowers from the garden. I brought them to my cheek, feeling the softness of their petals, taking in their gentle scent. Among them she had set a sprig of the lavender I had planted. I pressed them to my heart and kissed her, too.

"Thank you," I said.

I could not remember her name, for she was new to the abbey. I had kept apart from the novices, except at prayers. She knew who I was, though, for she curtsied as she smiled at me.

Jean Pierre was at my elbow then, handing me into my litter. His hand was warm on my arm, and I felt no lust from him. He felt my hesitation, and he waited, for it seemed he was a patient man as well as a kind one.

With one last look at the haven of my childhood, at the only haven I had known in all my life, I climbed into my litter and did not look back.

I raised my hand once to Mother Bernard. She smiled at me, though her face was wet with tears. The other women waved to me as if I were only going away for a holiday, as if I might someday return.

But my path was drawing me away from that moment onward. I had felt the tide of Fate before, when it had taken my daughter from me, when it had taken me from Henry forever. I knew that I would not be coming back to that place.

We were away from the convent within a matter of minutes, and it vanished behind me as if it had never been. I left the curtains of my litter open and gazed out at the countryside that I had not seen in almost twenty years.

Spring had come down like the sweet breath of the Virgin in Heaven, and the grass was touched with green where it grew by the river. The trees above our pathway swayed over our heads. I met Jean Pierre's eyes once through the open curtains when he leaned down from his mount to check on me, and I found myself wishing that our journey might be a long one.

My time in the abbey fell away from me as a dream does with the light of morning. Though in many ways I had lived a religious life, I had never taken vows and I was born for another fate. I knew well that my brother would find other, better political uses for me now that Richard had set me free.

As the abbey was left behind me, down the road that had no turning, I took in the sights of spring as if seeing them with new eyes. I was filled with joy at the thought of being among people again, of living in the world, all the good and ill that would come with it.

I was not afraid as I went to meet my future. I was simply grateful that I had one. At thirty-five, I was no doubt too old to bear children by now and would do my new husband, whoever he was, little good.

But the thought of wearing fine silk again, of having a lady to tend my bath and fireside, of dancing late into the night with men younger than myself, all came to me as ambassadors from my new life. I had been such a green girl when I was at Henry's court and so beset by pain, that I had had little time to enjoy myself. I vowed that this time my life would be different.

God seemed to hear my thoughts and sent me a messenger long before I reached Dover, where I was to take ship for Calais.

We meant to stop for the night at a monastery on the road from Bath, but before we reached that place, we were stopped by a great army of men on horseback.

They held lances and pikes, raised in a defensive position, but I knew how quickly they might be lowered to attack. At first, I thought them robbers and moved to draw my curtains closed, but I soon saw the banner of the Plantagenets waving above their horses' heads. It was Prince John's standard.

I laughed under my breath, wondering what mischief Eleanor's youngest son hoped to make by stopping me on my way to my brother. I did not laugh long, but rose from my litter without help, stepping between Jean Pierre and the man who faced him.

"Greetings," I said as if Jean Pierre was not

there. "Your lord does my brother much honor. But as you can see, I am already well guarded for my journey to Paris. Please give the Lord John my thanks for his kind regard."

The gentleman smiled down on me, grateful that I had intervened, for Jean Pierre had lowered the visor of his helmet and had challenged John's man to a duel to defend my long dead honor.

I had not heard the words spoken between them, but I saw the anger in Jean Pierre's eyes when he raised his visor once more and glared at me. I ignored him and kept my gaze only on John's man. No one would lose his life that night if I could stop it.

"Your Highness, greetings from Lord John, Prince of England. He sends you his regards and asks that you sup with him this night, along the river Avon. He has a pavilion set there for you, and all is in readiness."

Jean Pierre said nothing, but I could feel the heat of his gaze on the top of my head. I did not look at him but cast my eyes quickly over the men who surrounded us. I had a retinue of a dozen men, but John had sent sixty. I knew that my brother's men would have to fight to get away. I also knew that they would lose.

"I thank you. I will accept your lord's hospitality. My men and I will follow, if you will lead the way."

I thought in that moment Jean Pierre would vault down from his horse and throttle me. I met his eyes coolly and let him see the position I was in. I was only a woman under his protection. But I was also a princess of France.

In the end, he deferred to me, whether out of respect for me, or out of the desire to keep his men alive, I never knew. But I climbed back into my litter, careful to keep the curtains open so that all my men and John's men could see me. I sat straight and wished I wore a decent gown.

But I remembered the words of my father from my childhood. He told me that royalty came not from outer trappings, not from gold or jewels or silk, but from the mark of God, which shown from within. I had been chosen by God to serve France from my birth, and I would do it even here, even now, in this foreign place, among the soldiers of my enemy.

I had expected a military camp with a campaign tent pitched by a muddy riverbank, troops of men lined up beside it to show Prince John's might. I saw none of this as we rode into his camp. Instead, torches burned, making the twilight as bright as day, and as I stepped from my litter, fire-eaters and jugglers danced among us, shooting flames and scaring the horses.

I covered my mouth to hide my smile, and I met Jean Pierre's eyes as he swung down from his horse. I saw him forgive me in that moment when he saw the foolishness of John's servants. Surely a man who would send jugglers and mountebanks among warhorses was no threat to my person.

He was still angry at John's arrogance; I could feel his anger in his touch as he led me from my litter. He placed his body between myself and John's men, as if they meant to menace me. I knew that could not be John's aim, but I was touched at his single-minded devotion. His love for me was not just pretty words. Jean Pierre would truly have laid down his life for mine without thought or misgiving. I pressed his hand gently as he let me go.

Jean Pierre felt something more than courtesy in my touch, for he looked down at me, his eyes meeting mine. I saw a little more of his anger slide away as I stood in the door of the tent that John had prepared for me.

"I will watch the door," Jean Pierre said. "I will keep you safe."

I could not kiss him there, in front of all John's and my brother's men, though I wanted to. Instead I simply let my gaze linger on his face, hoping that he understood me. As I watched, his skin flushed red under his tan. I turned with a smile and stepped into the tent raised in my honor.

Inside, I was surprised that John was not there, waiting for me. Only women stood by, with heated water and a hip bath. Bathing sheets lay on a camp table, heaped high, and perfumes of every kind and clarity lay spread for my inspection, ready to be taken up when I called for them.

I turned myself over to the ministrations of those women, expecting country clumsiness at best and ham-fisted incompetence at worst. I was greeted with neither. Each woman moved, as good servants do, in the silence of a dance, taking my travel-stained gown from me, helping me carefully into the bath. Those women washed my skin and hair deftly and sprinkled both my hair and body with the perfume I selected as they dried me off. I had not been served so well even at Henry's court. I saw that these women had been trained not in France, but some land beyond, where silent service was not a courtesy, but offered as a lady's due.

They dressed me not in my own clothes but in a gown of the softest silk dyed pink to match the roses that sat on the table in my tent. I saw a bed beyond a screen, piled high with pillows and surrounded by braziers for warmth. I wondered if John thought to seduce me by the roadside. Though I had been the lover of a king, I was no milkmaid to be tilted in a field.

I set this thought aside and schooled my face to blankness. I would see John among his own people and take what came. I was a woman now, no longer a child and a pawn. I would make my own decision, whatever choice offered me.

Jean Pierre was as good as his word. He did not wash or change his clothes, but stood by the flap of my tent, guarding my life and my virtue. I touched his arm once in silent thanks before I followed John's man to a larger tent set down by the river's edge.

The flap of this tent was open wide to the night air. I breathed in the scent of the river, taken back once more to my time with Henry.

But no irises or daisies greeted me in John's tent. Instead, the table was covered in roses of every hue, roses in red and pink, yellow and white. I stood and stared, remembering how much I loved those flowers, and how little I had seen of them since leaving his father's court.

Prince John stood behind the great table, which had been set for two. He bowed to me, coming down from his throne to take my hand in his. Jean Pierre tensed behind me, but I stepped forward and met John as he approached.

John's face was narrow, as neither Eleanor's nor Henry's had been. His eyes were slanted like Eleanor's though, and a bit of her emerald green tinted their hazel hue. He smiled at me, and I saw a little of her in him. It was that small piece of Eleanor I spoke to, as I gazed into her youngest son's face.

"Your Highness," I said, dropping a decent curtsey. "You do me too much honor."

"That is not possible, Princess."

Prince John took my hand and led me to the other side of the table, seating me himself before taking his place beside me. I saw Jean Pierre's face flush with fury at the sight of only two chairs. Clearly, John expected my brother's ambassador to stand about like a footman, rather than treating him as the landed gentlemen he was.

I met Jean Pierre's eyes and begged him to say nothing. He must have seen my plea. He stayed silent.

John's footmen brought forth the wine and the meat to be laid in the trenchers. I saw then that there was only one trencher, and that we were meant to share it.

Jean Pierre raised his gaze to a point above

my head. He stood at military attention beside the door of the tent and kept his eye on every man that entered, and every serving woman. He was the only military man in the room, which set my mind at ease. As much as John seemed to be provoking him, I knew that I could keep them apart.

We sampled the first course without speaking. The meat was a fine venison stewed in mushrooms. I ate with relish, for I had had no such meat in the convent. I found myself pleased with John and his trappings, more than I had ever thought to be, despite there being no seat left for Jean Pierre.

When the second course was brought out, the footmen also brought a fresh wine, the light white wine from Anjou that I loved. I looked at John with new respect. My affinity for roses was widely known, but his spies were well informed indeed to tell him of the wine I drank.

I raised my glass to him in a silent toast. "So, my lord prince. What brings you to meet me by the roadside and to offer me such honor?"

"My Lady Alais, please let us not speak of business over dinner. Let us enjoy the good food and the entertainments I have planned. After that, we may talk together."

"As you wish, my lord. You are my host."

"Indeed, I am."

John smiled at me, offering me a bite of suckling pork from his knife, as Henry once had done. I took the tender meat with my fingertips and ate it slowly, watching John all the while. I saw the fire of lust light his amber eyes for the first time and I began to see the way his thoughts were tending.

Still, I said nothing as the last course was taken away and the fruit brought in. I kept an eye on Jean Pierre as the same jugglers and fire-eaters who had greeted us came in and performed once more.

Jean Pierre seemed to have turned to stone, so I drew my eyes and my mind from him. I knew that I needed to keep my wits about me, for John was cleverer than I had ever heard him given credit for.

The mountebanks were quite skilled and would have been entertaining had my thoughts not been tending toward John and his intentions. As I lifted my glass for more watered wine, I looked to see if a priest lurked in the shadows, ready to marry me to John then and there, but I saw none. I wondered if one waited just outside.

The entertainers left us, John showering them with gold. I raised one eyebrow but said nothing. In Henry's court, such people would have been paid, but in silver, and somewhere out of sight.

John turned to me as they left, raising one hand. In that moment, every footman and serving woman left us, until we were alone, just myself and Prince John, with Jean Pierre standing over us, as still as stone.

"My lady Alais, can we not speak in private?"

John's gaze moved pointedly to the count. I swallowed, praying that Jean Pierre would not draw a dagger from his boot and kill the heir to

England's throne then and there. The count still stood unwashed in the clothes he had worn on the road, though he had taken his armor off. As far as I knew, he had not eaten or drunk anything since we had come into camp four hours before. He stood unmoving, as if John had not spoken.

I met Jean Pierre's eyes then, and I saw him soften as he looked at me. His love for me would keep him silent and would keep John alive. I thanked him only with my eyes, but he seemed to understand. Jean Pierre relaxed just a little as he stood watch over me.

"Anything you have to say can be said in front of my brother's vassal," I said. "The Count of Valois has kindly come to guide me to the king, though he is soon to leave for the Holy Land, in the company of my brother, and yours."

At the mention of Richard, John's face was shadowed for the first time. His pleasant, bland expression fled, and I saw the darkness of his soul. I did not blink, for I had seen worse, but I knew now that I could not allow this man to have power over me, then or ever. I thanked God and the Virgin that Jean Pierre was there. I might need him to fight our way out; in the end, I knew that he could do it, and get us both to a horse, even if we were forced to leave his armor and my goods behind.

I forced myself to relax. It would not come to blows, if I could help it.

I prayed for my father the diplomat to look down from heaven and to bless my tongue with skill it did not have. Then I turned to face Prince John and schooled my looks to sweetness.

John was not pleased that I refused to dismiss Jean Pierre, but he hid his displeasure and the darkness beneath it behind a charming smile.

"Very well, Your Highness. If you lap dog would like to stay, by all means, let him."

I held my tongue and did not look at Jean Pierre. I could feel the heat of his anger from where I sat. But he was a man who kept his head in battle, and he kept his head then.

"Princess Alais, you have been ill used by my family."

I kept my own face bland, my smile pleasant. I could not believe that he would actually name his father to me.

"We will not speak of the late king, out of respect for you."

I thought that Jean Pierre might reach for the dagger in his boot in that moment, but he did not. I kept my eyes on Prince John.

John smiled at me, and for the first time his smile was oily, unctuous, as if he was certain he could convince me to bend to his will. I saw for all his talented spies and all the information he may have gathered, he did not yet know me.

"Richard has discarded you with no thought for your station or your rank. I have heard it said that he will not even return the Vexin when you go home to France."

I wanted to reach out and slap the smile from his face. I kept my hand still on the table before me. My rings gleamed in the lamplight. I was not a violent woman, but it seemed John was the one to bring out the violence in me. I breathed deeply and thought of my daughter in her grave in Winchester until the impulse passed.

"I am sure that my brother the king has seen to the disposition of my dowry."

I rose as if to go, and John caught my hand. I froze, and Jean Pierre took one step towards me before he stopped himself. I could feel his eyes on me. I knew that he would do nothing without my leave.

I had never had a man back me before, without regard or question for anything else. It was a heady feeling. I knew that if I asked it of him, Jean Pierre would strike the prince down, even if it brought the whole camp down on our heads. I smiled, strengthened by the man behind me.

"My lord prince," I said, "I thank you for your concern for me. My brother, Phillipe Auguste, thanks you. I will tell him of your concern, and of your wishes for my happiness when next we meet."

I forced his hand then, for he clutched me when he meant only to charm. John released me at the mention of my brother's name. I knew that for the moment, my brother and Richard were allies. It seemed that John knew it, too.

John had meant to use me to shore up his power against their alliance, until a better day came, as one always did for the likes of men like him. Men without honor could afford to wait. The wind would always blow their way once more.

"I would offer you honorable marriage, my lady Alais. I would offer you this kingdom, all that you survey, if you would pity me, and become my bride."

I saw in that moment that this move was not just a political one. The prince was moved by my beauty, but more importantly, he was drawn by the fact that I had once been his father's whore, and his brother's plaything. He wanted what neither his brother nor his father would ever have again. In this, he wished to conquer them both, as well as conquer me.

If he married me, John hoped also to force my brother's hand, so that the valuable county of the Vexin might pass to him, shoring up his position as the landless, younger son. Just as John did not know me, neither did he know my brother.

At such a blatant disregard of his express wishes, Phillipe August would go to war until all John knew and held dear was driven into the ground. Phillipe Auguste would leave off all talk of the Holy Land and wars for Christ. He would turn all the force of his will and all the might of France on ruining the man who sat before me.

I looked down at John and pitied him. He was a man born to live always in the shadow of his betters. I knew I had already won. I was gracious in victory, as my brother never would have been.

"My lord Prince." I spoke softly. I looked at him, my face bland, my eyes clear of malice. "You do me too much honor. Whatever my own feelings, I am but a weak woman, called home by my brother the king. I cannot defy him, this night or ever. Your lordship must look from me, and honor another."

John sat listening to my words. He swallowed them, as he had no doubt taken in much bitterness before. I thought for a moment that he would fight me even then. But he knew that he was beaten, and not by me. I was simply reminding him of what he already knew. We were both pawns on another's chess board. And no doubt, we always would be.

He rose and bowed to me, the gallant knight once more, though he had never fought in battle and, as far as I knew, never did.

"My lady Alais, forgive my impetuous words. I have been overcome by your beauty. Please convey to your brother my deepest regards. See to it that he knows that he ever has a staunch ally in me."

I stepped back from the table and curtsied deeply to him, as if he was already king. "My lord prince, it is my honor to be your messenger. And know this: after this night, you will have a friend and ally in France."

I knew no such thing, nor could I make such promises. But John's position was so weak, with both his mother and his brother allied against him, he would grasp at any straw. He bowed over my hand deeply, as if I had promised him a kingdom of gold. When he rose once more and met my eyes, I saw that though he strove to deceive himself, he had failed.

"I thank you, my lady. Be my guest this night. Stay amongst my men and let them guard you. In the morning, they will escort you to the dockside, where you will board your brother's ship for home."

"I thank you, my lord prince. I am ever in your debt."

John smiled and this time his smile was genuine. He went so far as to lead me by the hand to the door of the tent, which was tied open to the night air over the river.

"I will have someone send a meal to your tent, for your lap dog."

Jean Pierre had crossed the tent beside me. At those words, he turned and met the prince's eyes. I had seen men give such looks over their shields on the tilting yard. Such looks meant that, if they did not kill their opponent at arms, it would not be for lack of trying.

I said nothing more but took Jean Pierre's arm and drew him from the prince's presence. He loved me, for he walked away. He sent only one more look to John over his shoulder. I said a prayer in my mind to the Virgin, and she heard me, for I got Jean Pierre back to my tent and the flap closed with no blood shed.

Once in my tent, neither of us spoke. I watched him, drawing off my gloves as I did so, casting them down onto the table beside the roses. Jean Pierre did not move, except for a muscle that jumped in his cheek. I stayed silent.

Before long, women came into the tent with food and more flowers. They set Jean Pierre's meal on the table. I saw that it was the same dinner the prince and I had eaten, though it had now grown cold.

The women also brought in the roses from John's table so that soon my borrowed tent was filled with the scent of flowers.

Still, Jean Pierre said nothing. I nodded, giving the women leave to go.

"Will you eat, my lord?" I stepped to the table and began to cut the food for him, serving him on a bronze plate that had been set down for that purpose. I took up the bronze pitcher to pour him a glass of wine.

He reached out, his hand as quick as a striking snake, and stopped me. "You will not serve me."

I met his eyes and raised my other hand, placing it over his. Something in my touch was his undoing. He sat down then, heavily, as if he had run far in armor. I drew his meal toward him and set his wine beside his hand. I mixed a little more with clear water and poured a glass for myself. When I tasted it, I found it was still the sweet white wine I loved from Anjou.

I sat beside him, keeping my hand over his. Jean Pierre ate then, slowly, for he was hungry. The road had been long, and the night's doings had left him weary. He met my eyes as he finished his meal and I saw that his pain had risen to meet me.

"I am sorry," I said. "Forgive me for bringing you here."

Jean Pierre did not answer but lowered his lips to my hand, where it lay on the table between us. He kissed my skin, the warmth of his lips filling my senses until even the scent of roses faded and there was nothing left but him.

"Let me love you," he said. His voice was so low, I thought he had not meant for me to hear.

I looked at him, and he raised his eyes to mine. I saw that he wanted me to hear him, and to obey.

I knew myself to be as weak and wanton a woman as I had ever been, for I kissed him, long and lingering. He rose from his chair and drew me with him until my body was pressed against his. His hands rose into my hair, drawing it from beneath the veil I wore, until my curls spilled over his palms and down my back.

He sighed deeply and released me. I leaned against him, both of us breathing hard. I said a prayer to the Virgin that She might guide my steps. I still felt weak, and selfish, wanting nothing more than to lay down with this man and damn the cost, whatever was. But I listened for the Holy Mother and, as always, found that I knew the answer already.

"I cannot lie with you," I said. "I belong not to myself, but to my brother. What honor I have left must be given to him."

Jean Pierre said nothing. I felt the hope run out of him, as water from a broken jar. I stayed by him, leaning against him, taking in his strength, shored up by him as I had been by no other man, not even my father.

"I love you, Alais."

I could not answer him. I felt my own love rise from my heart into my throat where it lodged, unspoken. I clutched him close, my touch my only answer. He stroked my hair.

We did not sleep that night. I lay on my borrowed bed and he sat beside me on a chair drawn close. We did not speak but watched the fires in the braziers burn down as he held my hand. He did not move to touch me in any other way as the fires surrounding us turned to ash.

4

MARIE HELENE

JOHN WAS AS GOOD AS HIS WORD. HE SAW ME OFF himself and gave over ten of his men-at-arms to accompany us. Jean Pierre rode close to my litter all that day, in case of ambush or kidnapping. But even when we came to the dock at Dover, still John's men did nothing. They escorted us as far as the ship, then bowed to us and went away.

Jean Pierre and I sat together under an awning on the deck. I was not sick as I had been as a child. Even the dangerous waters of the Channel did not frighten me any longer.

As we sat under an awning on the deck, Jean Pierre brought me fresh melon cut from the rind and sweet wine. He sang for me, very low, so that none of his men might hear. They all could see that we were taken with each other, and with my reputation, no doubt they assumed we were lovers already. These men were careful to look the other way, for they were loyal to him as much as to my brother and would follow Jean

Pierre to the Holy Land and beyond. I was glad that he would have them to guard his back.

When we docked, I was sure that I would be wretched. Though I was returning home to live a life of a great lady, to make an alliance to shore up the power of France, I found I no longer wanted it. I wanted only Jean Pierre, to feel safe with him as I had with no other man.

Though he said nothing, I saw in his eyes that a part of him would have denied the Holy Land and the Crusade he had sworn to fight. He might have turned his back on all of that for me had I been free.

But I was not free. My ties to the throne of France were as strong as they had ever been. Now, as a woman grown, I knew the cost of war. I knew that once again, I would lay down my life and the lives of my unborn children to make an alliance for France. I wished, when I looked at Jean Pierre, that I had not been born a princess of the realm.

I was sad when we docked at Calais, but my sorrow soon was tempered. For I found Marie Helene waiting for me. I had not seen her in over twenty years, since I had been sent back to the nunnery. After my disgrace, she had been married to a man not of her choosing.

I was in her arms before I could speak, my tears wetting the fine silk of her gown and kirtle. She held me so tightly that I thought my ribs might bruise. It was as if the dead had been restored to me. I had never thought to see her face again this side of Paradise.

Her eyes were as blue as they had ever been. Even her golden hair had hardly faded, but gleamed bright against the dark blue of her wimple. She met my eyes, leaning hard against me.

We did not speak, and it was a long while before I found my voice. We simply stood, clutching each other by the quayside. Jean Pierre's men-at-arms stared at first, then looked away, horrified to see a princess of the blood behave with such open emotion. Even then I did not pull away from her, but I made an effort to stop crying.

Marie Helene drew a soft kerchief from her sleeve and wiped my eyes with it. "There now, my lady. There is no need to weep."

I laughed when she said that, for tears were on her face as well as mine. I took Eleanor's linen from my sleeve, the kerchief emblazoned with the queen's crest. I moved to wipe away Marie Helene's tears. But when she saw the queen's coat of arms on that kerchief, she recoiled from my hand. I thought for a moment that she might spit on it in her hatred. But the moment passed with only a hideous look on her face, as if she had eaten something vile. I saw this look for what it was: loyalty to me. So, I put my kerchief away and wiped her face with her own.

Jean Pierre watched all this in silence. The rest of his men turned away to regard the water, their boots, or the mud along the roadside. But Jean Pierre looked only at me.

I knew him well, even after so short a time. I

saw that he was glad I had a friend to stand by me at court, when he himself could not.

With my arm around Marie Helene's waist, I leaned over and kissed her cheek.

"So," I said to her. "You are like a phantom risen from the ground. How long do I have you with me?"

"For as long as you will have me, my lady."

I was surprised and showed it, for I knew she was a married woman. She had never written to ask me to call on the king to bring her away from her husband, so I had always assumed that she was happy with him. Or, if not happy, at least content, as most married women were.

I saw a sorrow in her eyes that she did not want to speak of, so I turned to Jean Pierre. "Marie Helene, I present to you my escort and protector, Jean Pierre, Count of Valois. He has stood by me on the long road to France. He has stood by me against even my enemies."

Marie Helene met his eyes, and I saw a gleam of recognition there. At first, I thought she only saw what he meant to me, but in a moment, it was clear that they knew each other.

She curtsied and he bowed, almost in the same breath.

"My lord count," she said. "I greet you. You are welcome to this place."

"It is my honor to see you again," was all Jean Pierre said, before he took my arm once more. So, we walked then in silence to my litter, with Jean Pierre on one side of me and Marie Helene on the other.

Marie Helene climbed in first, with a

footman to help her, but Jean Pierre handed me into it himself. He was reluctant to take his hand from my arm. We had grown used to being together on the ship and now neither of us could bear to part.

"I will escort you to your brother's side," he said, his voice low, so that no one else might hear him.

Marie Helene heard and turned her face away, as if to offer us privacy.

"We sleep tonight in the Abbey of Saint John," he said. "Tomorrow, we will take a barge on the river Seine towards Paris."

We stood together a long moment, until even his men began to look to him, to see when we might leave. That was when I knew that our borrowed time was up.

"I thank you," I said.

Jean Pierre heard the true meaning of my words, for when he met my eyes, his heart was in them. He did not kiss me, as we both would have wished, but leaned down as if to bow to me. Instead, he kissed my hand where it lay on his arm. Then he drew back and let me go.

I closed the curtains of my litter, so that the prying eyes of his men and my brother's might not see me. I leaned back against the cushions, feeling suddenly tired and sad.

Marie Helene took my hand and warmed it between her own. She did not speak, for we had only the heavy curtains of the litter to shield us. But I knew that she had seen how things were between Jean Pierre and myself, how I loved him, and how like all the loves of my life, it was doomed to fail.

So, we rode to the abbey in silence, her hand in mine.

Sorrow of her own rode Marie Helene, darkening her blue eyes to indigo. This sorrow weighed her down, despite her strength and the joy of our meeting.

I kept her hand in mine until we were alone in the abbot's rooms, warm water in the hip bath, and the door shut firmly behind us.

She helped me undress, and I bathed. She washed my long hair. It had never grown as long as it had once been in my youth before I cut it in mourning for the death of my daughter.

I sat by the fire, and Marie Helene dried it slowly, spreading it out on a swatch of linen. Bread and fruit sat on a table beside us. If the tapestries had been new, and if the room had wooden floors, I would have thought myself back at Windsor, before Henry had ever seen me.

I sat in my shift in the firelight, the door to the abbot's rooms locking out the rest of the world. I almost expected my little white dog Bijou to come running out from beneath the bed, to circle our ankles, begging to be picked up.

Marie Helene smiled as if she could read my thoughts. I had forgotten that there had once been a time when she could.

"Bijou always missed you."

I buttered a slab of bread, placing a bit of cheese on it before I handed it to her. She blinked to see me serve her, but then she remembered how I had done so from time to time when we were together years before. My years in the abbey had reminded me that we are all servants in the eyes of God.

Marie Helene took the bread I offered her, and I poured us each a cup of wine. The goblets were of blown glass from Germany, finer workmanship than I had seen since I left my father's court. I raised my wine to my lips and felt the smooth warmth of the watered Burgundy flow down my throat. I knew myself back in France truly in that moment, with the taste of that fine wine on my tongue.

I sighed and settled back in my chair, tension leaving me that I had not even known was there. I had been guarded so long, even in the Abbey of St. Agnes. Always I had known that I was on foreign soil. Now I felt myself truly safe for the first time in years. I knew this safety to be an illusion, but it was an illusion I cherished. I was only a day's ride away from my brother, and Paris. One day's ride from home.

"Perhaps I will get another dog, once I have settled with the man my brother has chosen for me."

"So, you come home to marry?" Her eyes were grave. Her bread lay on the table before her, uneaten.

"Phillipe has not told me so. But I can think of no other reason to ask Richard to let me go."

"And the Count of Valois? He has come only to fetch you?"

"Yes."

"And you love him?"

I did not look away from her. Though it had been many years since we were parted, she knew me still. "I do. But I will let him go."

"For the good of France," she said.

"For the good of my brother, and his throne. My life is not my own. It has never been."

Tears rose in her eyes, and I saw that it was not for me that she wept. I took her in my arms, and she stiffened. I could feel her pride and her need to harbor her strength. But some wall gave way within her, and she wept while I held her.

"The Count of Valois was there when my husband died. Gregory was killed in a tournament. No one else moved as quickly to his side. Jean Pierre tried to save him but could not."

Her voice was soft, but I could hear the bitterness beneath it. Gregory had died, not in war and honorable bloodshed, but in the pointless games that men played to amuse themselves.

"He was struck through the breastplate. I did not know that there was so much blood in a man's heart. Gregory was dead before I could get to him. His blood covered the tiltyard. They tried to keep me back, so that I wouldn't see, but I made it past them. As quick as I was, I was still too late."

She stared past my shoulder into the fire. "I

did not think to love him, when Queen Eleanor sent me away."

There was no help for her but time and its passing. And in the dark watches of the night, even time's softening distance would bring little comfort.

"I am sorry," I said. "I am sorry for your loss."

Marie Helene offered a slight smile to comfort me. The sorrow in her eyes did not fade or change. Her hand was cold in mine. "My son is only nineteen, but he is strong. The king has given him the land, in Gregory's place."

Her voice broke again when she said her husband's name. I pressed her hand, and she did not say anything more. I said a prayer to the Virgin for the soul of her husband. I would have knelt, but I did not want to take my hand from hers.

When I opened my eyes once more, her smile held a touch of its usual light. Marie Helene knew my long silences well; I spent such moments in prayer, both for the dead and for the living. I had many souls within my keeping.

"Thank you," she whispered.

"You will see him again," I said.

I remembered the touch of my daughter's hand as it had once come to me when I was working alone in the cloister garden, the warmth of her presence somewhere just behind me, where I could not see. I looked at Marie Helene with the certainty my daughter had given me. She saw in my eyes that I did not tell empty lies to placate her.

"I pray every day that you are right."

I sat with her in the firelight and watched the candle burn down. We stayed that way all night, with her hand in mine.

5

PHILLIPPE AUGUSTE

THE MORNING FOUND US ON THE RIVER, SETTING out to meet my brother. The sky was blue overhead, blue as it is only in France.

Marie Helene was pale but looked better than she had the night before. Though we never spoke of her husband again, it gave her comfort to speak of him that one time. I understood her. I had not said Rose's name except in prayer in almost twenty years. Some sorrows are treasures, never to be handled by another.

The Count of Valois looked in on us under our velvet awning, but he did not sit beside me, as I wished he might. The weight of other eyes rode him, for not only his men traveled with us now, but courtiers sent by my brother. For a moment, like the foolish girl I once had been, I feared that he no longer wanted my love, now that he knew he could not keep it. But he brought me wine once, and watered it himself, with his own hand.

When I took the wine he offered, he met my eyes. I saw then that I was not alone in what I felt, though he would never speak of it again. I felt that loss even as I looked at him, but it gave me comfort that he shared it.

River travel was swift, though we went against the current. The rowers knew their business, and as their great paddles lifted into the air and down again, I felt the wind on my face.

The warmth of the day seemed to cheer even Marie Helene. I caught her smiling with almost the same light in her eyes that had shone from her when first we met at Eleanor's court, before we had gone to Windsor, before Henry had ever seen me.

The standard of my brother flew over the palace on the *Ile de la Cité*. I breathed in the air of my native city and watched as fishmongers scrambled by the quayside to see the royal barge as it passed.

I raised my hand to them and a cheer went up, a cheer that spread along the riverside up into the city proper. More people gathered to see my ship come in; I smiled at them and stood so that they might see me better.

I moved to the front of the barge, and the Count of Valois rose to join me, offering his hand to steady me against the motion of the ship. I savored his touch, though I made sure that it was hidden by the wool of my cloak.

My brother had not come to greet me at the quayside, having other things more important to attend to, such as the welfare of the kingdom and the movement of the armies of his enemies.

But my brother's people stood to welcome me, though the men-at-arms let none of them gather too close. They called to me, and one woman tossed flowers from a high window near the river's edge. The flowers fell into the water below and slid past the barge I stood on. I raised my face and smiled, waving to her with my gloved hand.

She did not seem to see my woolen cloak or my linen gown, nor care that I wore the same gown I had worn for two years in the nunnery. She seemed not to mind that I wore no silk or brocade as a princess of France should. That woman and the rest of the crowd saw only my father in me, and the sacrifices we both had made all our lives for their good, to keep the fragile peace.

For though men of wealth loved war better than wine, the people of the cities and the farms needed peace to keep their families safe and fed during the harsh winter months. They needed the peace my father had done his best to keep in order to be free of fear and death, at least as free as anyone on this earth can ever be.

I saw that knowledge in that woman's face and in the faces of the people that lined the causeway. I stepped from the barge, heedless of the guards that surrounded me and raised my hand once more to my father's people.

They seemed to know something of my sacrifice. As I stood on the steps leading to my brother's palace, my father's people honored me for it, as those among my own class did not. The people cheered me, calling my name, and I waved to them. We might have gone on standing there, basking in the pleasure of one another's company, but the Count of Valois took my arm in his and led me away.

I watched as my brother's courtiers and men-at-arms frowned and muttered when he touched me without my leave. Jean Pierre's love blinded him to the fact that my position had nothing to do with me and everything to do with the power of my brother.

I was soon glad of his protection, for my brother's men surrounded us on all sides, cutting me off from the people of the city. I could smell the heavy scent of unwashed bodies, and I turned my face to Jean Pierre's cloak. He drew me ever closer and kept me under his arm as we were pushed through the press and into the palace gates.

I lost Marie Helene in the shuffle as I was led into the darkness of my brother's keep. I could still hear the cheering of the people as I went indoors.

I knew that they cheered not just to see me, looking younger than my years, despite my dowdy clothes. They cheered also for the peace my brother kept, for the holy war he would soon wage in the Levant, and for the warmth of spring that had come finally on the heels of a long winter. I was glad that I could be an excuse for them to bask in the sunshine before they went back to their daily work.

Jean Pierre stepped away from me once we

had room to breathe. My brother's men fell back and stayed silent as the count looked at me. I saw that he wished to speak, but we both knew that anything we said would be carried at once as tales to the king.

So, Jean Pierre said nothing, but led me into a chamber at the center of the palace, up a winding staircase, and into a long hall. I did not remember the room at first, until I saw the windows high above my head, and the sunlight that filtered through them like the grace of God.

I stood in that sunlight, and watched the dust dance over my head, as it had done once, long ago. In that same room, I had been named Countess at the age of eight. In that room, I had first learned that I was to be sent away.

My brother stood at the end of the hall by his throne. There was little to distinguish him from the men around him, only the power of his stance and the gold fillet he wore on his brow.

I moved away from Jean Pierre, leaving him and my brother's men-at-arms behind me. I walked alone up the long hall to the dais, where the king waited for me, with three young men ranged about him.

I did not look at those men, but only at him. All my childhood training came back to me as if I had never been away, as if I had not been in exile almost all my life. I remembered my father standing in that very spot, wearing a brocade gown, ermine dripping from his sleeves, his face shadowed by the crown he wore.

I curtsied, then knelt, making the same obeisance I had been trained to as a child.

Phillipe surprised me. Instead of waving me to my feet, he stepped away from his companions and helped me stand.

"Sister." He embraced me, kissing me once very formally on each cheek.

I had not expected such warmth. We had not seen each other since he was a very small child. I thought it likely that he had no memory of me at all, except as a pawn he had fought over with Richard and Henry once, long ago.

"You have not aged," he said. "I have heard of your beauty all my life, but I thought it only a fairy story."

I felt blood rise in my cheeks and tears come into my eyes. He was tall, as our father had been. As I looked at him, I saw that he had our father's eyes.

"You are kind," I managed to say without weeping.

He saw that I was close to losing my composure. He placed himself directly before the men behind him so that they could not see my face.

"I possess many qualities, sister," he said. "But kindness is not one of them."

There was great strength in him. As I looked into his eyes, I saw that he was older than he looked, as I was. His face was smooth and unlined in spite of the time he spent in the sun, riding to battle, and on the hunt. His eyes were the same piercing blue our father's had been, but there the resemblance ended. As I blinked my tears of sentiment away, I saw that his blue eyes held the look of a hawk. I, among others, was his prey.

Phillipe's voice took on a lacquered formality. "Alais, Princess of France and Countess of Berry and of the Vexin, may I present William of the House of Bellême, Count of Ponthieu."

I expected to see a middle-aged man step forward, balancing his paunch or a doddering toothless grandad, wiping drool from his chin. My brother had chosen neither kind of man for me. My betrothed was a bright-faced boy with blond hair and smooth skin. He was little older than my daughter would have been, if she had lived.

If he had seen twenty summers, I would have been surprised. William of Ponthieu carried himself with the confidence of a man who has acquitted himself well in battle. But the beard on his chin was so light, it almost had not grown in yet.

Surely Phillipe did not mean to betroth me to a boy almost half my age, while I was wearing nothing but dark linen from the nunnery?

My horror must have shown on my face, for the boy smiled wryly, bowing over my hand. William kissed my fingertips where they were covered by my linen gloves.

My brother talked on, using a great many words to say nothing, speaking of the realm and the war to come in the Levant. He gave a gracious speech of how he needed strong vassals like the Count of Ponthieu at his back, to keep the peace while he was away. I hoped desperately that I was mistaken. Phillipe had not brought me home to marry this boy. But the count had been briefed as I had not. He did not let go of my fingertips.

My brother raised his hand over us, as if in benediction, as if he were himself a priest. "Once you are married, you will stand beside my sister and hold the realm of France in peace."

Even I knew this for so much nonsense. Phillipe would never leave me as regent at the side of this untrained boy. I stood in silence, looking at my brother as at a stranger. As indeed he was.

In that moment, the only man in the room that had sympathy for me was the boy himself. Even as my brother spoke, the boy glanced at me sidelong, as if to say, "Well, whatever comes, we are in this together."

I tried to step away from him, but William held me firm. His strength flowed into me where his hand grasped mine. I wondered, for the first of many times, where this boy found his self-possession.

I was not to know the answer to the riddle of his soul for years, if we ever truly know another. But that day I had a glimpse into his strength of will that gave me pause. I had known kings, and strong men had been in my life since birth. As I looked into the eyes of that boy, I saw that he was one of the strongest.

My brother left us then, and the other men went with him. I turned to look behind me, to see if Jean Pierre was there. But he had been sent away, along with my brother's men. I stood alone in the king's hall, forgotten.

My future husband smiled down at me. Whatever Fate would bring us, on that first day, he was my friend.

"It is a shock, Your Highness, and not the first you'll have, now that you're back among the living."

"We considered ourselves among the living at the abbey, my lord."

William of Ponthieu laughed, and I found his laugh infectious. It made me smile, too.

"If you call that living. I prefer to be in the world. For better or for worse, you cannot shut yourself away from life. I think you will find that is true, the longer you are out in the world among us."

I did not want to argue religion with him. I was still stunned by the suddenness of my fate coming upon me. When he saw that I would not speak, William turned toward the door. Marie Helene had come for me.

"Your waiting woman is here," he said. "I will leave you. But know this, my lady. You have nothing to fear from me, now or ever."

He spoke as if taking a solemn vow. I nodded once, as if accepting his fealty.

Then the boy was gone, and Marie Helene was beside me, holding me up. Without her hand under my arm, I did not know if I would have been able to stand.

"My lady. Come away. We can't have you standing in the middle of the court of France wearing that linen gown."

• • •

My brother's women entered my chamber laden with gowns in silk and brocade, and soft linen shifts to go under them. I had just dressed once more in the gown of a princess when the king's summons came.

The messenger led me alone down winding corridors to a room deep in the center of the palace. It was a smaller room, nothing as grand as the throne room where I had been before. I stood alone in my brother's bedchamber.

The bed was hung with heavy brocade drapery. Though the bed was different and stood along a different wall, I recognized the room as my father's.

I looked for the *prie dieu*, where Papa and I had prayed so many times, that God might send France a son. The *prie dieu* was gone and an embroidered screen stood in its place.

Phillipe sat at a table in the center of the room with wine beside him. A brazier burned at his elbow, for it was always cold in our stone palaces, even in spring. He read over a document, then signed it, before handing it to a waiting scribe. The boy bowed, a clerk little older than twelve summers. My brother watched him go, and then he turned to me.

"Sister, you are welcome to this place."

I curtsied but did not kneel. I waited, but in spite of his informal tone, he did not ask me to sit down.

He poured himself more wine but did not offer me any. I was surprised that he would think such things would offend me. I had been too long away.

I knew how little he thought of me. I had seen the man he had chosen to pledge me to for the rest of my life.

Phillipe watched me in silence.

"Brother," I said.

His back stiffened at this informal address. The king's power was based on the respect of others, including mine. And at court, the walls had ears.

I began again. "My lord king, will you not reconsider my fate?"

He smiled, and I saw a little of his charm, the same charm he had turned on the page who had just left us. I knew it for what it was, a false smile and false warmth. He often used it to gain his own ends with ease, and no doubt he thought he could do so with me.

As I looked at him, I saw nothing of my father in him. For an awful moment, I thought I might weep. But though my father had been good, he had not been strong. My brother made a better king.

Phillipe met my eyes, his hand still on his wine. He raised his glass to his lips and drank as if I were no more than a servant. My anger rose unbidden, my control threatening to slip even after so many years of discipline, yet I held my tongue.

"I do not hold your fate, sister. Only God does." His smile deepened then and I saw that he meant to mock me. He had heard of my religious convictions, and that my faith, like our father's, was a true one. Phillipe believed in nothing except himself.

"Is there no one else?" I asked. My voice was almost a whisper so that I would not forget myself and shout.

"The marriage contract is already signed."

I wanted to plead for my life, for my future. I wanted to ask for mercy, though I knew it was futile. My brother would simply mock me to my face for being a coward. Clearly, he already thought me a fool.

"He is half my age," I said. "Can you find no one more suitable? Surely our House has not come to this."

I closed my mouth to keep myself from saying anything more. Phillipe looked at me as if I were a problem he had long since solved. He did not reprimand me or send me from him. The lying charm fell away from his eyes. He set his goblet down.

"William of Ponthieu is good man and has served me well," Phillipe said. "He stood by me when few others did." My brother rose, and I saw that he would soon dismiss me. He had more important matters to attend to before he went into the great hall for the evening meal.

"His family is an old one, and his lands stand near the Vexin. He is young, but he will hold the land he has inherited. I will not have to watch my back while I am in the Levant, for he will defend it. Your marriage will seal that bargain, no matter how young he is."

I thought of Jean Pierre and the way his hand felt on mine. I remembered the peace I felt when I was with him. I remembered my youth and all the years since, lost in the prison of that English nunnery. I thought of all my years to come, given over into the keeping of a boy, when Jean Pierre loved me as I loved him.

I knew not to mention Jean Pierre. To do so would bring his death, or worse. My father's eyes stared out of Phillipe's face, but he did not know me any more than I knew him.

"I have given my life for France. Has She not had enough of me?"

I felt his hand on mine.

Phillipe's hand was warm but bore no calluses from riding or from war. His skin was as smooth as my own, but I felt the strength behind it. "The kingdom of France is not done with you. Not until you are in the grave, sister. And you know it."

"Yes," I said. "I know it."

I thought of our father then, and I was ashamed. My privileged life as a princess, eating when others starved, being cared for always, was bought at a price. This was the price. I had been born to make an alliance to serve the good of France. Though I was old and tired, I had not been released from the vow I had made years ago, kneeling at my father's feet. I would never be.

Phillipe left me then, and I stood alone as the last of day faded into shadow. His page came back in and stopped short, surprised to find me still there. He called at once for a footman to lead me back to my borrowed room.

Though I wished to be gone from that place,

I waited until the man came to fetch me. I had thought of this palace as my home throughout the many years of my exile, but I could not find my path through the maze of corridors on my own. I had been so long away.

6

A WEDDING

My wedding day dawned bright with no hint of clouds. From my window above the city, I watched the people as they carried their wares, some to the market, others to the riverside. I wondered what it was like to be free.

I thought of Jean Pierre, and whether I might send word to him without my brother knowing. I remembered the only letter I had ever written, the ill-fated letter to my father, pleading with him to push for my marriage to Richard.

That letter had brought about my ruin and sealed my fate. Eleanor had intercepted it, and Henry had taken me as a lover the next day, ruining my marriage and the treaty bound to it. I had learned a hard lesson. Any letter I wrote for Jean Pierre would be taken directly to my brother.

Marie Helene kissed me and brought me a glass of my favorite wine.

"You must dress, Your Highness. The wedding is in an hour."

"Yes. I know it."

My gown was the best of the new clothes brought to me by my brother's women, a dark blue silk that set off the darkness of my unfaded hair. Phillipe had sent sapphires from the treasury, so that I would not be without jewels on my wedding day.

Marie Helene dressed my hair with gold and sapphires. When I looked at myself in the silver mirror that was part of my dowry, I saw another woman reflected back at me.

We walked together in silence to the chapel near my father's rooms. Marie Helene was the only woman who walked with me. My dishonor lived still in the minds of my brother's courtiers. None were there to watch me swear my oath with the Count of Ponthieu.

There were still songs sung of me, of how my beauty had conquered a king. But no one in my brother's court forgot that, though once I held a king, I had failed to keep him. And that failure was all that mattered.

The chapel had high stained-glass windows. The light that slanted in from the east made prisms of color along the stone floor. There were no witnesses but my brother, the priest, and Marie Helene.

There was no mass on my wedding day, no feast, and no guests. We skulked through the ceremony as if God Himself might not take notice of it.

I met my husband's eyes as he leaned over to

give me the kiss of peace. When his lips touched mine, I caught the scent of rosewood. I wondered if my brother had given him that perfume.

His eyes were clear as he drew back from me, and there was no pretense in them. Perhaps he shared my horror at this clandestine wedding, at the fact that my brother was so ashamed of me that he did not have me married properly, with guests and celebrations, but as an afterthought, before he rode to war.

None of these thoughts showed on my face, for I had sworn never to show weakness in front of my brother again. Phillipe seemed to admire this. He smiled at me as we turned to face him in the shadows of that chapel once our oaths were taken.

My husband and I moved as one, kneeling before my brother. I did not look at William, but knew that he would speak for us both, as was his right from that day forward.

"We swear fealty to you, my lord king. Know that you have staunch allies in us. You may turn your back on Ponthieu, for we will always guard it."

I kept my eyes modestly lowered, as a good wife should. But his steady voice soothed me, as did his strong arm under my hand. Whatever would be between us in the future, in that moment, his strength gave me comfort.

"I accept the renewal of your vow. Now rise and give us the kiss of peace."

William rose first, then helped me to stand. He turned from me and embraced my brother.

My husband clung to the king. I saw the truth of their relationship in that moment but did not let it trouble me. The king had many lovers. That my husband had been among them should not have surprised me.

They held each other longer than was seemly, but no one else was there to see it. The priest had already withdrawn behind a screen. He had more important duties to attend to, a mass to perform for all the court in less than half an hour.

Phillipe released my husband and turned to me. I offered my lips in the formal kiss of peace. Phillipe kissed my forehead instead, as if he were the elder, offering me a blessing in my father's stead.

"Peace be with you, sister, now and always."

"And with you."

I was careful to keep the irony out of my voice. All the court knew that he left within the month to take ship for the Levant. Phillipe and Richard were to journey there with Leopold of Austria. As brother kings in Christ, they were to take back the city of Jerusalem from those who held it.

Phillipe held us both with his eyes for one moment more, and then he left us without another word. If he had not been king, I would have thought his leave-taking abrupt. As it was, he had more to concern him than the likes of us.

I turned to my husband, certain that he knew what we were to do next, where we were to go. But William did not look at me. His eyes did not leave the king.

Phillipe's stride was purposeful and steady, the stride of a man who had seen an onerous task done. He walked out of the chapel, his cloak swirling behind him. He did not look back.

I saw pain in William's eyes that he was too young to mask. Love for my brother lingered there, and the sharpness of loss. I took my husband's hand.

For the first time that day, William looked as young as his twenty years. He was unmoored; my brother had cut him adrift. I saw then that Phillipe had not witnessed our wedding for my sake, but for his. William did not know where to turn, naked need still visible in his eyes.

I took a step closer. Whatever came between us after, in that moment, he could turn to me. "Where do we go now, my lord husband?"

My voice seemed to draw him back, to where he was and what we were doing there. The strength came back into his eyes, as well as gratitude. William lifted my hand and kissed it, his lips lingering not in desire, but in fealty. "Home, my lady. We are going home."

I did not tell him that his home was not mine. I had no home on Earth save the love I had just found in Jean Pierre's eyes. But I smiled and let my husband kiss my hand.

William's lips still lingered on my skin when Jean Pierre entered the chapel. He had run up the stairs from the courtyard below. We were in the high chapel, where only courtiers could come.

Jean Pierre stopped his stride, breathless. He

looked only at my face, seeing nothing else. "You are married, then?"

The silence that followed was so thick that I thought it would smother me. The stones of the chapel floor were cold under my felt shoes. The light from the high windows struck Jean Pierre's face.

William took in Jean Pierre with one glance. He saw more than he ever spoke of. Only minutes after we had bound ourselves one to another until death, William stepped away from me and offered his arm to Marie Helene.

She moved away with him, keeping her eyes from my face. They went together to the altar, where they looked at the fine glass above the golden cross. I kept my eyes on Jean Pierre.

"You are married." This time he did not ask the question.

"I am."

He swayed, but then drew himself up straight. He spoke as if he could not stop the words from flowing from him, as he could not stop his heart's blood from painting the stones at our feet. "I tried to get an audience with the king. I would have asked for your hand. I would have given anything- "

"It is already done."

He reached out to me but drew his hand back at once, as if I were a fire that would burn. Touch was something we could no longer permit ourselves.

William came back to my side, as if he knew I needed him. He took my hand and let me lean on him. He met Jean Pierre's eyes. The man I loved faced my husband without flinching.

"You are always welcome in our home," my husband said.

It was all I could do to stand my ground, even with my husband's hand on mine. But William's words stayed with me.

I remembered them later when I was alone. When I finally understood them, I knew what our marriage would be.

Jean Pierre said nothing but bowed low. He would never permit himself to put one foot on my husband's lands, much less break bread at his table, or sleep under his roof.

I met Jean Pierre's eyes, saw his honor reflected there and his devotion to his duty.

I saw his love for me written on his face as Scripture on a page of vellum. I prayed to the Holy Mother that he saw mine. Jean Pierre bowed his head so that he would not have to watch us walk away.

I looked for him as I stood by the river. I did not board my husband's barge, though all our baggage had been loaded. Only when the tide was turning did I take my husband's hand.

I stood at the edge of the barge and looked back at the palace. My brother did not come down to see us off, nor any of his people. But at the last, with the sun high above my head, I finally saw Jean Pierre on the river's edge, staring back at me.

He did not wave, nor did I. We watched

each other across that distance, and I wondered if we would ever see each other again. He would leave for the Holy Land, for the war my brother waged there. In that place, an infidel's sword might cut him down and end his line forever. He was the last of his father's family, him and one lone sister who I now would never meet.

As I looked across the wide water, I prayed to the Holy Mother that Jean Pierre might be kept safe. That She might take him into Her Hand and protect him when he was far from me.

I hoped he knew that I prayed for him though, as a man of action, he thought little of prayer. Jean Pierre raised his hand just as we came to a bend in the river.

My hand went up in answer, but the river had turned, and the current carried us away from him. The men-at-arms were staring. William took my raised hand and led me away.

He helped me to a chair bolted to the deck under an awning. I sat alone, my heart bleeding. I had lived long enough to know that though my wound pained me, I would live to bleed longer. Marie Helene came to sit on one side of me and William on the other. I roused myself from my pain to look about me, to see the boat that carried me into my future.

My husband's barge was more luxuriously appointed than the one my brother had sent for me. The cushions were new and deep, the wood of the chairs and the railings polished to a high gloss. Fruit and bread had been set out, along with my favorite wine from Anjou.

William spoke to me, his voice low, his own pain pushed to one side. He made polite comments about the beauty of the day and the freshness of the food. He poured the wine himself, though he did not taste it.

I knew that I must rouse myself. I was no lady in a song of love, to lie pining for the man I would never see again. I was a princess of France, and I had struck a bargain both with William and with God. For the rest of my life, I would honor it.

I raised a grape to my lips and ate it, so that William would know that I valued all he had done for me. He smiled to see me eat. My husband said nothing of all that had passed in my brother's chapel, nor of what he had seen by the riverside. He spoke evenly, calmly, as if it were any other day, as if both he and I had not had our hearts ripped out and left on the quayside behind us.

"I will leave you now. If you have need of anything, ring this bell, and my man will see to your comfort."

William raised one hand and a man of forty stepped forward and bowed as low to me as if I were a queen. I forced myself to be gracious. At my nod, he retreated into the shadows cast by the silk-lined hangings above our heads.

I was surprised to see William command men so much older than himself. As if I were reading his thoughts in a book, I saw that he had much to say to me. It would wait until we were alone, with the bedroom door closed behind us.

As he kissed my hand, his lips lingered. I

wondered if he had not touched me before because he had not wanted to take a liberty.

When William rose once more to his full height, I could no longer read his eyes. He left us with my favorite wine and pears set down between us and went to speak to the captain of his ship.

William checked the trunks my dowry was stowed in, to see to it that they were well secured. My new gowns had been packed as soon as they were shown to me and placed in trunks along with bolts of fine cloth and jewels.

It was strange to see my husband's standard flying over our heads. I had grown so used to seeing my father's *fleur de lys*, and the lions of Henry Plantagenet, that I had come to think of them as the only standards in the world.

The men on that barge wore my husband's colors of red and gold. Though a boy, William had power enough to command an army.

His men-at-arms and their families had served the House of Bellême time out of mind. I had always thought my family the oldest, the one to inspire loyalty – indeed, the only family worth serving. The House of Bellême had just as long a lineage, and as much pride, as the royal House of France.

We spent our wedding night in a monastery outside of Rouen. It was a small house, endowed by William's great-grandfather. The monks were solicitous, and happy to see us. We dined on mutton and fresh greens from the garden. I was surprised when William ate his vegetables with such relish. At court, such things were cooked to a pulp, if they were ever eaten at all.

"I am open to new things," he said.

We dined alone, for Marie Helene had been given her own room. She helped me take off my jewels and brushed out my hair, laying my brother's sapphires in their casket, locking it carefully.

"I wonder if I must send them back," I said.

"No." William spoke as he stepped into the room. "They are yours now."

Marie Helene left us. Her hand lingered on mine. I saw the knowledge of my pain there, a mirror of her own. A man I had known for a few days was not a sorrow to rival the loss of a much beloved husband. I pressed her hand once before she drew it away.

The door closed behind her. I stood by the bed wearing only my linen shift and a thin shawl. I saw hunger in my husband's eyes. But William turned from me at once and spoke of the food he had ordered for our dinner. I wondered if I had deceived myself. God help him, I was old enough to be his mother.

Though I sat across from him in the firelight all evening, he did not look at me again. In addition to my pain over the loss of Jean Pierre, I felt my age for the first time in my life. I wondered how I would be able to bear a marriage with a man so much younger than myself. I reminded myself that ours was a political alliance and to set aside my vanity.

When our food was taken away, we lingered

over our wine. I looked toward the marriage bed, but my pride would never allow me to ask him whether he would share it. Perhaps our marriage was to be one of convenience only, though surely a man as young as he was wanted children.

A tide of shame rose in me. I was so old, who knew if I could still breed? The shadow of my age haunted me. For the first time, I thought what our marriage might mean to this boy, and the future of his House.

"Alais, come here."

It was the first time William ever used my given name. I sat with him on the great bed that the abbot had blessed for us. We both knew our duty, whatever our personal feelings. We must lie together at least once and bind our alliance in truth.

I waited for him to touch me, as Henry once had done. All thoughts of Jean Pierre, I pushed to the back of my mind, where I could lock them away. I prayed to the Holy Mother to help me with this, and She answered.

She took pity on me, for my pain lifted. All I could smell was the dust from the fading tapestries in that tiny room. The scent of the roses in John's tent faded, as did the memory of the night I had spent holding Jean Pierre's hand.

William took my hand in his and turned it over so that he could look onto my palm. He stared at it so long that I thought to make a joke that he had turned gypsy and wished to tell my fortune. When he met my eyes, the pain I saw there took my breath away.

"Alais," he said again. "Lady. We have wronged you."

I felt a touch of hope. I thought of Jean Pierre, and of how I might send word to him. "The priest was a fake," I said.

William laughed, the shadows chased from his eyes for the space of a breath.

"No, my lady. The priest was real. It is I who am false."

I schooled my face to blankness and reined in my thoughts.

"Lady, I am a man with a taste for other men."

I knew this already. He and my brother had been lovers. William loved my brother still. I wondered why he was telling me this.

"I see that you understand me." William cradled my hand in his, as if it were made of spun glass, as if it and I might both break if he breathed too heavily.

"You prefer the company of men," I said.

"Yes."

I had seen the light of lust in his eyes when he first came into the room, when he found me in my shift and little else. I was old, but my body was still slim, my breasts high and my thighs firm, for I had only been brought to childbed once. I had seen desire his eyes before he damped it down and turned away.

I knew in that moment why my brother had joined us in marriage. I was too old to bear children and this boy had no inclination to father any. My brother wanted the boy's line to die out for some reason.

"William."

He flinched at the use of his given name, but his hand tightened on mine.

"I have done much in my life that I am not proud of. I was forced to things in my youth that I would never have done in good conscience."

He flinched as I spoke of Henry, even in this oblique way. But I knew that if I did not speak of it now, I never would. Some things needed to be said before we went on.

"I will never judge you, in this life or the next. Your soul is between you and God."

"So, you think I am damned then?"

I heard youth in his voice for the first time, and I grasped his hand in both of mine. "You are not damned. No more than any one of us. We are all sinners before God. We are all outside His Grace."

William kissed me, his lips warm and soft on mine. I felt his breath catch in his throat. I wondered what man had been able to convince this boy that he could look only to men for pleasure.

"I cannot love you, even once" he said. "It would be a lie, a promise of something that I cannot give."

His hand was warm on mine. I felt my new life receding from me, the life I had sworn to live. A lady who kept to her place at her husband's side out of duty, but whose duty was fulfilled. If we never consummated the marriage, it could easily be overthrown.

I thought of the blue of Jean Pierre's eyes. I remembered the warmth of his hand on mine.

He would have married me and kept me safe. I had thought when I wed this boy that I would be beyond my brother's reach for the rest of my life. I saw now that this hope was just one more illusion, like all the rest. I would have cursed fate, my brother, and William, but I had lived too long. I knew what came of cursing and of bitterness. Eleanor had taught me that.

I rose and stood close to the lamp, so that William might see my face and know that I was not lying. "Husband, I have sworn that your honor is mine. And so it is, until my death. I am strong enough for this. Believe me when I say that I have faced worse."

William knelt at my feet and hid his face in the folds of my shift. I caressed his golden hair and let him weep. His truth weighed heavily on him, and now he could lay that burden down.

I looked into the fire as I held my young husband. I thought of the look on my brother's face as he had left us in the chapel. He had known what he was leaving me to.

7

ALL THAT IS LOST

WILLIAM DID NOT SLEEP IN MY BED THAT NIGHT but, despite my entreaties, curled up in his cloak and slept on the floor like a dog.

He was gone when I woke at dawn and Marie Helene came to rouse me. "My lady, I have something to confound them."

I saw the bladder of pig's blood hidden under her cloak, and I laughed.

"Lady," she hissed. "Be still. The monks will hear."

I stifled my laughter with difficulty and helped her to spread a little false blood on the cold sheets of my marriage bed. Marie Helene had expected the sheets to be mussed, and my husband's bolster to have been dented with the weight of his head.

She saw in a moment that I had spent the night alone. I could not speak of it, even to her. She knew me well, even after all those years, and did not question me.

"They will think me a virgin indeed," I said.

Marie Helene hid the bladder of pig's blood the moment before the monks' servant came in with wash water and my breakfast.

"Your husband says that he would like to show you the cathedral in the city, before he takes you home."

Her accent was thick, not the court French I was used to, but I managed to understand her. "Give my husband my thanks. I will not be long."

The door closed behind her after she had taken one long look at my newly soiled sheets. My reputation had preceded me, even in this place, for her eyes widened before she went away.

"Let her spread that tale," Marie Helene said. "Let them make songs about that."

I looked at those sheets, another lie that my life was built on. Then I turned away. Marie Helene already had buttered bread for us, and a slice of pear rested on the tip of her knife.

We rode in a litter into the city of Rouen. I had little use for cities outside of Paris, but the town was built all of stone, close to the riverside. I kept the curtains of my litter closed until we stopped in front of the cathedral. To my eyes, it could not compare to the churches of Paris, but even I could see that it was beautiful.

I climbed from my litter without waiting for my husband's man to hand me out. William was off his horse and at my side in a moment. His true strength shone clear from his eyes when he met my gaze without flinching.

"My lady, I thought you might like to see the church before we journey home."

"Thank you, husband. That is kind."

Beyond the pain in my voice, he heard that I had agreed to go along with the farce of our marriage without complaint. I put my pain aside and kissed his cheek.

I stepped into the church alone.

The shrine to the Holy Mother shown with candles in its alcove, set back from the long aisle. I left the sunlit day behind me. I lit a candle for my daughter, as I did every day, and at every shrine for the Virgin I ever came to.

I knelt before the Holy Mother and it seemed I felt the warmth of my daughter's presence with me as I prayed. I lay my pain before Her, and my loss of Jean Pierre, and the futility of my marriage.

The longer I knelt there, the more I began to feel that I was not alone. Indeed, it was not just the memory of my daughter who had come to comfort me. I heard footsteps behind me, the slow and thoughtful tread I remembered well.

As I crossed myself, his voice spoke to me as from a dream half-forgotten. It was as if my thoughts had conjured him, as if my prayers had made him rise from the very stones of that old church.

"You still pray for her," he said.

"Every day."

I rose to my feet and turned to face him. Though it had been almost twenty years since I had seen him, he still looked the same to me. His hair glinted red where the sunlight touched it from the windows high above our heads. His eyes were as blue as they once had been, and their fathoms as deep, too deep for me to see my way to the bottom of his thoughts. He held himself as he always had, controlled and kingly. He had been born to be a king, as the rest of his brothers had not.

"Richard," I said. "You are welcome to this place."

I was well rewarded for my audacity, for he smiled at me. Though he was forty now, his smile was as sweet as it had been the day we met, when I was a girl of fourteen. After all the time that had passed, I wished he reserved that smile just for me.

"I am glad to see you, Alais. Your brother mentioned that you were traveling through Rouen. I had hoped to see you before I went away."

We had both been raised to control our emotions, and their expression. But the warmth of his eyes held a shadow of his old love for me. That sweet warmth brought me comfort, though I knew we would never speak of it.

"You are for the Levant and Jerusalem," I said.

"God willing. Jerusalem will have to be won."

"If it can be done, you will do it."

I spoke with faith, but I spoke the simple truth. He frowned at first, thinking perhaps that

I flattered him, as many had done all his life, and as even more did now that he was king.

I simply stood and looked at him, memorizing his face, though his was a face I would never forget, even on my death bed. Something of those we love remains with us after they are gone. So it has always been for me.

Richard seemed to see something of my love for him in my eyes. He smiled at me, his frown melting away as if it had never been. "You forgive me then."

"For what, Richard?"

"For dismissing you before the whole of Europe, Alais. Surely even locked away in your nunnery, you heard of that."

I looked to see if he was mocking me, but he stood sober, his smile gone. I reached out to touch him but stopped myself. My gloved hand hovered between us until I thought Richard might reach out and take it in his own. He did not. Finally, I lowered my hand to my side. "There is nothing to forgive."

"It was policy, Alais. I would never--"

"You would never freely choose to shame me before the whole of Europe, no matter what I've done. Richard, the pain between us is past, buried long ago. I have made my peace with it. Please do not think on it again, not for my sake."

Tears had come into his eyes. He could not speak, so I took it on myself to speak for him.

"It is good to see you again, Richard. I hope God guides your steps in the Holy Land."

"And my sword," he said, trying to regain control of his features. I watched his battle with himself and, as always, he won. Henry never had. Though Richard would not make as good a king as his father, he was a better man.

"God guide you in all things." I raised my hand, this time in blessing. Tears rose in my own eyes.

He saw them, and they were his undoing. Richard turned away from me. I saw him hesitate before he went. He had to fight himself again to keep from touching me. I felt his pain from where I stood, and I wished I could take it on myself and shield him. He was bound for Cyprus before he went to the Levant. There he would meet the princess from Navarre whom he had chosen to marry. Always, policy ruled the life of a king.

He walked away from me, then stopped, framed in the wide doorway of the church. Eleanor stepped into the light from beyond the door. I watched as she took his hand. Richard seemed to take comfort from her touch. She could help him as I could not. He turned then and looked back at me. I hoped he could see my face in the gathering gloom, that he was not alone in his pain, that I loved him too.

Richard left me then for the last time, stepping out into the bright sunshine of that spring day. Eleanor stood in his place for a long while, but she did not smile at me in triumph. Even from that distance, I saw that she was full of sorrow and of the knowledge of all that had been lost between us. Perhaps the presence of her son's living pain touched her as it always had, as my pain did not.

Eleanor raised her hand to me. It was the last time I ever saw her. Her white hair had begun to come loose from her hood, and the sunlight struck it, so that it shone like electrum in the shadow of the doorway. We stood for a long moment, simply looking at one another before she walked away.

I felt her going as keenly as I did her son's. The silence of the church folded around me, as final as the grave my daughter lay in. I stood in the gloom of that church, the candle I had lit for my daughter flickering on the altar beside me.

My husband was at my elbow. He stepped up in silence. I had not even heard him come into the church. I did not turn to him but stared past the doorway, to the sunlight that waited beyond. I wondered how long I would have to stand there before I could be certain that Eleanor and Richard had gone.

William stood quiet beside me. I thought for a moment that he would not speak, that he would respect my sorrow as I had respected his pain the night before.

"You love him," he said.

I did not seek to shield him as I might have done. He had not asked about Jean Pierre, and I knew he never would. But to love a prince was a different thing, and I had loved Richard longer than this boy had been alive. I could lie about many things in the name of duty, but I would not lie about this.

"I will always love him." My words hung between us, cradled by the silence that followed.

No monks came to tend the altars, no priests

99

came to hear confessions. No one entered the cathedral from the front door. We stood alone. For the first time while in a church, I could not feel the presence of God. In that moment of inner darkness, my husband reached out and took my hand.

"I loved once," he said simply.

Something in his solemn eyes gave me the urge to strike him. As young as he was, how could he possibly love as I had loved, carrying the weight of loss for so many years?

But then I remembered. I was fourteen when I first saw Richard. I had loved him then as I loved him now. I closed my mouth over any other words I might have said. "Let us leave this place. I am tired of the dark."

William tucked my hand into the crook of his arm. He led me out of that cathedral into the bright light of morning. It would soon be noon. We would ride on to his lands in Ponthieu. We had tarried long enough in Rouen.

Though a groom and our men-at-arms stood close, it was my husband who raised me to my saddle, as Henry once had done long ago. His hands lingered on my waist as he set me on my horse, and I thought there might be a quickening between us.

But his touch moved to my foot to check the length of the stirrup, and the moment was gone as if it had never been. I wondered why a man so young would turn from women so completely. I drew my mind away from that. I did not understand the thoughts of men, and I never would. He had respected my privacy. It was the least I could do to respect his.

We left Rouen as the morning burned away in the warmth of the noon sun. We did not speak, but rode close together, going slowly, for it had been twenty years since I had last ridden a horse, and my pace could not be fast. William reached across the distance that separated us and took my hand.

The leather of his glove covered the kidskin of mine. I was surprised to see how small my hand looked in his, and how protected I felt in that moment as he rode beside me.

8

IN MY HUSBAND'S HOUSE

I HAD NEVER HAD A HOME BEFORE, SAVE FOR MY father's palace when I was very small. Though the Abbey of St. Agnes had been comfortable, it had also been a sort of prison, and religious life eluded me, for all my earnest prayers. Perhaps I would make a home for myself among my husband's people.

As we rode into the sunlight of the afternoon, I saw that William's country was full of growing things. Trees towered over us like sentinels, whispering as we passed. Their varied shades of green called to me; I had never seen so fine a forest in England or anywhere.

William saw my love for his country in my eyes. He began to tell me of his lands at Bellême, how much the land yielded in a season, how his people were healthy and prosperous. He sounded like a country farmer speaking of his home, not like a count who had served my brother for years at court.

Though I knew little of farming and of the

daily care of the land, the life he painted with his words seemed peaceful and full of joy. Perhaps I had found a place to be free of the ties that bound me, a place where I might grow roses and learn once more to be content.

The forest yielded to vast fields of barley and wheat. Though it was early in the year, the land was covered with bright green grass that swayed in the wind. There were farmers in the fields, and they did not stop and kneel as they would have done had we been carrying my brother's standard. Instead, they waved and doffed their caps to my husband, who waved back as if they were his friends.

"We are coming closer to my lands here," he said. "The people have seen me ride through on my way to court. They know me."

We stopped to eat in a field that lay fallow. A tent had been set up to keep the sun off our heads, but three sides were raised so that the breeze would cool us as we ate.

Marie Helene sat at our table and dined with us as if she were family, for truly she was the only family I had left. This was another gesture that raised my husband in my esteem. I kissed his cheek before he went to fetch the horses, and he blushed as if he were a boy in truth.

We rode onto his lands just before the sun began to slant far into the west. William raised one gloved hand to shade his eyes and showed me the new crops that had been planted, a new strain of wheat from Flanders, one that never would have been tried while his father was alive.

"It may keep more children and old people

alive this winter," he said as he looked out across his fields.

I saw that he did not say this to gain favor with me but was simply speaking openly from his heart.

"God willing, my lord."

He quirked an eyebrow at me. His liking for God and the church was tenuous at best. "It is in His hands, is it not, lady?"

I smiled, knowing that he teased me. Despite the pious mutterings of many, few actually knew the grace of God. I had only glimpses, though I had sought it all my life. "Indeed, my lord. As we all are."

William turned from me then, and I changed the subject. "I would like to plant a garden of roses, if I might. The soil here looks to be good for all growing things, and I learned a great deal about roses in my last years at the abbey."

He was delighted to be able to offer me something within his power to grant. "You may have all the gardens you wish, my lady. I would indulge you in all things." He waved to his lands around us, as if offering them to me.

The sweetness of the gesture touched me and I took his hand. We were riding close together, for the track was narrow, though well laid.

Something shifted in his eyes when I touched him. The shadow passed over his face for a moment and then was gone. I had overstepped, but I could not be sorry for it. William took his hand away from me as we rode into his castle bailey.

The house at Bellême was stone, as all the Norman castles are, as all the castles of my childhood had been. His bailiff was a good steward, for the stones of the courtyard had been washed, and clean rushes laid down.

The servants of the keep stood in the courtyard as we rode in. The household was well run, for they had posted a look out, and had seen us coming.

I had never been mistress in my own house, though Mother Bernard had trained me to it as a child. I had learned how to run a household when it still looked as if I would be allowed a decent marriage, before Henry ever saw me. I hoped some of those lessons would come back to me.

As I greeted my husband's servants, I felt as if Mother Bernard stood by, approving my soft voice and calm gaze, traits she had often praised in me as a child. My husband's people curtsied to me, some awkwardly, some with grace. I could tell within a moment which worked in the buttery and which served at the high table on feast days.

One little girl offered me a bunch of handpicked wildflowers from the roadside. I bent low and gave her my hand. She smiled at me as Rose might have done had she lived, and the light of her smile followed me into my husband's house.

There were no speeches, for we had traveled far that day. Holding my hand in his, my husband said only, "My lady wife."

His people bowed to me, then rose and went about their business as we walked into the keep.

My husband's housekeeper greeted us in the great hall. She had been with the family many years, since before William was born. She smiled at him affectionately, and he took her in his arms, lifting her off her feet. "Maisie! You are a sight for sore eyes."

"Ah, you've been too long at court, my lord," she said.

Her piercing blue eyes took me in as he set her down. Despite her jovial smile, she missed nothing. I was glad I had worn a new gown from my dowry to honor my husband's house. Maisie curtsied with grace. "My lady, you are welcome. I trust you will find everything in order."

She was a little afraid of me and of the changes I brought to what had been her household. I admired that she fought so valiantly to hide her nerves. The gentle hand of Mother Bernard was on my arm as I smiled at her. I knew it would take weeks, if not months, to win her over.

"Thank you, Maisie. I have no doubt I will."

She led me through the main hall, with William trailing behind us over the rushes. I caught the scent of rosemary and cloves. The trestle table was well scrubbed, and the chairs by the fire were filled with plump embroidered cushions.

Maisie took me the long way to the staircase, so that I could see everything and know that she had nothing to hide. If I had asked her, she would have led me on a tour of the laundry and the buttery.

I would leave those things to her, but I wanted to ask about the kitchen garden. I would never feel at home until I had planted something myself.

She led us up the wooden staircase to the floor above the main hall. All the while, William followed behind us, saying nothing. I praised each room, each display of her housekeeping. Even Eleanor's household had not been run so well.

Maisie had saved the best room for last. She opened the great wooden door with a flourish and stood back to let me pass. I caught my breath, for it was the loveliest room I had ever seen.

The bedchamber's floor was a wide expanse of polished wood, stretched larger than any room I had ever slept in. The windows were set with glass through which the last light of the day shone.

On each wall, tapestries hung in brilliant blues, yellows and greens. Flowers and birds were worked in bright colors. A unicorn knelt in the center, close to a clear pond. It gazed at its own reflection, lowering its horn to the water to purify it.

I almost crossed myself at the sight, so beautiful was that work of art. I could feel the presence of Christ reflected in the image. The calm, clear eye of the beast looked out at us, as if to say that we had only to repent. We were forgiven already.

I drew my gaze from the tapestries and looked at the rest of the room. The last of the afternoon sunlight slanted across the floor. The windows faced south, letting in the sun both afternoon and morning. The soft light transformed the tapestries around us, until they seemed almost to come alive.

When I turned from the windows with their beveled glass and their view that led far down to the river, I saw the bed was draped in satin.

I had not seen such costly material since I was at Henry's court. I stepped forward to touch it, to see if it was real. The satin was soft, smooth under my hands as nothing else had ever been. I swallowed tears as I turned to my husband. William had outfitted this room as if a queen had come to live there.

Maisie saw my tears and slipped away. William and I stood alone in the light of the fading sun.

"These rooms were my mother's."

"They are beautiful. My lord, the expense-"

William raised one hand to silence me. I thought for a moment that he would extend his hand and touch my cheek. But he did not. His gloved hand stayed in the air between us.

"My lady, you honor our House. My mother, had she lived, would be pleased to have you here, among us." My husband lowered his arm. We stood looking at one another across what should have been my marriage bed.

Marie Helene came in, directing the servants with my trunks. "Place them there for now," she said, gesturing beneath my windows. "There should be enough light to unpack before sundown."

"I will send candles." William walked out of my bedroom and did not look back.

Marie Helene caught my eye and smiled at me, as if her smile might heal the sorrow I felt over my marriage. "Lady, your bathwater is boiling in the kitchen. I have not seen such a well-run household since the queen's. I did not even have to ask for it."

As she spoke, two women came in with a wooden tub draped in linens. Trailing them was a line of women carrying water in great urns. They set the bathtub between two braziers, then filled it. One woman offered to stay and attend me, but Marie Helene sent her away.

"It is good to be in a civilized country again, is it not, my lady?"

Marie Helene knew me well, even after all the time that had passed. England had always seemed a wild country, a place apart. Truly, I was glad to be home.

We kept silent after that, as she left me to my own thoughts and slipped into her own. The day since my marriage had brought a new home and a great deal of pain. My husband honored me but wanted nothing further from me. I bled for what might have been with Jean Pierre. And I had seen Richard for the last time. Marie Helene was the only woman left alive, save Eleanor, who knew what that had cost me.

Marie Helene stayed silent, her hands gentle on my hair, for indeed, there was nothing left to say.

9

JEAN PIERRE

THOUGH MY HUSBAND NEVER TOUCHED ME BUT
to take my hand to lead me into dinner, I found
his home a welcoming place. The house had
been without a mistress since his mother died
three years before. But Maisie had run it
beautifully ever since, so there was little for me
to do but to sit in the sun and smell the green
things growing in the garden. I would sit, taking
in the sight of the river as it wound round its
bend, down the hill from the castle keep.

Each day was peaceful in its simplicity.
William knew I did not like to hunt, so he never
invited me to ride out with him and his men. He
was an avid hunter and came back with venison
and boar from the forests. His lands were vast,
but I had no interest in exploring them.

In those first days in my husband's house, I
waited to see what might come next. So much
change had come upon me so suddenly that now
I waited for it to show its face again.

But as the month of May passed, and June

came to us with its afternoon rains and its sunny mornings, I began to trust that I was where I would always be. No force would come from the court to tear me away from that place and from the peace I had found there.

I began to take more interest in the running of the household. Maisie took my suggestions easily, sometimes even gratefully. I did little to change the way she ran things, but she took confidence from my interest. She carried herself with more authority. It gave her pleasure to say, whenever she ordered a task done, "As my lady would wish it."

Marie Helene would smile, offering no suggestions, though she had run a great house for over twenty years. She was retired now, she told me, and would not lift a finger in this life again except in my service.

As time passed, the sorrow in her eyes lifted. My husband's country soothed her as much as our renewed friendship. The land all about us seemed to have been left under an enchantment, as if such things as armies and courtly love, warfare and strife had never been seen or heard of there.

I knew this to be false. My father had fought battles nearby to keep the Vexin from the English. After his death, my brother had fought again to defend what was left of my honor.

But all evidence of such warfare was gone as if it had never been. Fields of grain and flowers grew on land armies had once ravaged. I went walking in those fields alone one morning when Marie Helene was too tired to rise from her bed.

As I walked, I was grateful for the silence and the rising wind. The wind in my face always made me feel free, as if I were on the sea or flying, as I sometimes did in dreams. This sense of freedom was an illusion, but after my life of sacrifice, I had come to cherish my illusions as the children I would never have.

The sun had come up over the trees beyond the river, and I stopped to look out over the water. It was at least twenty feet to the other side, and the land beyond the river belonged to my husband as well.

By the river grew irises and daisies, the same flowers that had flourished long ago by the river near Windsor. Henry had woven me a crown of flowers and placed it on my head. I stood with my memories, looking out over the river, when Jean Pierre came to me.

"My Lady Alais."

The sound of wind and moving water had concealed his footsteps as he crossed my husband's lands to stand beside me. I knew this, but in that first moment, I felt as if the Virgin had opened Her Hand and given him back to me. His horse stood close by, munching grass.

We looked at each other, the sunlight burnishing the gold and copper of his hair. His eyes were a cerulean blue. It had been only two months, but already his eyes were a deeper blue than I remembered.

"Jean Pierre," I said.

He knelt in the grass before me and took my hand. I looked down at his bared head. His hair covered his face in a curtain of gold. He clutched my hand as if he were drowning.

I knelt beside him, and his arms came around me, all thought for my marriage forgotten. I clung to him, and he to me, in silence, except for the wind and the water that moved beside us and around us, with no thought for us or our pain.

We did not move for a long time. It was he who remembered himself first. He rose to his feet and drew me with him. He would have stepped back and let me go, but I still clung to him.

"My lady," he said. "I left my men at the village one mile hence. I am leaving for the Levant, and I could not go without seeing you again."

"Come to the house," I said. "My husband is kind and will welcome both you and your men."

"No." His face was as dark as if I had asked him to step into Hell. "I cannot linger. I should not be here now."

There were many things I wanted to say to him, things that now could make no difference. When I spoke, I meant my words as a blessing, but they sounded hollow in my ears.

"God be with you when you go to war. My prayers will be with you, always, wherever you are."

Jean Pierre held me, but he would not let me come too near. He breathed in the scent of my hair once, then set me back from him. I saw in his face that my nearness pained him, so I did not cling to him again.

We stared at each other, his hands on my arms. I did not come close to him again, but I could not take my eyes from his face.

"I have heard a rumor at court that your husband cannot love you," he said.

"For once, the rumor is true."

A muscle leaped in his jaw. In that moment, if my brother had been standing there, Jean Pierre would have taken the sword he wore and run him through. He breathed deeply, his hands flexing on my arms. Even in his fury, he was careful not to bruise me.

"I have sworn to go on Crusade with your brother, the King." On the last word, he looked as if he would spit, as if he tasted something vile. But something in his tone gave me hope for the first time since my benighted marriage. I watched his face as he spoke again. "If I live, I will come back to you."

We stood in the tall grass beside the river on my husband's land, the sun rising behind us. I took in the blue of his eyes and the curve of his cheek and felt for the last time the strength of his hands on my arms.

"Do you understand me?" he asked.

"Yes," I said. Tears were rising in my eyes, though I had long since trained myself not to weep – they rose despite my training, despite all my hard years of self-denial. My longing for him rose in my throat, and I closed my lips so that I would not speak of it.

Jean Pierre bent his head and kissed me once, fiercely, so that I would remember. "I will come back for you. But do not wait for me. I want you to be happy."

I did not tell him that I did not know what simple happiness was. I had only begun to know it for the first time in my life while in his presence. I had known love and lust and loss, but what lay between us was something new, something pure, as pure as my first love for Richard. Our parting was hard enough for him, without proof of my pain added to it. I did not speak the words that rose to my lips but swallowed them. I spoke others instead. "I will do my best to be happy."

He saw my tears, and they were almost his undoing. He drew me close once more, though it pained him to offer me comfort. I clung to him, and his arms closed safe around me, shutting out the world for the space of a breath. But the world cannot be shut out. Like the wind and the river, it moves on, and we must move with it.

"Give me a token, something to take with me when I go."

I had heard of such things. I had even seen it done once or twice at Eleanor's court, where the art of courtly love had been honored above all things, even God.

I had nothing about me except the kerchief I kept always in my sleeve. It bore the queen's crest, Eleanor's coat of arms.

I pressed the soft linen into his palm. He wiped away my tears with it. Then his lips were on mine. He tasted me once, a temptation he could not turn from. But I felt his reluctance even before he pulled away from me. He would not force me to break my wedding vows when he could not stay.

I could taste his love for me on his tongue. I had nothing else to give him. Only my lips for half a moment, and that bit of cloth, and even it belonged to another. It did not even bear my crest.

Jean Pierre drew back and looked down at me, as if to memorize my face, as I had once tried to memorize Richard's.

"I love you," he said.

"And I love you." I did not weep again, knowing it would be years, or never, before I saw him again. I did not want his last sight of my face to be of me weeping.

He smiled at me. "Your love will be a light in dark places." Jean Pierre moved to leave, but his hands refused to let go of my arms. He kissed me once more on my forehead. His lips were light, like the touch of a feather against my skin. "Stand here until I go. I want to remember you this way, with the sun behind you, shining on your hair."

I said nothing more, but stood still, just as he bid me. He looked at me one last time, took in his fill, then turned away. He walked away from me, the sunlight turning his hair to burning gold. He did not look back.

I watched him move to his horse, tethered by the riverside. He rose onto its back in one fluid motion, then turned and raised his hand to me.

I waved to him, as if he were going only for that one day. I watched him ride away, his body moving with his horse as if they were one flesh.

He was gone from my sight too quickly, and I was left by that river alone.

But I was not alone. Even then, I felt the Hand of the Holy Mother on my arm, keeping me from despair. I had promised him that I would be happy. I wondered what that word truly meant, and if I could ever learn the skill of daily joy.

I knelt in the tall grasses, the sun rising above my head. I felt the Holy Mother's hand on me as I prayed for Jean Pierre. I asked the Mother to lay Her hand on him, to protect him when he was far from me.

I stayed kneeling, the wind in my hair, the sun shining down on me. That was where Marie Helene found me. She had heard from my husband's men that Jean Pierre had asked for safe passage onto William's lands. He had not come up to the castle keep.

She said nothing but offered her hand to help me rise, then led me back to my husband's house. I leaned on her for the first few steps, but soon stood alone. I was strong enough to support my own weight.

I went straight into the chapel, where I stayed on my knees. I did not come to the great hall for the evening meal, but prayed for my father, for my daughter, for Eleanor and Richard, for Henry, and most of all, for Jean Pierre.

I was alone after Vespers. The priest had gone to tend other matters behind the arras that led to his private rooms. Still I stayed, after the songs were silenced. It was there on my knees that William found me.

"You are praying again," my husband said.

I raised my head but did not rise when he spoke. My knees burned like fire beneath me, in spite of the cushion I knelt on. Marie Helene had been kind enough to bring it that morning and, after an hour, when she saw that I meant to stay, she left me and went away.

She came back to fetch me every hour, and every hour she saw the look on my face and went away again. She knew me well. Nothing short of the Second Coming of Our Lord would move me.

I faced my husband, pausing in my prayers, for I was tired. I knew that the mortification of the flesh was not to appeal to God, for He had no use for my pain. It was to appeal to me, to remind myself of the suffering of Our Lord, to remind myself that even now, alone, with all my dead gone from me, my suffering was not in vain. Our Lord had walked there first.

I met William's eyes. He stared down at me, and for once he did not smile. He was not a religious man and like most at court, he did not understand religious feeling in others. All our lives, the knowledge of God's love was a gulf between us, a gulf we never bridged. We had many other things in common, but never that.

"You must not stay here," he said. "I did not marry you so that you could go on being a nun."

I raised one eyebrow. He had the courtesy to blush, but he did not turn away.

"I am here praying for the souls of the dead," I said.

"You are among the living, lady. You need to have a care for them." He offered his hand to me, and I took it.

I let him raise me up. He had to catch me, for my feet and legs were numb and would not hold me. He half carried me, supporting all my weight, as I regained my balance. The pain was worse once I was standing, and I welcomed it.

William saw this in my face, and his eyes darkened, even in the candlelight of that dark chapel.

There was a step leading to the stone altar. William helped me sit on it, then knelt at my feet. He drew my shoes from me and massaged my feet and calves until the fire of my pain was so strong that I thought I would lose my breath. Still, he did not stop until the pain receded and the blood flowed unobstructed once more.

"It is foolish to do such things," he said. "It is dangerous. You could hurt yourself with too much praying, Alais. Your blood must flow properly. You no longer have just yourself to think of."

I did not look away from him, nor did I speak.

He sat down beside me and took my hand. "I know that Jean Pierre of Valois was here this morning."

"All the keep knows of it, my lord."

"Is this why you kneel and hurt yourself on this stone floor? Out of guilt?"

I did not answer.

"Lady, I may be young, but I know a little more of the world than you. Trust me when I say, you have nothing to feel guilty for."

Tears rose in my eyes. I blinked to hide them, but he saw them anyway, and his voice softened. He caressed my hand. "Alais, I know you love him. There is no shame in that."

I turned my face away, but William turned me back, so that he could meet my eyes. "You knew nothing of me when you met him. We do not choose those we love. Love comes to us."

I saw that my brother still haunted my husband as he sat beside me in that stone church, holding my hand. His gaze turned inward, until he remembered me, and why he was there.

"You soul is in my keeping, now, Alais. For better or for worse, you are my wife. I would have it be for the better. I would have you be happy."

I sighed deeply and leaned my head against his chest. William was wise, despite his youth, and as I relaxed my guard, I offered a trust to him given to almost no one else.

His arms came around me. I wondered for the second time that day what happiness was, and whether I was worthy of it.

"No more long hours of prayer," he said.

I knew myself and knew that I could make him no promises. But I stayed silent, leaning against him. His arms stayed around me. I was tired and thought that I might sleep.

William drew me to my feet. When he found that I could stand, he did not let me go. "You must promise me, Alais. You must promise me that you will try to stay in the land of the living."

I met his eyes. Their blue depths stared back at me, unknowable.

"I promise to try."

He smiled at me. "That is something."

William carried me up the back staircase, the one that wound in a spiral to keep out invaders. He did not put me down until Marie Helene opened my bedroom door to him. He carried me past her, to my satin draped bed, and it was there he laid me.

"Good night, my lady. I will see you in the morning."

Something about his face, the youthful hope that lay there, quickened my heart. His hope shone on me, and I remembered a time when I was not hemmed in by sin and loss, when I too had been as young and as free from sorrow.

I took his hand before he could leave me. William bent down, as if I were his maiden aunt. I pressed my lips to his in thanks. He did not pull away.

His smile faded. "Good night, my lady." He bowed then and left me.

Marie Helene came out of the shadows and closed the door behind him. She did not ask questions but fed me a dinner of bread and cheese before I slept, still dressed in the gown I had worn that morning on my walk down by the river.

10

DUTY

"Alais, we will soon celebrate the Feast of the Assumption of Our Lady. Peasants and lords alike will flood our borders to rejoice with us."

I stared at William, my embroidery forgotten. I did not know what to say. It was clear he was not asking my permission but telling me of a plan he had laid down long ago. Perhaps it was a tradition there to honor the Holy Mother on that day.

"There will be dancing, and songs sung in your honor."

"There need be no songs for me," I said.

"Lady, I will sing the first of them myself."

William left my room as suddenly as he had come, and Marie Helene raised one eyebrow.

"Songs for you?" she asked. "And he will sing the first of them?" She was often silent, but I had forgotten that her sweet serenity and soft blonde hair hid a sardonic wit and a mind that missed nothing.

I laughed. It felt good to laugh for the first time since Jean Pierre had left me.

"I have no doubt his men will be dutiful and obey him in this. God knows what songs they can come up with, between now and the Feast Day."

On the first night of the festival, after spending the day in jousts and buying trinkets at the fair, the gentry and the nobles gathered in my husband's keep. We ate a meal of venison and suckling pig, with large displays of flowers from the garden on the trestle tables in the great hall.

I sat by William's side at the high table. A few couples from my brother's court sat with us, those too old to travel on Crusade with the king. But younger men took up the tables nearest us, just below the dais. At the end of the meal, as the fruit was brought out and passed among the company, my husband rose to his feet. A young man at the lower table stood with him, a lute in his hand.

The company seemed to know what to expect, as I did not. I was sipping my wine, watching the servers to see that the fruit was handed around with grace. When I turned back, I found not only my husband but everyone in the hall staring at me.

William bowed. "For my lady."

He took my hand in his and kissed it. Without letting go, William sang the sweetest song I had yet heard. It began with soft lines about the passing spring, and how it faded all too quickly into the heat of summer. The song then turned to the time of year when the heat of summer began to give way to the cooler breezes of autumn, while the last of the summer roses were still in bloom. William likened me to one of these. Even as his song faded, he drew out a deep red rose and offered it to me. I took it, tears rising in my eyes.

William bent down, and kissed my cheek, while the young men at the tables below us stamped their feet and shouted. I hid my face. William sat down beside me and took my hand in his, so that I could not hide. I sat, exposed to view, as three more young men stood to sing my praises. They sang just as sweetly, but none moved me to tears as my husband had.

After the singing was done, musicians began to play in earnest, and the lower tables were cleared away for the dancing. I rose, expecting my husband to lead me out in the first measure. Instead, William caught my hand, and gave it to another.

"My lady wife," he said. "I present Gerald of Anjou. He has been my companion-in-arms these many years. He has asked if you might favor him with the honor of a dance."

I hid my surprise. Though I was convent-raised, my first training had been at my father's hand. I smiled graciously at Gerald without seeing him. I saw only that he was an attractive young man, a little older than my husband, and that his smiled did not quite reach his eyes.

Gerald led me into the swirl of dancers, but not before I first saw William smile at a youth who came to sit beside him, in the chair opposite mine.

"My lady fair," Gerald said. "Your husband would have me cheer you. When you are sad, the whole party grieves with you."

I looked away from my husband, who now sat talking with a youth of fifteen. I listened to the laughter all around us, both at the high table and lower tables in the hall. I felt a searing pain, like a hot brand in my belly.

My longing for Jean Pierre was so strong in that moment, I thought the floor might open beneath me and swallow me whole. But it did not. I breathed deeply and made sure that I did not lose my place in the dance. I had found since coming to my husband's house that it was one thing to live alone in the confines of a nunnery, away from prying eyes and the poison of gossip, but quite another to stand alone among my husband's people, those I did not know, those who, despite their songs written to my fading beauty, did not know me.

As I looked into the eyes of the man who danced with me, I saw that he lied prettily. No one felt my sorrow but me.

Gerald was not as young as I had first thought. As I studied his face, I saw his age in the lines around his eyes. He was at least ten years older than my husband. His brown eyes were merry, but beneath that cultivated warmth was a world weariness that I had not seen before. He seemed not at all intimidated by my silence or the fact that I had been born a princess of France.

His hair curled across his temples where his barber had cut it too short, trying to keep with the fashion. It was his hair that made him look younger than he was. His eyes gleamed with more than mischief as he looked at me.

There was a pause in the dancing. As I looked across the hall, I found my husband watching us. William raised his goblet to me. I turned from William then and met the eyes of the man who held my hand.

The dance changed, and Gerald lifted me with one hand, as all the other dancing men lifted their partners. Gerald was stronger than most, or perhaps he was simply bolder. He lifted me high, almost above his head, so that for the space of a breath, all my pain and humiliation was forgotten. There was only him, his hand that kept me from falling, and the dark brown of his eyes.

Gerald set me once more on my feet. As the dance ended, he led me back to the high table. William was gone, as was the youth he had been speaking to.

I met Gerald's eyes. He did not grin or cajole me. He did not feign ignorance or indifference as he sat down beside me. He did not speak but drew his chair much closer than good manners warranted. I took in the sight of this young man, all the while wondering where Jean Pierre was, if already he had taken ship for the Levant. It had not been a month since I had seen him last. I did not know if I would ever see him again.

I could not think of him and do as my husband wished. So, I pushed the thought of the man I loved to the back of my mind, into the chest where I kept the memories of all my dead, all those who were lost to me. I closed the lid and locked it.

I found that I could not smile, but my voice was cheerful when I spoke. "Gerald, you are welcome to my husband's court. You and your lady wife."

"My lady countess, I have no wife. I am as free as the air we breathe."

His voice was as pleasant as mine and beneath his surface lay warmth. I was almost certain that he wished me well. If I had asked him to, I think he would have backed away. But I did not. I took the wine he offered me and drank. "How fortunate for you," I said. "Few of us can say the same."

We did not speak more but drank our wine in silence. I took in his scent, and found I was not repulsed. He smelled of cloves, and of the thyme we had eaten at dinner. He saw in my eyes that, though my husband had asked him to court me, he would get no further with me that night.

Gerald rose to his feet and bowed in the same moment that Marie Helene came to fetch me. He took my hand in his, but this time he did not kiss it. He met my eyes, and I saw that he was not a fool. He would not lie or try to deceive me with sweet words that he did not mean. I was grateful for that.

"Good night, my lady fair."

"Until tomorrow, my lord Gerald."

He smiled at his sudden rise in rank, but

even then, I saw irony reflected in his eyes and knew that I would be able to deal with him. Gerald left me with a bow, backing away from me as from a queen. Marie Helene took my arm.

I smiled to reassure her, as if to say that though I had been handed once more, from one man to another, it did not cause me pain. Her own eyes held a sheen of tears. She had always been able to weep for me when my own tears had dried up. I took her hand in mine.

As we left the hall, all my husband's men bowed as I passed. I nodded to them, but Marie Helene looked neither right nor left, drawing me out of there. Gerald stood apart, his gaze on me. He stared but did not smile, and I saw the strength of his intention and that his duty was not distasteful to him.

Marie Helene took me to my room where the braziers burned with the scent of lavender. The tapestries' unicorns and flowers were shadowed by the low light from the candle.

I sank into my chair and felt the cool wind blow in from the river. Marie Helene sat down beside me.

"William wants me to take a lover," I said.

"He has selected one for you and left you to him."

"He wants an heir."

Marie Helene choked on bitter laughter. "Lady, I think myself hard, then I hear such a thing from you."

She said nothing of Jean Pierre, and neither did I. If my husband had told me of his desire for an heir, it would have behooved me to know it sooner. Jean Pierre might have broken his oath and stayed with me.

As the breeze caressed my hair, I thought of the last time he had touched me by the river. I wished, if I were to enter into sin, that he would be the one to come with me.

This thought was wicked, and I crossed myself against it. I did not know what political alliances William wished to make. I did not know anything of his affairs, only that they could not be simple, for he had been at court too long. If my husband wanted an heir, even by another man, it was my duty to give it to him.

Marie Helene and I sat together beside the fire until its light began to burn down. Then she put me to sleep in my great marriage bed that was too large for a woman as small as I.

Adultery, even sanctioned by my husband, was still a sin. I had lived long enough to see the cost of folly. I had walked the path of sin before. I had buried my daughter and lost my honor as well as the husband my father had chosen for me. But I did not lie to myself, even those many years later. There had been joy on that path, too.

I could still remember the weight of my baby in my arms. The joy of that hour with my daughter had been worth all the pain before and since. As I sat by my window on that fresh summer morning, I knew that I wanted to feel a child of mine in my arms again.

I went to William's rooms for the first time

since our marriage. I went early, before he was out for the hunt. I scratched at the door and his man let me in, bowing only once before retreating behind a screen.

I looked around my husband's rooms and saw that his tapestries, while well made, were not as fine as mine. I saw that his bed was large but draped only in linen. He had given me the best of everything in the household, as he had given it to his mother before me. The curtains of his bed were still drawn, and I wondered if the youth from the night before still lay behind them.

"Husband," I said. "I would speak with you."

"And I with you, wife."

William raised one hand, and his man drew open the curtains of his bed and tied them back. I saw then that the bed was empty, and the tension went out of my neck. I lowered myself into the chair William offered.

We sat in silence as his man poured us each a glass of watered wine. A look passed between them, and William's valet left without a backward glance.

The door closed behind him. I did not touch my wine, and neither did William.

"My House is an old one," he said.

When he did not speak again, I realized that he waited for some acknowledgement from me. I had known of the House of Bellême and its ancient lineage even as a child.

"Yes," I said.

"I am the last of our line. My father's House, and all that went before, ends with me."

I felt the heavy hand of my father on my shoulder, as I had when I was a child. I remembered the weight of my father's crown, and how it shadowed his eyes even as he looked at me. The sin of adultery was something I would have to accept and be shriven for. My father had taught me to face the worst when he sent me away.

"You cannot do it yourself?" I said.

William looked at me. His pain stared back at me, the pain I had first seen in him on out wedding night, and never since. "I cannot."

Without an heir, there was no doubt that my brother would take the Bellême lands for the crown upon William's death. The House of Bellême would end, and their name would go down into the dust.

"Is Gerald to your liking?" William asked. "He is my first choice. I have known him many years. But if you cannot bear to touch him-"

"I can bear it." I rose then, because I knew I could not continue this discussion.

William stood when I did and took my hand. I flinched, then held myself very still. He did not speak, and I forced myself to meet his eyes.

"I am sorry, Alais. It is one more way in which I have failed you."

I moved away from him, and he let me go. As I stepped into the hall beyond his door, I saw the youth from the night before. William's wash water was in a bowl between his hands. For a page, this work was lowly, and beneath his station. I saw in his face that he loved my husband and brought his wash water simply to be near him.

My heart softened at the sight of that boy, and some of the bitterness that threatened me slipped away. He smiled at me, hopefully, as if I were his ally. I could not bring myself to be cruel to him. Nothing between my husband and myself was his fault. I nodded and went on my way.

As I turned the corner of the hallway, I saw the youth waiting outside my husband's door. I watched as his face lit up when my husband's voice called for him to enter.

At the evening meal, Gerald brought me a bundle of flowers he had picked by the riverside. They were wrapped in ribbon, and by their disarray, I could tell that he had prepared them himself.

He smiled at me, his eyes warmer than they had been before. Marie Helene saw the flowers he brought and turned her back to us discreetly, as if we were not surrounded by my husband's cohorts on every side. I accepted the distance she gave me and turned toward the man who would be my lover.

Gerald caught my eye over the petals of those flowers. This time he did not smile, but held my gaze, so that there could be no question between us.

"Will I do, my lady fair?"

I raised one eyebrow and stared him down. I

had never accepted impertinence, not even from a king.

He did not look away even then, nor did he apologize. He raised my hand to his lips and kissed it, first the back, and then the tips of my fingers. I sat very still, the heat of his mouth on my skin. He met my eyes, and his tongue flicked once against the warmth of my palm.

"Sir, you forget yourself, who I am, and where we are."

He did not smile or take his gaze from mine. He did not let go of my hand. "My lady fair, I forget nothing."

I did not try to take my hand from him again but let him hold it. I thought to look down the table, to where my husband sat with his own paramour. I thought to glance at the lower tables, to see if anyone noticed Gerald touching me. But I found I could not. I simply stared back at him, taking in the fire banked behind the chestnut brown of his eyes.

"You have not answered me." His eyes did not leave mine, but held them, as he held my palm in his own. "Will you have me, lady, or will you leave me pining?"

I smiled; like Henry before him, this man pined for no one. I saw that our way could be made easy by falling back on the language of courtly love, and its easy lies.

"I would not leave you to mourn me in darkness," I said.

Gerald laughed. He had not expected such a response from the convent-bred likes of me.

Tales of my time in the nunnery had

reached him, as had tales of my misdeeds. Clearly, he thought me too sheltered to know the ways of the world. He did not know that my soul had been forged, not in the cloister, but in Henry's court. Of course, there were few left alive who knew that. How could he, a man and a stranger, be expected to know anything of me?

And yet, as he looked into my eyes, he seemed to find something in me that no one else had ever seen, not even Henry. He saw the place in my soul where softness gave way to flint. Those who loved me never saw it. As he did not love me, nor I him, he could see it. And it made him smile.

"So, if darkness is not to be my fate, when and where might you favor me? Shall I bring more blossoms? Shall I sing of my love for you?"

I raised one brow, but he did not mock me. His own soul was hard, forged in the fires of my brother's court. In that, if in nothing else, he was my equal. My soul had its measure of hardness, too.

"Tonight, if you are free," I said.

He laughed again, but his eyes darkened with desire. "There is no need to chase you then, or to win you with song and deed?"

"There is only one deed worth mentioning between us, and it needs no songs sung of it."

I rose then, my trencher untouched. I did not stay for the dancing that night and knew that others in my husband's house would take note of it, and of who left soon after me. But I found that I was beyond shame. What I did, I did for the House of Bellême. Perhaps, for once, there was a bit of twisted honor in that.

William's eyes did not leave me as I stood. It seemed that I felt his gaze on me even after I had left the hall. As all things of this world, it soon fell away, and I was alone, walking to my rooms unencumbered.

There were no servants to greet me as I made my way down the torch lit corridors. They were all at the feast, or outside dancing at the bonfire. I could hear their shouts and laughter through the thick walls. William was a liberal lord and looked the other way on feast days, when the men and women in his service made merry with the lords and ladies. He looked the other way, as did I, so long as the work of the day got done.

I opened the door to my rooms. Marie Helene had seen me leave the hall and had not moved to follow. My husband's court was a world away as I stood in the firelight and waited for Gerald to come to me.

I had not been in my room half a moment, but he appeared in the shadows. I had not yet had time to draw the door shut.

Gerald came in after me, pulled the door closed behind him, and drew in the latch. He was far bolder than I had thought him to be, with his sweet songs, his poems, and his flowers.

He took me in his arms as if I had never been a princess of France. He touched me as if he had never heard of my brother, as if I did not have a husband two floors below. His grip was firm and brooked no refusals. Any refusal I might have offered, he had given me the chance to voice before. Now there would be room for none.

In this, he reminded me of Henry, so I was smiling when he kissed me. His lips were firm and warm and did not wait long to part over mine. He tasted of the mulled wine he drank at dinner, and of the bread he had eaten before he came to me. I had eaten little but did not feel the lack of it. My stomach fluttered with fear and with desire. He seemed to feel them both as I trembled under his hands. He drew me to the bed.

The first time we touched could not be hurried, but neither could it be delayed. He was gentle, for he seemed to know that it had been a long time since a man had touched me, but he did not hesitate or linger over long.

I felt myself quickening beneath him on the soft covers of my bed. It was as if I stood outside myself and watched another woman respond to the touch of a stranger.

Gerald laughed a little when it was over. We lay together, our breaths catching in our throats, and he kissed me.

"Still waters run deep, I see," he said. I heard the compliment in his tone, and I smiled.

"I am simply happy that I remember the steps. It has been a very long time for me."

He kissed me again, and his breath was sweet on my cheek when he pulled away. "They are steps I would dance again, my lady, if you are willing."

So, we spent the night in sin, adrift on my

marriage bed, in a world of our own making. Too soon the morning light brightened my windows from dark blue to gray.

Gerald lay still beside me, his arm thrown over me in sleep, his breath even for the first time in many hours. I did not sleep but lay alone in the knowledge of my sin. I knew myself not only to be an adulteress, but foresworn. Yet I could not confess the sin and free myself, for I did not repent.

I prayed for a repentant heart, even as I lay there, but it did not come to me. Instead, I heard birdsong from my window and knew that a new day had come. No servants had entered to trim the lamps in my room, so it was certain that all the household knew of my disgrace and were gossiping about me as they lit the first of the morning fires.

I felt no shame as I lay there, my lover close beside me. I thought of my husband. It should have been him lying against me in our great marriage bed. Instead a stranger had waked the desire within me, a beast that had slept for years. The lust of the night before had warmed my bones. I was not as old as I once had thought.

I lay in the morning light, the soft breeze from the river coming through my windows. The bedsheets against my skin felt like another caress. I knew myself better from that night's work than I had through many hours of prayer.

I wondered if God and the Virgin would take pity on me, and hear my prayers for the dead though I was now in a state of sin, unworthy to plead for anyone. Never a day went by, but I lit a candle for my mother, my sisters, my father and my daughter. I would still pray that day, light the candles, and take Mass. God would hear me or not, as He chose. I could only pray for His mercy.

For as I watched the sun come in, its golden light covering my bed, I felt nothing but triumph.

PART II
MY FATHER'S DAUGHTER

11

A CHILD

Marie Helene had not come in early as she usually did, and I dozed a little past dawn, and woke with a smile on my face. Gerald was still with me. I had half expected him to steal away when I was no longer looking, but he smiled down on me, raised on one elbow. He had a look of pride about him, as if I were a mountain he had long wished to climb. I had seen the same look once or twice on Henry's face when we had first been together, so long ago.

I turned my mind from Henry and from any thought of my husband downstairs. I blinked the sleep from my eyes and let my new lover kiss me.

"Good morning, my lady."

"So, it is, my lord."

He flushed at the courtesy I paid him, for he was not high-ranking enough to be the lord of a princess of France. "I must go, Countess, before your ladies come in."

He kissed me again and rose gracefully. I saw that he was in no hurry to leave. For men, a

141

sexual conquest was something to be savored. Unlike women, they did not have to be discreet.

I was not ashamed of anything we had done, so I did nothing to hurry him away. I sat up, drawing my shift over my head. I left the ribbon at my throat untied, and my shift hung down past one shoulder. I must have made a fetching picture, for he came back to me then, his hose still dangling in one hand.

Gerald kissed me deeply, his need to dress forgotten. His lips were still on mine, his hands running up into my hair, when my women scratched at the door. They could not come in, for it was still latched tight.

He pulled away from me as if I were a fire that had burned him, but I only laughed. "Will you open the door, my lord, or shall I?"

He was flattered by my tone and by the false title I gave him. He was no fool, but I have never known a man who was not warmed by flattery, except perhaps my father, and he was a saint on earth. A king hears too much of false flattery to be taken in by it.

Gerald let my women in, and they kept their eyes averted as they went about the business of bringing my wash water and fresh fruit for my breakfast. I let them work but held Gerald by his sleeve. He looked down at me, surprised that I would touch him before servants, but our time together was something my husband had wrought. Sin or no, I was not ashamed of it. I drew him down to me and kissed him.

He kissed me back, his lips soft and warm on mine, tasting of the honeyed wine he had drunk upon waking. He offered me the goblet and I took it, downing it to the last drop. Gerald had the grace to flush as my head woman curtsied before us, her eyes on the floor.

"My lady, will you need anything else this morning?"

"No, Maude. Another flagon of honeyed wine, but that will be all."

She curtsied again and left us quickly, the rest of the women trailing in her wake. The youngest one, a girl who could not be much older than ten summers, looked at me around the edges of her veil. I winked at her, and she smiled back, clearly surprised that I would so easily meet her eyes. One of the older women looked back and saw where the girl's gaze was tending. She hustled the little one out, closing the door with an emphatic thump behind them.

I looked down at my rumpled shift, my breasts soft and half visible beneath the white linen. My hair curled down my back and my legs lay beneath the rumpled bedclothes. A more wanton woman was not to be seen in Christendom, at least not in my husband's household.

I laughed then, a laugh from my belly, the kind of laugh that was never allowed in the nunnery, the kind of laughter I had forgotten myself capable of. Gerald forgot his embarrassment as he looked at me. In a moment, his lips were on mine again, and I was tasting his sweet heat, feeling it flame into desire between us.

Before that heat could truly take fire, there

was a knock on my door. It swung open before I could tell the intruder to go away.

Gerald stiffened beside me, and drew himself to his full height, as if the king had come upon us in my bedchamber.

It was not my brother the king who entered, but my husband. "Good morning, wife."

I watched William carefully for any sign of displeasure. I thought in the first second I turned to him that I saw a flicker of sexual heat behind his eyes. If it had turned into a flame, I would have ordered Gerald out and had my way with my husband. But the light disappeared like so much smoke, and for a long time after, I wondered if I had seen it at all.

"Good morning, William."

Gerald still said nothing but stood frozen, as if he wished himself far from my side – anywhere but where he stood. My husband was wearing his sword, and Gerald's lay across the room, on my table underneath the window. My lover faced my husband unarmed, before he had even finished dressing.

William's gaze never strayed from my face. Gerald might as well not have been in the room, for all the attention my husband paid him.

"You are welcome, husband. Will you have breakfast with us before Gerald takes his leave?"

Gerald turned his eyes on me, and I felt the sting of his anger like a slap against my cheek. He had no rights with me as he seemed to think he did. He had agreed to this bargain, as I had. I owed him nothing beyond courtesy. I kept my gaze on my husband.

"I have eaten already, wife. I thank you. I am here only to invite our guest to ride with me this day. We hunt in the southern forest if he would join us."

Gerald mastered himself and his anger. "My lord, it would be my honor."

"Good. Then do not let us keep you. I know you do not want to hunt in the same clothes you wore to my table last night."

Gerald's gaze darkened. Something passed between them that made me think that they had once known each other better. I saw in that moment that they had once been lovers, and now we had come to this.

I leaned back against my pillow and surrendered. No matter how old I was or how jaded I thought to become, I would never be a match for men brought up among my brother's courtiers.

Gerald drew his gaze from my husband, their silent communication finished. I thought that he would leave me without another word, but instead he turned and lowered his lips to mine. I could taste nothing of him in that chaste kiss, but the gesture moved me, that he would dare such a thing in front of William.

"I will see you this evening, lady, if it be your will."

I pushed my husband from my thoughts and focused on my lover's face. "I will be happy to see you tonight, my lord."

He took more from my tone than I intended, for he seemed heartened by it. He rose, taking his hose and jerkin in hand. He drew them on without another word, and I marveled that any man could dress himself so quickly.

He bowed first to me, then met my husband's eyes and bowed to him. William was as unruffled as if they had met in the garden and not beside my marriage bed. He bowed to my lover, but only from the neck, as befitted his rank. Gerald left without another word, and my husband closed the door behind him.

"Will you rise today, lady, or stay abed?"

I listened close for rancor in my young husband's voice. All I could hear was a note of light teasing.

"Indeed, husband, I will rise. But I believe I will have a glass honeyed wine first."

My husband must have met the serving girl on the stairs, for he held the flagon I had asked for. William poured a glass for me and one for himself before he sank down on the edge of my bed. I felt a last frisson of regret that he did not want me as a woman, but I let this regret pass. As we sat together, I wondered if perhaps we might be friends.

"So." William sipped his wine, handing me a bit of bread to sop in mine. "All is well with you this morning, my lady?"

For one horrible moment, I thought that he meant for me to share details of my night with Gerald, perhaps even to reminisce about times of his own. But my good sense prevailed almost immediately, and the tension slipped from my shoulders like water from an overturned glass.

As I drank my wine, I saw in his face that he was concerned for my welfare, that on some level, he regretted that our marriage was a sham, as so many other marriages were.

I did not chastise him for loaning me out. If my womb quickened, it need never happen again. "I am well, my lord. I thank you."

William looked at me for a long time, no doubt searching my face for some sign of displeasure or ire. I had learned self-control in a harder school than his house, for he found nothing. I drank my wine, finishing the bread he had given me and found myself wishing for more. William leaned over and kissed me, his lips warm and dry on the soft skin of my cheek.

His lips lingered for the briefest moment, and half my mind thought to turn and kiss him in truth. But he stood then, crossing the room in three long strides, setting his untouched wine down on my table.

"I am headed for the southern forest, near the village, my lady. There is a boar and her piglets ranging there that need killing."

"God ride with you, husband."

He quirked a smile at me, his eyes lit with the certain knowledge that God did not exist, that religion was a fairy story told to children and peasants. Most in Henry's court had thought the same, and I saw now that this certainty was held by the people at my brother's court as well. And yet many of the young men had gone to free Jerusalem from the infidel. I did not understand the minds of men.

"Good day, my lady."

He was gone without another word, his short cape swirling behind him. He left the door open, and I saw Marie Helene standing beyond it. She looked drawn and pale, as if she had not slept.

I beckoned, and she came to me quickly, closing the door firmly behind her. I saw the sorrow in her eyes, and I knew it was for me. I realized then how much she must have loved her husband and how much she must miss him.

I held her in my arms her while she shed the tears that I could not. "There is no reason to weep. I am a rich woman, far better off than most."

When she drew back to dry her eyes on the kerchief from her sleeve, I saw in her sorrow a hint of what a true marriage was like. She wept for me, that I would never know it.

Gerald stayed in my husband's house for a fortnight and we played at love every night, far into the dawn. We often went down by the riverside during the long afternoons and made love among the irises that grew there. If anyone from the castle or the fields saw us, no one ever told me.

Gerald left me to travel to the Levant, as Jean Pierre had before him, but this time I felt no pain at the parting. I wondered as I raised my hand to him and watched him ride away, if this was how a man felt, when he could finally be free of a woman. Pleasure in the memory of the time spent, but also relief that it was over.

With Gerald gone, I went back to my quiet ways, praying daily and going to Mass, though the sin of adultery still rested on my soul. My husband's guests had long since gone and Marie Helene and I resumed our long walks by the river. As fall came on and the heat of August faded into September, I found myself grateful for my quiet life. My time with Gerald seemed like a sweet dream that I had just waked from.

The dream lingered, however, for as September drew to a close, the mornings found me bent over a silver bowl at dawn.

Marie Helene, now my bedfellow again, held my hair back when it slipped from its ribbon. I had forgotten the misery of early pregnancy, but it came back to me as I leaned over the heavy bowl, unable to eat a bite of bread until noon or after.

On the third day of this, I met Marie Helene's eyes. We had not spoken of my sudden illness, though all the household knew already.

"Lady, I think there may be more to this than the fish you ate on Friday."

I laughed at her, my nausea fading. When it did not come back again, I reached for the cup of water and the willow bark twig Marie Helene had laid at my elbow.

I cleaned my teeth and chewed my mint, remembering when I had done the same at Eleanor's prompting, before going to see the king. I pushed these memories from my mind and all the helpless fear they engendered. I was a woman grown, mistress of my own household. As long as my husband stood behind me, I had nothing to fear.

The entire reason I had taken Gerald to my bed was to quicken my womb with an heir for

Ponthieu. Surely, my husband would remember this and not turn from me. Though, in my years at court, I had learned that a man's whims were worse than any woman's.

I saw in Marie Helene's face that she feared for me. From my clothes press she drew out my most somber gown. After she dressed me, we knelt together and said a rosary for the fate of my unborn child. When we rose again, I turned to her.

"I will go and make my confession."

She said nothing, but only looked at me. She knew that I had not been to confession since I first lay with Gerald in my marriage bed.

"When I have done this, I will go and see my husband."

She wrapped her slender arms around me, as if she might shield me from fate. I felt the fear in her touch. I knew that she, too, had visited the past. Her mind was back among my enemies, among the people I had loved. Henry and Eleanor, who had used me and betrayed me, then left me in a nunnery to rot.

I blinked at the darkness of my thoughts. They were another thing I must do penance for.

"Do not fear for me, Marie Helene. William will not turn from me."

"He could put you aside for unfaithfulness."

"He will not. I promise you."

I made my way to the chapel, schooling my thoughts to God and to repentance. I would not carry a child with a mortal sin on my soul. It was for the child's sake and not mine that I knelt in the church that day and confessed myself to the priest before the morning mass. He heard me out, though I shocked him to the core, for he was a simple country man who had seen nothing of the court or its ways. He listened to my litany of sins, and it was the horror in his eyes that brought home to me the sin that I had done.

He gave me no penance, saying only that the sins themselves were penance enough. He absolved me before I rose and prayed with me for the life of my child.

A fever came and took that priest before the winter was done, but I have remembered his kindness all my life. He was one of the only true men of God that I have ever known.

I came to my husband's rooms while he was still out hunting deer. His man bowed to me and let me in without question. His eyes were gentle, and I found myself sorry that I had never taken the time to learn his name.

"Your Highness, you honor us with your presence in this house."

I searched for signs of mockery in his face, for all the household knew of my condition. Some of the maids had known before I did. I had lost count of the days between my monthly courses and had only known my fate when I began to sicken in the mornings.

The knowledge of my disgrace was in his eyes, but he also honored me for who my father had been, and for who my brother was. As I looked at him, I saw that he also honored me for myself. He knew the nature of my relationship with my husband.

He brought me a cushion and I leaned back against it, for my back often ached. I drank the warm posset he brought as well and wondered where my husband had found such a kind man to serve him. I was about to ask when William came in, and his man left my side to go to his.

"Thank you, Georges."

His man withdrew without a word, and my husband and I were left alone.

I set my posset down and stood, for as always, I knew my duty.

I knelt to William, my head bowed. "Husband, I have done you wrong. I have slept with another man, and now I carry his child."

"A child?"

The warmth in his voice made me raise my head, and I saw the same joy mirrored in his face. I smiled to see it, but I stayed on my knees. When I did not rise, he came to help me stand. Only when I continued to kneel did his face darken.

"You kneel to no one in this house. You are a princess of France." He offered me his hand, and this time, I took it.

I was surprised as I always was by the strength in his grip and the steadiness in his eyes, a centered certainty that I had rarely seen even in kings. When I was on my feet, he helped me back to my chair, handling me carefully, as if I were made of spun glass.

Once I was seated, he drew another chair up beside me and took my hand again. "You are also my wife. I would see you kneel only in prayer."

His words touched me, and I felt the easy tears of early pregnancy rise in my eyes. I tried to blink them away, but they fell too quickly. William reached over and dried them gently. I knew then that whatever his proclivities, whatever had made him turn from me, he would not turn away from my child. He would not leave us in disgrace.

When my tears were dried, he pressed my hand, then offered me the posset I had left on the table between us. I sipped it and found it still warm in the good pewter mug his man had served it in.

We sat a little longer in silence, then William decided that it was time to make me smile. "Wife, I would not have you down on your knees even in prayer very often. But when you do, pray for my soul, as I have need of it."

I laughed when he said that, and he leaned back in his chair, well rewarded. I thought that he would leave me then, but we were in his rooms, not in mine. It would be for me to leave when I could gather the strength. I had been more frightened than I had realized when I knelt to ask his forgiveness.

"Your brother will be angry," he said.

I did not answer right away but thought of what he said. I knew that my marriage had more than one purpose my brother had hoped to satisfy with my union.

In case I was in any doubt, my husband explained it to me as gently as he had wiped the tears from my cheeks. "He hoped to take the land of my fathers for the crown. Now your son will have it."

"God willing," I said.

He touched my hair, where it curled loose beneath my veil. For a moment, I almost thought that he believed in God.

"God willing," he answered me.

MY SECOND DAUGHTER

ONCE I TOLD WILLIAM OF MY DISGRACE, MY pregnancy seemed to smooth out like a sea after a storm. The waves of nausea ran their course. I was able to eat again in the mornings and felt almost like myself.

I saw little of William after our talk in his rooms. But whenever I did see him, whether in the corridor leading to the main hall or at the large trestle table where we ate our evening meal, he always smiled on me, and asked after my health and that of the baby.

When we spoke together it seemed that all the world listened, waiting to hear some breath of further scandal, some indication that he would cast me off as the harlot they knew me to be.

But though William was never warm to me during the first pregnancy of our marriage, he was never cold either. He walked a line somewhere in between, so that I wondered, as did everyone around us, what his true thoughts and intentions were.

After a month of this, I decided that I did not care. I had my own life and child to think of. As with my first pregnancy, I found myself serene even in the face of disapproval, but I did not feel the close connection with my child that I had once felt with Rose. My daughter swam in me, surfacing against my flesh, and then swimming away from me again. I touched her hand with my own and was grateful that she thrived, though her mother was a sinner and undeserving of such a gift.

As punishment, my heart did not warm to this baby as it had to Rose. I regretted this, and I prayed on it, but there was nothing I could do to change it. God was silent, as He always was, and the Holy Mother did nothing to warm my heart, either. I was alone, separate from my child.

Even as I sat on the birthing chair in my chambers, I did not feel joy at the thought of this baby. The midwife stood by, coaxing me to do my duty, and my aging body obeyed her.

Marie Helene was at my side, silent, remembering, as I did, that other birth that had ended so badly. As this baby was pressed down the birth canal toward the light of her new life, I felt certain that, though she was not the child of my heart as Rose had been, she would live.

Her birth was quick, though bloody, as all births are. When the women had washed the blood from her and the midwife handed her to me, I was shocked as I had been the first time by how heavy she was, like a lead weight in my arms, more substantial than my idea of her had ever been.

My daughter looked up at me, blinking in the first light of her new world. I smiled down at her, tears on my face. Marie Helene gripped my hand beneath the blanket, careful as always never to be too familiar when others were nearby.

This care was forgotten in a moment as the other women bustled around my room, opening the shutters to the light and air outside, clearing out the musky scent of birth as they took away the afterbirth to be burned and buried.

Marie Helene gazed down into my daughter's face, openly weeping. "My lady, she has the look of her."

I blinked tears away and tried to see what Marie Helene saw. I looked for my lost daughter in the face of this one. All I saw was a child, her eyes closing now in much needed sleep, her face red from her ordeal, her hair the dark brown of her father's.

I could not say such things to Marie Helene, who seemed to find her own lost children in this one. I kissed my daughter's forehead and gave her to Marie Helene, who held her as if she were as precious as spun gold. As I gave the baby over into my friend's care, William came in and stood at my bedside.

I could feel the heaviness of sleep gripping me, leading me down into the dark. For I was old and tired. No matter how much of my youthful looks I had kept, I could feel the difference keenly between this birth and my first.

The remembered loss of Rose was like a raw wound in my side, which pained me every time I drew breath. It was as if some warrior had pierced me with his sword, leaving me to bleed to death on the field. As my husband looked down on me, I wished nothing more than to collapse into oblivion, to wake to a better world. A world where my daughter Rose was still living, and where Richard, not Henry, was her father.

Young as he was, my husband was also wise. He seemed to see something of my sorrow in my face. He could not have known of Rose, except what he may have heard at my brother's court. Scraps of whispered rumors, rumors of a long dead scandal flogged to life only when my brother had need of them.

Though William could have known nothing of my pain, he had compassion for it. He leaned down in front of all the women in that room and kissed me full on the lips. There was no lust in his kiss. Only love, as if he might lend me his strength, as if he might take my pain on himself, freeing me of it forever.

He knelt beside me, smoothed back my hair, and let me weep. "My lady," he said, loud enough for others to hear, "What would you name our daughter?"

I wiped my face with my hand until Marie Helene leaned over and handed me a cloth. I started to dry my own tears, but William took the kerchief and did it for me.

I found my voice, wondering if some of his strength had indeed infused me. I felt less like dying, and falling out of the world that I lived in.

I looked at my daughter, who now lay in her father's arms. He had risen and taken her from Marie Helene, once my tears were dried.

My daughter blinked at me once, looking displeased to be called by any name. I searched my heart. I knew who had stood by me all the years of my imprisonment in the nunnery, who had sent letters every month, though her husband forbade her. The woman who had comforted me all those barren years, when I had thought never to look on a child of mine again this side of Paradise.

"Husband, her name is Marie," I said.

Marie Helene wept, gasping, her face contorted with sorrow and joy together.

William raised my daughter so that he could look into her face. "Little one, we name you for Marie Helene, your godmother here on Earth, and for the Holy Mother in Heaven. May She look over you all the days of your life. May She guide and protect you when your mother and I cannot."

I wept when he said that, for in my just-birthed state, everything moved me. It was generous of him to take her as if she were truly his own. Indeed, the household wondered after that day if perhaps she might have been his in truth, that he and I had lain together, and they had simply not known it.

Marie slept then, and Marie Helene took her from my husband's arms and handed her to the nurse. We had found a healthy girl on my husband's estate, and she took to my daughter from the first as if she had birthed her. I thanked God for that, for I knew that I did not have the heart to feed another child of mine from my own breast. I was grateful that the privilege of my high birth let me turn from it.

My room was cleared, the shutters pushed back from the windows so that the flow of air was unencumbered. I sat up, grateful for the smell of the fresh turned earth from the fields down by the river. It was late in the month of May, the month named for the Blessed Virgin, the one woman who had stood by me and guided me all my life.

I took in the scent from the fields, wondering how I could take it in from my high window, even in my marriage bed. As my husband's women bathed me and dressed me in clean linen, I knew that this blessing, like all others, came from Her.

It was not long before the women left my rooms. Marie Helene sat beside me and held my hand. As tired as I was, I could see that she longed for my daughter.

"Go to her," I said. "She needs one of us, and I do not have the strength."

She moved to go, but I clutched her hand. "You must stand for her in my place with the nurse and the servants. You must watch over her as if she were your own. Promise me."

I could see that at first, she thought my words were just so much air, so tired was I from my ordeal. It had been many hours since I had slept. But she looked into my face and saw that my eyes burned, and not with fever. She knelt beside my bed, though the floor was hard, with no rug beside me. "Lady. I swear it."

She has never failed me; in that, as in all things, she has always been faithful, a friend far better than my deserving.

My daughter thrived, drinking that peasant girl's milk. My own milk dried up quickly, and I lost the weight I had gained in carrying her.

I saw my daughter every day. Marie Helene was always with her, for she loathed to be parted from her, even when the girl was feeding her. So, I saw less of my friend in those days and took to walking my husband's lands alone again, seeing him only at dinner.

Mother Bernard's garden still thrived at the Abbey of St. Agnes, and she was kind enough to send me seeds and cuttings when she could, though the cuttings rarely survived the salty journey across the Channel. I had planted the first of these seeds when I had come to my husband's land. Now the mint and thyme grew high, and my lavender promised to come in well the next year.

I sat in my garden, where a willow grew by a small pond. This garden was not walled and looked down the slope of the land to the river in the distance. After my daughter was born, I sat there often, taking in the summer sun, and eating the first of the strawberries straight off the vine, always careful to leave enough for the kitchen servants to gather, to be served later with cream.

One morning, after I had been churched a week or more, my husband came to me in that garden, a letter in his hand. I rose from my bench when I saw him, but he raised one hand, and I sat again. At first, I thought he meant to sit beside me, but he stood with the morning light in his eyes, passing his letter from one hand to the other.

"Your brother sends news," he said.

Whatever the news, it had sent my husband back to another time, a time when he had waited for letters from my brother with joy. Such was no longer the case between them. I watched as my husband fought himself, striving for mastery over his pain.

In a moment, his struggle done, he met my eyes and held out the letter to me. I took the vellum from his hand and held it close to my heart. I did not read the letter but kept my eyes on my husband's face.

"The king sends his regards, wife, and asks after your health, now that our daughter is born."

I listened for irony in his voice but heard none. He had accepted my daughter as his own. He sat down beside me. The wind moved in his hair, pushing it away from his face, the soft blond strands caressing his cheek. William's eyes were as blue as the summer sky, and as clear. Not for the first time, I wished that more lay between us than respect, and our empty marriage vows. I took his hand in mine.

William smiled at me, allowing me to draw him away from the pain he bore, as he had drawn me from mine on the day my second daughter was born. We sat together in silence, listening to the wind as it rose over the land from the river, and to the birdsong in the trees above us. I thought that we might continue that way for some time, my brother's letter forgotten. I should have known better. Over a year later, my brother held sway over my husband more than I would ever know.

"He has declared that he will be the child's godfather and has sent his gloves for me to wear during the ceremony."

I said nothing, though this was passing strange. I had heard of marriages done by proxy, but never of a godfather sending gloves to a child's baptism. But Phillipe was just home from the Levant and could not be expected to take the time away from court to come for my daughter's christening.

Marie Helene was just finishing the lace on Marie's gown. Now that I was churched, William had set the date for the christening for the Sunday after next. Marie Helene was to stand as godmother, and now the king would stand before God as her father.

"Does he seek to show us his displeasure in some strange way, that he offers to attach his name to my disgrace?"

William frowned at me, his pain over my brother's letter forgotten. "Wife, I will not have you speak of disgrace and our daughter in the same breath. She is a blessing from God and will bear my name all her life until she is married, no matter who her father was."

I felt stung by his vehemence, all my self-recrimination swept away in his pure fire.

"Your brother seeks to honor us, as if he had made a true marriage between us."

We sat in silence, the song of birds in the willow above us the only sound. I opened my brother's letter and read the calm and steady words, words which no doubt had been dictated to a scribe.

I read it only once, then handed it back to my husband. He made no effort to hide its dearness from me but folded it with care and placed it in the bag at his waist. He sat once again beside me, the waves of his sorrow and misery showing on his face.

I took his hand, but I knew that my touch offered little comfort. He left his hand in mine and we sat, palm to palm, until the morning gardener came to water the basil. William left me then, striding away without a backward glance, like a man who felt no pain, a man who mourned nothing and no one.

13

TO COURT A KING

WILLIAM HELD MY DAUGHTER IN FRONT OF THE priest, wearing the King's gloves, standing before God in my brother's stead. I stood back, though I had given birth to her. As Marie Helene and my husband flanked the child, I felt as if my dead had gathered before that altar with me, my father, my daughter Rose, and the mother I never knew.

As I watched my second child brought into the family of God, I thought of my mother. She had not lived to see me christened but had died the day I was born. And yet I seemed to feel her presence clearly on that day, more than any other. She had not come to stand with me at my wedding, nor did she stand with me at any other child's naming day. But on that day, late in June, I felt her hand on mine as my husband held the child who was not his and claimed her as his own.

There was a feast that day, though my daughter was not present. After she was baptized and blessed, Marie Helene took the baby to her rooms and watched over her as the nurse fed her and put her to bed. So, I was alone at my husband's table, seated at his right hand. He shared his trencher with me. We said little, content with the peace between us, both satisfied to listen to the wild talk all around. For many of his young friends were back from the Levant, rich with loot, bringing gifts to William of silk and spices. One even brought a bolt of deep blue damask, so that my women might make a gown for me.

We listened to these young men talk, and I felt my age. My husband seemed to see something of this in my face, and he smiled at me.

"Lady, you are as fair as the day I met you."

I smiled back. We had been married a little over a year at this time, and he had not known me long. "And you are as valiant, husband."

William made no secret of his distaste for war, a distaste that never brought him censure. My brother had used this distaste to his advantage. Knowing that William would not ride off to war, Phillipe had married him to me.

He took my good-natured teasing for what it was, bringing my gloved hand to his lips. He opened his mouth to respond in kind, perhaps a joke about my hair, which still curled against my shoulders, unencumbered by a wimple or veil, but the words died in his throat.

For we heard a raucous cheer as young men at the end of the high table raised beakers of wine. A man stood among them, toasting my brother. "To the prowess of our King, who throws down all his enemies!"

Another cheer went up at this. William signaled the servers to bring more wine, though he did not raise a glass himself. I, too, sat in silence, to listen for what came next, for it seemed to me that there was something ominous in the tone of these celebrants. I did not have long to wait.

"Richard, King of England, is caged behind bars!"

A roar went up from the crowd, this time from the lower tables. William gripped my hand and I felt his strength through the kidskin of my glove. It seemed that a hole had opened in the floor behind me. If I were to breathe too deeply, I would fall into it.

"This may be only a rumor, love. Let me find out the truth of it."

William's breath was warm on my cheek, as he leaned over to whisper these words in my ear. He gestured, and one of his young men came forward to draw back my chair.

"Lady," the young man said. "You are grown weary with these festivities. Let me escort you to your women."

I had none, for Marie Helene was in the nursery. Gregory waited silently for me to stand, solicitous; his blue eyes were warm on mine. He was my husband's current favorite, and I could see that there was kindness behind the beauty of his face. William, when allowed to choose for himself, always chose well.

I rose to my feet, the floor receding

dangerously as I stood. I caught the edge of the table, and William's hand came under my elbow, steadying me. I saw in his eyes that he wanted to escort me to my rooms himself but could not leave his own hall.

I pressed his hand. "Thank you."

Gregory took my arm from my husband's grasp and bowed to me, leading me carefully away. There was a door behind the dais which the servants used to bring in more food and wine to the high table. Gregory took me out that door, quickly and silently.

No one noticed us. Indeed, no one seemed to notice that I was gone at all, so bent were they on celebrating my brother's triumph. Gregory brought me into my room and helped me sit. He placed the brazier by my chair at the window and even went so far as to bring a lap robe, as if I were his elderly aunt.

"My lady, what else can I do for you?"

I looked into the deep blue of that boy's eyes; he could be no older than seventeen. I saw no pity in his face, only kindness. William was always good to the young men he chose to grant his favor and they, in their turn, were good to him. I found myself drawn into their circle of protection for the first time in my marriage, and the welcoming warmth of it made me want to weep. For I was an outsider, and always would be. My husband's true life was locked and veiled against me. I saw this more clearly than I ever had as I stared into the blue of that boy's eyes.

"I am well," I said. "I thank you."

He bowed, holding my hand to his forehead

in an antique gesture of fealty, which touched me even as it burned. Gregory left me then, and I sat alone, my thoughts bent on my husband and his lover, and on Richard, who was not free, but was trapped in some foreign castle as I was in this marriage that my brother had wrought.

I sat by the window, waiting for word.

When William could, he came to me himself. He entered my rooms without knocking and closed the door behind him. I stayed where I was, an embroidery frame forgotten in my hands.

William smiled to see me at such work, for he knew how I loathed it. He did not smile long but drew another chair to sit close beside me so that he might take my hand.

"There is news, wife, underneath the noise and bluster."

I schooled my face to blankness, all the hard lessons of my childhood returning. William admired this show of strength. I felt his admiration in the touch of his hand. I had laid my gloves aside and the warmth of his touched soothed me as he spoke of Richard.

"Alais, Richard was taken prisoner this winter as he passed overland through Vienna, on his way home from the Levant."

"He was set upon by robbers?"

"No, wife. He was kidnapped by his brother king, Duke Leopold of Austria."

I listened to those words, but it seemed I could not take them in. I could think of nothing but my brother's face as he had looked on my wedding day, when it seemed as if he loved me.

"And what share does Phillipe have in this?"

William flinched at my words, but to his credit, he did not shrink from them. "It is said that the king Phillipe is behind Richard's continued imprisonment, that he sends Leopold gold to keep Richard where he is."

I did not speak but sat with my husband's hand on mine. The afternoon was waning. As I looked from my window, I saw that the blue of the sky was beginning to darken. Before long, dusk would fall.

"Talk of such gold is rumor only."

I did not rebuke him for defending his old lover. I could not yet feel the pain of my brother's betrayal. It would be many days before I felt that. I sat in silence, listening to my husband's words, feeling nothing but the gentle wind on my face.

"I know that Phillipe has sent word to the Holy Roman Emperor, asking that the Pope turn a deaf ear to any pleas from Richard or his mother to let him go."

I thought of Eleanor and of how she had not wanted her favorite son to go on Crusade at all. I thought of Henry and all the times he had railed against the foolishness of foreign wars and their drain on the treasury. Foreign glory, he said, was too expensive.

"And the Pope agrees to this, in spite of the fact that Richard fought valiantly against the infidel less than a year ago?"

"Yes, wife. Richard fought the infidel. But he did not win."

The sting of this truth was like a needle

behind my eyes. I felt my hard-won calm dissolving. William gripped my hand, but there was little he could do for me.

The pain passed, as with an outgoing tide. I took my next breath slowly, gingerly, as if the act of breathing itself might cause me more pain. Through all this, my husband held my hand.

"I must go to my brother in Paris."

"He will not listen to you."

"I know. But still, I must go."

"Richard of England and Aquitaine left you in disgrace, discarding you in front of all of Europe." Suddenly, William's voice was full of anger and loathing for a man he had never met.

"I know," I said. "That makes no difference. I love him. If there is anything I can do for him, I must do it. I must try."

William swallowed all other objections that he might have made. He knew well what it was like to love a man who did not love you back. We sat together, neither of us saying a word as the sun began to set beyond the fields. The shadows in my room lengthened until the servants came to light the tapers and build up my fire.

William stayed with me even then, calling for bread and cheese to be brought to my rooms, along with my favorite wine. The taste of that wine burned me. It was the same wine that Richard's vineyards grew in Anjou. I drank it down, in memory of him and all he meant to me. I drank it because my husband brought it to me, knowing only that I loved it.

. . .

I left for Paris the next morning. William did not come with me, but neither did he try to make me stay. I did not take a trunk, only a bag tied onto the back of one of the horses. I would ride a horse myself for swiftness until we came to Rouen and the river.

Marie Helene kissed me before I went, handing my daughter to me so that I might see her face. Marie was sleeping, but she woke when I touched her. She did not cry, though I was unfamiliar to her now that she no longer rode within me. She blinked and looked up at me, as if seeing me for the first time. I smiled down on her and kissed her forehead.

She seemed to take this gesture for the blessing it was, for she smiled at me for the first time. That small smile touched my heart, and I felt tears rise in my eyes. I smoothed her hair where it feathered along her forehead. She would not have my curls it seemed, but her father's straight brown locks.

"She will be here when you return, my lady."

Marie Helene's voice was soft in my ear. I met my friend's gaze, tearing my eyes from my daughter's face. "She is beautiful, Marie Helene. How is it that I have not seen that before, but only now, when I am going away?"

Marie Helene handed the baby to the wet nurse who was standing by. She took me in her arms then, and held me close to her heart, so that I could hear it beating. "It is because you lost your first child, lady, and still feel the sorrow of it. But perhaps it will be easier now."

I kissed her cheek but did not speak. She released me, and I turned to my horse.

She was wrong. The loss of Rose was never made easy, not by Marie or any of my living children to come. But after that day I could look upon my second daughter and see her for what she was, a unique miracle wrought by God, just as Rose had been.

I was thinking these things, fighting off my misery and the despair that threatened as I turned to go on my errand of mercy, when my husband caught my arm.

Looking up at him, my eyes wide, I must have seemed frightened, for he drew me close and kissed me in front of the whole company. "My lady wife, Godspeed and His blessings on your journey."

I blinked, surprised into a smile, for I knew well that my husband had little truck with God, or His blessings. William lifted me onto my horse and winked at me, his back turned so that others could not see.

I rode out of my husband's keep, his standard flying above me, six of his men-at-arms flanking me as if I were a queen indeed. I rode in state all the way to the river, my back straight, my gloved hands firm on my horse's reigns.

I had learned to ride a little more since coming into my husband's country. I had decided that it did not suit a princess of France to seem too timid, no matter what her age. I was grateful now that I had taken the time to learn, for the road back to Rouen was longer than I remembered. I had crossed that country only once before, after my wedding day.

It was half a day's journey to Rouen, and we stopped in the same monastery where my husband and I had spent our wedding night. I was housed in the same room, though that night I slept little. I stared into the fire, trying not to think of the tradition of the cold marriage bed that we had started in that room.

Instead, I prayed for Richard, that he might be delivered from his enemies, even though those enemies were my kin.

When I rode into my brother's palace keep, the men-at-arms saluted me but asked no questions. I saw immediately that my husband had sent a rider to tell my brother of my coming.

Phillipe did not emerge from the darkness of his castle to greet me himself, but his steward was quick to welcome me, bowing deeply, as people no longer did at my husband's house.

I was taken to the same room where I had slept before, and given wash water and women to serve me, since I had brought none of my own. I could see that the court servants were scandalized that a princess of France would travel by horse instead of by litter, without her husband to attend her.

They laughed behind their hands that I had not brought my own women to serve me, along with deep trunks of gowns. Of course, they did not know why I was there. No one knew but my brother. My husband had not told him in his letter, but I had no doubt that the reason my brother kept his throne, and kept peace in his own lands, was because he was rarely caught unawares. Phillipe was still young, but he saw far.

I waited in my rooms but received no summons for an audience. I thought at first that I might go down to dinner in the great hall, but no woman came to lead me there, and as I looked at my rumpled gown, I knew that I could not face my brother's court that night.

Instead, I dressed in a decent gown of black and wrapped my father's rosary around my waist, where the diamonds, pearls and amethysts caught the light from the candles. I knew that I could find the chapel, for I had a rare sixth sense about such things. I could find nothing else in strange places but was always was able to find my way to God.

I went out without a lady to escort me, since only serving women had come to me since my arrival. My reputation and honor were long since spent, so I thought nothing of it as I strolled alone down the wide, torch-lit corridor of my brother's castle.

I thought of my father as I walked, and I felt his presence with me, guiding me, telling me where to turn, and what stairs to take. This fancy served me, for I came to a small chapel, half hidden beyond the rooms where the court lived and played.

I stood in the doorway of that chapel and saw that it was well tended, though no one was there now but an old priest sitting in the

Presence. He stood and bowed to me but knelt again almost immediately. I could see that mass was never sung there anymore, for my brother had greater places to hear mass, large cathedrals where all might see him. This was a private place, a silent place, where a man could come before God with none to know it but him.

I remembered suddenly that my father had brought me there once when I was a child. He had brought me to that chapel to take mass when he was between queens. With no wife to chide him and to keep him from me, we had knelt together on our cushions before the altar, and heard mass sung for us alone.

I genuflected before the Host and came to kneel behind the priest. He did not turn to look at me again, but left me to my prayers, as I left him to his.

Though it had been many years since I had knelt without a cushion, I still remembered Mother Bernard's trick of folding my gown beneath my knees. I knelt a long time, going over the litany of my dead, saying prayers to the Holy Mother and to God, that their souls might be safe in heaven.

When I was done, I stood, my knees creaking from being on the hard ground. The priest still knelt before me, as if I had never come in. I stood a while longer in the Presence of God, until the priest rose, crossing himself, and stepped back behind a screen without a word or a glance at me.

I heard a footstep behind me, and I turned, thinking one of my brother's women had found me. It was not a servant, but the Count of Valois who stood behind me.

"Your Highness."

He did not bow, but stood and looked at me, as if I were a river of clear water, and he had walked out of the desert, longing for a drink.

"My lord of Valois." I remembered myself enough to drop a small curtsy. I lowered my gaze, wondering why he was there. Once again, he had appeared from nowhere like magic in a fairy story.

"I heard that you had come to court, but I did not see you in the hall."

"No," I said. "I am at court only to see my brother."

We stared at each other as if we had never been parted. I had taken a lover and borne another man's child, but now that Jean Pierre stood before me, I felt as if nothing had changed between us. He was the same as when I had last seen him by the river on my husband's land, with the sunlight in his hair.

The need to weep rose in me from the ground at my feet. Tears I had been trained never to shed in front of strangers, in front of anyone, came into my eyes. I turned from him, searching for the handkerchief I always carried, the one that bore Eleanor's seal. But then I remembered that I had given it to him. I did not carry one of my own anymore, as I had no more need to weep.

He was at my side in a moment, his hand on my arm, with no thought for the fact that I was a married woman or a princess of France.

I had a fanciful notion that he might kiss me, as I looked into the clear blue of his eyes. They reminded me of my husband's eyes at first, those eyes of agate that looked only on my brother with love, and on myself with respect and kindness.

But in that moment, I saw that this man was nothing like my husband. When he looked into my eyes, he wanted all of me. He raised his hand to my cheek and brushed my tears away with his fingertips. His touch was gentle, the soft touch of a moth. His hands were callused, and the hard pads of his fingers made me weak. I leaned into him. It had been months since a man had touched me, and I hungered for it.

I was sure that he would kiss me, but Jean Pierre had a mind for where we stood even if I did not. He took a step back and I swayed as if to follow him. He caught my arm and held me back.

I saw then that the priest had come out to tend the candles at the altar and had stopped in his business to stare at us, to see what new mischief the king's wanton sister would make, even here, in the house of God.

The count took my arm and led me away, as if it were his right. I knew that word of our connection would be spread throughout the court by sunrise. I prayed that it would not make my brother turn from me before I had begged his mercy.

Phillipe was unlikely to grant mercy in any case; a king was rarely free to be merciful. But for all the darkness that had passed between

Richard and me, and for all the good that had not grown between us and never would, I would still speak for him, even at the gates of hell, if my voice could do him any good.

Jean Pierre knew where my room was and took me there, for servants were easily bribed in my brother's house. He opened the door for me. I stopped just inside and held up one hand.

"You can come no further."

He did not protest. He looked down on me, his feathered hat jaunty on his head, his eyes dark where the shadow of the hallway covered them, hiding his thoughts. But then he leaned forward and the light from the candles in my room fell on his face. I saw that he still loved me, even after all this time, even though his love for me had brought him nothing, barely even the touch of my hand.

He smiled then, and I saw that he liked me as well. This was welcome knowledge. For in my father's house, which had now become my brother's, I was surrounded by enemies. Most courtiers thought nothing but ill of me and were amused by the dark turns my life had taken.

In that place, which held only memories of all that was gone from me forever, Jean Pierre stood with me. I knew in that moment that he would stand by me for the rest of his life, whoever's wife I was, even if it brought him the displeasure of the king. I saw in his face that he valued me for myself. He was the only one in my life to value me so, except Marie Helene. And perhaps Richard in the first moment we met, so many years ago.

"Good night, Your Highness. I will bring you to the king on the morrow. Do you have anyone to sleep outside your door?"

I smiled at this. As if he thought my brother's house a den of thieves, from which I needed guarding.

"I have no guard, but I do not need one. This door has a sturdy lock."

"Have you any women to attend you?"

"I did not bring one, for I wished to travel light. The palace women have lit my fire and brought water and wine. I will do well enough until morning."

This did not satisfy him, but he did not have the right to say anything more. He kissed me once, hard on my closed lips, then stepped back, as if he did not trust himself to touch me further.

"Close the door and lock it, Highness. I return in the morning, to see that you are safe and well."

"Good night, Jean Pierre."

At the sound of his name on my lips, a smile lit his face. The year and more that we had been apart had been hard on him, harder than I would ever know, and for reasons that he would never let me see. Some men are born for war, and some men join in battle against their better judgment. Jean Pierre was one of the men that carried the scars of battle not on his body, but on his soul.

He bowed but did not move away. I closed the door and locked it. I waited a long time, but I did not hear his footsteps when he left. The door was thick and might have muffled the sound. Or he stayed by me and guarded my door until the sun began to rise, and the servants began to stir. I slept well that night, feeling more protected and cared for than I had since I was a child, before my father had sent me away.

14

THE MEETING

I DID NOT SEE JEAN PIERRE THE NEXT MORNING. When my brother's women brought in my wash water and my breakfast of fruit and cheese, he was not lurking in the hallway.

The pastry in my brother's house was as light as I remembered it from childhood, and it seemed to melt on my tongue. When I returned to Ponthieu, I resolved to ask William if we might find a Parisian chef retire to the country and cook for us.

This thought only lingered as long as the pastry did. I turned my mind to the king as the palace women helped me dress. I wore a veil, though I could not bring myself to wear a wimple. The women's eyes spoke of my lack of virtue, even as they cast them down.

I had long since grown used to the censure of others, so that now I hardly noticed it. I thought only of how my brother might see me as I came to plead for Richard's life. If my brother's allies did not poison Richard one night, being mewed up indoors would kill him.

I knelt in prayer before I went to my brother. I asked God to guide me and for the Holy Mother to give me eloquence. I remembered the time I had pled for my own freedom before my wedding, and how I had failed. I pushed this thought from me to leave my mind clear, that I might seek God unencumbered.

I was at peace when I stood again and found one of my brother's footmen waiting for me in the doorway. He said nothing but crossed himself when I did. I took this for a good omen and smiled at him. He returned my smile shyly before leading me away.

I was taken not to the great hall, for my brother would not be there so early in the morning. Nor was I brought to the throne room at the top of the curving stairs. I was taken instead to my brother's private rooms where my father and I had often knelt in prayer when I was a child.

I stood in the gloom as my brother dismissed his manservant. Phillipe straightened the sleeves of his gown, drawing them down to cover his wrists. The door closed, sealing us away, but as always with a king, I knew that others were no doubt listening and waited for his attention just behind the door.

I was grateful to my brother for seeing me alone, so as not to humiliate me. For I could see in the first moment that he would refuse my request. If he had meant to grant it, he would have seen me formally, in public, so that his largesse would have witnesses.

As it was, he sat at his own table, wine and cheese laid out. He offered a chair to me and went so far as to have his man draw it out before he sent him away.

I sat with my brother and watched as he ate. He had yet to speak a word but only waved in greeting before turning to his breakfast. Some wine had been poured for me, but it was a heavy red, and I did not touch it.

"Brother, I have come to ask a boon of you."

Phillipe smiled at me. I had caught him on a good day, for he seemed delighted by my lack of hesitation and my lack of fear. He leaned back in his chair, enjoying the moment between us, and his power over me. He knew that to ask him for anything cost me more than I would ever say.

"Indeed, sister. And a boon that brings you here yourself, unescorted, not three months after you have delivered your husband's heir."

I heard his amusement at my disgrace, and irritation that I had defied him by giving birth to the next Countess of Ponthieu. But I knew he bore me no ill will for this, for not only had he stood as Marie's godfather, he had sent the princely gift of a gold cradle that no one in their right mind would ever set a child in.

So, nothing more was said of my daughter. He simply watched me and waited, knowing already what I would ask.

"Let Richard go," I said.

Phillipe laughed out loud then, his warm voice echoing off the wood paneling of the chamber. The tapestries were down for cleaning, and his voice carried well, for he had been trained to give orders on the battlefield.

"Sister, I do not have your errant lover up my sleeve. He is not a prisoner of France. Indeed, he is my brother king. He is being held at the pleasure of the Holy Roman Emperor. Surely even in the wilderness you live in, you have heard this much?"

"Brother, do not insult me. We both know the emperor holds him at your request."

"You give me more power than I have, Alais."

His eyes hardened and for a moment I thought he would order me from him, that my audience had ended before it had even begun. But he remembered our father and the ties of duty that bound us. He knew that my youth had been given in the service of France, as even his had not. For he was not a woman, bound to obedience, but a man who could act and think for himself.

Phillipe paused, taking a long, deep sip of wine. When he spoke, his voice was calm, all trace of laughter gone. "Even if it was in my power, I would not free him, Alais."

I saw in his eyes a moment of private pain which he did not mean for me to see. I would not have recognized it, had it not reflected some of the pain I felt myself. He, too, loved Richard, though he would never own it. He, too, had once been close to him and had lost him, as I had.

It was this pain I spoke to and not my

brother the king. "Phillipe." I kept my voice low, my eyes downcast. "Can you not take pity on him, for my sake?"

The window that had been open to his soul fell shut. It never opened to me again in the same way, though over the years I came to know him a little better. My brother was a hard man. It was this hardness, this strength, which answered me.

"Let me be certain of what I am hearing. When you first were betrothed, Richard left you to the devices of his mother and the mercy of his hell-spawn father. He did not lift a finger to save you, even when you were his contracted wife. But you have come here, when he is less than nothing to you, when you owe him nothing but contempt, to plead for him with me." Phillipe did not ask this as a question but stated it as fact.

I raised my eyes and met his gaze, unblinking. "Yes."

He sighed and rose from his chair, his wine and breakfast forgotten. He paced the room, but it was small and confined him, so that he soon stopped again. I had the impression of a beast in a menagerie, some great mountain cat that had been caged and now wanted only to be free. Nothing of this desire for escape was reflected in his voice when he spoke, for my father had had the training of him. He knew his duty, as I did.

"You know that he has married that Spaniard? And surely you have heard, that when he was in the Levant, he took a Muslim whore?"

"I have heard."

This infidel woman was only whispered of – as an aberration even stranger than Richard's rumored taste for young men. I had heard this rumor and let it pass from my mind as quickly, like water running out of a broken jar. For as always, anything Richard did was nothing to me compared to the love that lay between us. I would carry that love with me to my grave and beyond, past the gates of Paradise.

"And still you plead for him. Sister, you are too good for this world."

I frowned, for I thought that he mocked me. I saw almost immediately that he did not, that he looked at me with a calm, unwavering stare. After a long, considered glance, he looked away. Goodness was a commodity worth nothing.

"We are all sinners before God, brother."

Phillipe waved away my talk of religion with one hand. "Whatever may or may not be true about the state of Richard's soul, he is too dangerous to let live. And yet we cannot kill him outright, for he is an anointed king. I think our solution is a rather elegant one."

He walked to the room's only window, a small slit that let in little light. He stood, looking beyond it to the courtyard below. Phillipe spoke to me as if in a dream. "Richard has his eyes set on France. He could not conquer Jerusalem. If he is released, he will come here. He will try to conquer us."

"He will not, Phillipe. He loves you."

My voice seemed to reach him, for he blinked, drawing himself back into the room, back from whatever road his mind had taken.

He turned to me then, and I saw the bitterness in his face. He did not try to mask it. For the first time I saw how deep it ran, and how much he once had loved Richard.

Phillipe's face was hard when he answered me, his eyes shadowed, and not just by the indoor gloom. "Whatever love there was between us was spent and lost, long ago."

We stood together in silence. There was no comfort for such a loss, and I offered none.

"If Richard comes back, he will come with an army. He may even turn his eye on your corner of the world, sister. He would destroy your peace. Surely you do not want that."

"He would not make war on us. Our house is bound to his, and his to ours."

"He would, and he will. That is why I pay Leopold to keep him where he is, where no harm can come to him, or to us."

When my brother openly admitted the truth, I saw that all my words had been in vain, so much air to warm the space between us. I wished for my father at that moment as I set the thought of Richard aside and reached for my brother's hand. "I love you, Phillipe. You serve and sacrifice for us all. I am grateful."

Tears came into his eyes, as hard as he was, as weary. He said nothing but raised my hand to his lips and held it there for one long moment. When he spoke, his tears were gone, and his voice was even, as if his emotion had never been. But still, he held my hand.

"And will you leave us, sister? Do the pleasures of the country call you quickly away?"

"I am meant for a quiet life. I will return to my husband before the sun has set."

Phillipe drew his hand from mine. "I will send you with an escort and with ladies to attend you. You must think of my state, sister, if not your own. A princess of France cannot gad about the countryside with six men-at-arms and no retainers."

I knew his censure for what it was, care for my wellbeing that he could voice no other way. He was a hard man, and sometimes a cruel one, but I saw then for the first time that he loved me.

"I must be about the business of the kingdom, Alais. I have no more time to devote to talk of your lovers and their whereabouts."

He moved to leave me. I could hear his courtiers gathering outside the door.

I stepped toward him and kissed him quickly, before he could get away. "Come to us at Easter, brother."

He let me kiss him and did not pull back. "My time is not my own, sister, as you well know. But I will be there, if I can."

Only then did I think of William and of how it would hurt him to see my brother again. But I looked to my brother and his loneliness. There is nothing like a crown to keep a man from those who love him. I had seen it in Henry and in my father, too.

Phillipe left me without another word. He did not look back. I stood a long time in his room, the cloying scent of sandalwood burning in the brazier.

I moved to leave. I meant to send word to

my husband's men-at-arms that we would leave with the tide. Only then did I see movement behind the screen in the corner.

A tall man emerged, with a weasel's face and a sly smile. At first, I took him for an assassin and thanked God that my brother had already gone. I looked behind the screen and saw a chair hidden there. Whatever warmth my brother felt for me, he had known that this man was listening to every word.

I felt this betrayal like a sharp thrust of a dagger in my side. But the cut was not deep, for I had been betrayed before, and by those closer to me.

"So, princess, you come to ask for my brother's freedom?"

When he stepped closer to me and into the light of the lamp, I saw that it was Richard's brother, John. I remembered how this man had waylaid me in England in an effort to marry me before I could return to France, but all illusion of courtly love had been stripped away from him now. His face held nothing for me but contempt.

I stared at him as if he were a bug that would soon be crushed beneath the heel of my shoe. I thought to leave, but he placed himself between me and the door.

Though John sought to menace me, I knew him to be a weakling and a coward, so I was not afraid. I had been done more harm than he could conceive of by his betters.

He smiled at me, and I saw a little of Henry in the line of his jaw, and in the slant of his eyes,

I saw traces of Eleanor. Of Richard, I saw nothing.

"Richard is better off where he is. Perhaps he has a fat German woman to keep him warm at night." When this clumsy thrust did not touch me, he went on. "Or perhaps he has taken a young page to his bed. Your husband could tell you something of that, no doubt."

I called on all the training of my childhood to keep my face impassive. Anger rose hot in me, and I took a deep breath of the incense-scented air. The room was too warm, and the air, too close.

I moved to walk past John, but again he blocked my path. This time he stood so close that I could smell the cloying perfume he wore under his gown. I did not gag but stepped back reflexively.

He smiled, thinking that I moved away out of fear, and not out of loathing. "You could always cast off your husband as my mother did. And take a new one."

I took a shallow breath, wanting to reach for a handkerchief to cover my nose and mouth, but I no longer carried one.

John stepped forward, his eyes on mine. As I watched him, his gaze slipped lower, down my gown with its modest front drawn close over my breasts, past my waist to my thighs, where they were hidden beneath the silk of my skirt. I almost laughed to think that this man was rumored to be a womanizer. But then I thought of Richard and of how he had no heir. This man would be king, if Richard died with no son to succeed him.

I felt the pain of that, as if it were the death of my own son I had just heard of. As I stood there, it seemed I could hear the sound of our unborn son's laughter. I could almost hear him on the stairs as he came into my solar and see his happy face shining as he brought me some boyish treat, a flower from the garden or a strip of leather from the tilting yard. This boy's face was before me, the son I would never see, his father's blue eyes shining, his father's dark red hair around his shoulders like a lion's mane.

I staggered under the weight of this pain, my hard-won impassivity shattered. Like the animal he was, John scented this, and caught my arm before I fell.

The stink of his perfume mingled with the scent of sandalwood in the brazier. I thought that he would kiss me in that moment of my greatest weakness, hungry to score another victory over me. But John seemed to remember who I was and who my father had been. He was my brother's ally, but he had heard us speak. Perhaps we had seemed closer than we were, for once I gained my footing, he let me go.

John's gaze met mine, all lust burned away. Only calculation remained in the light hazel of his eyes. "Remember what I offer you. You might put your husband aside and marry me."

I saw that he thought to dazzle me, as if I had never had the throne of England offered me before. I remembered Henry in that moment and his strength. I seemed to feel him with me, his power flowing into me with my next breath. Henry had been cruel and had used me for his own amusement, pride and pleasure, but he had loved me. Henry loved me enough in the end to let me go.

I took strength from my memories, from the scent of apple wood burning on a September fire and the color of maple leaves just beginning to fall. It seemed I could feel Henry standing behind me, a wall against which I might lean, a wall against the machinations of his youngest son.

"Remember, princess. My offer stands. Richard will not live forever." John turned and left me.

The scent of his perfume lingered in my eyes and on my skin. I found the chamber pot and retched into it. I had never been made sick by the mere presence of a man before. I could never again breathe in the scent of sandalwood without nausea.

I left my brother's chamber, but my memories of Henry were still with me. I seemed to feel his arm under my hand as he led me down the stairs and back to my room. I entered my room and turned to look for him, to see if perhaps his shade had returned from Hell to lead me.

My fancy was put aside like so much smoke, for there was no one. Only myself, alone in an empty room. I rang for my brother's women, that they might pack my things. I was going home.

15

HOME

I DID NOT SEE JEAN PIERRE AGAIN UNTIL THE
royal barge was halfway to Rouen. The sun was
beginning to set over the Seine, dazzling my
eyes. The water slid away beneath the polished
wood of my brother's boat. The silver cast of
the sun along the river reminded me that there is
beauty in the world.

I was downcast on leaving Paris, as I always
was. The interview with my brother and the
confrontation with John had only made it worse.
As I turned my thoughts toward my husband's
house, I found that though I missed Paris and
always would, I would never miss the court. For
better or for worse, I was content in the country,
where politics could do me no more harm.

The fresh air of the river raised my spirits. I
leaned back against the cushions of my brother's
shaded bench, listening to the stamp of the
horses behind me.

When coming to Paris alone, I had hired a
barge from Rouen and had flown my husband's

standard. Now I rode in the royal barge and my husband's coat of arms flew proud beneath the standard of the royal house of France.

I sighed, taking in the beauty of the countryside around me, letting go the horror of my time at court. The taste of bile was still in my mouth from my interview with John, so I called for wine. It was Jean Pierre who brought it to me.

I knew in that moment that my brother had sent him in my train, a parting gift and, perhaps, an apology. The only apology I was ever likely to receive from the king. Perhaps Phillipe truly would join us for Easter, if he was generous enough to send the man that I loved away with me.

I looked up at Jean Pierre, my eyes dazzled by the sunlight, until he sat beside me, the wineskin in his hand.

"Shall I pour you a glass, my lady?"

I smiled at his boldness and his ease with me. No one else seemed to see me as I was and not a reflection of my father or my brother. I took the wineskin from him and tipped it back, drinking deep.

Handing it back to him, I caught his eye. Jean Pierre could have looked no more surprised if I had leaned over the side of the barge and lapped water from the river. I started laughing then, a low belly laugh that left me gasping. It had been many years since I had laughed like that. Whatever else might lie between us, he had given me that.

He smiled but did not laugh himself. He

looked at me sideways, as if I were a woman he had never seen before, but one he liked the look of. I leaned back against the cushions of my brother's barge and let the pain of leaving Paris slip away with the outgoing tide.

I had done what I could, as little as that was. Richard was a man among men and would have to fend for himself. I put all thoughts of Richard aside, along with those of my brother and the hideous John. I turned my eyes to the sunset and to the cathedral of Rouen, where it gleamed in the fading light.

"They are to build a new church," Jean Pierre said, trying to cover his surprise at my ease with his wineskin and my sudden laughter.

I had drunk straight from such a skin only once before, long ago, walking with Henry under the apple trees of his hunting lodge.

I tipped Jean Pierre's wineskin back again. The taste of the warm red wine on my lips, combined with the warmth of the sun on my skin made me remember the part of myself that I had rediscovered in Gerald's arms. I realized that I would not return to my old ways of the nunnery within my husband's house. I would forge a new way, this time on my own. I would take Jean Pierre as a lover, if he was willing.

Something in my brother's eyes, as well as the dark loneliness of his court, reminded me that life was fleeting. As I looked at Jean Pierre beside me, sweet desire rose in me at the sight of his strong shoulders encased in the leather of his cuirass. I also felt my love for him rise in me like a blessing. The sin of living with joy, if sin it was, was something I would learn to accept.

As he raised the wineskin to his lips, Jean Pierre caught my eye on him. He faltered, blinking, as if struck by a bright light.

"I would have you take supper with me, if you are willing."

He stared at me, and at first, I thought he was going to dismiss my offer out of hand. I was married still. Perhaps his own sense of honor gave him pause. But his eyes met mine and held them. He drank, lowering the wineskin to the bench between us. I felt the weight of the gaze of my brother's men on us and knew it would not be worth his life for him to touch me there, under the open sky.

So, I smiled instead, so that he would not misunderstand me.

He swallowed hard, the wineskin forgotten, though he still held it in his hand. "It would be my honor, my lady."

I laughed for joy; it was the second time he had made me laugh that hour. He smiled a little, but I could see that it cost him something, that inadvertently I had broken a solemn moment between us.

I hid my hand beneath the silk of my skirt. The fashion at court was to wear skirts so long and wide that the skirt alone held material enough for one of the dresses I had worn at the convent. I slid my hand across the cushion I sat on, under the soft smoothness of my silk gown, until my hand caressed his thigh where the high boots met the hem of his tunic.

He stopped breathing, and I drew my hand away. He was careful to keep his face averted from me, looking out over the water and the town before us. I saw the line of his jaw, and how the muscles tightened there as if he wished to speak.

"I will ask for venison and mulled wine," I said.

Jean Pierre did not respond, nor did he look at me, and I wondered if I had been too bold, too much like a harlot. We had docked by that time, and the gang plank was down. I saw the monks standing in a row like birds, bobbing in their black gowns, ready to greet me. I rose and took one last look at Jean Pierre. He met my eyes now that none of the other men could see his face. He sent me a look of such pure longing that it made my heart sing.

"And fruit," he said. "Ask for fruit."

With a smile, I did not speak again but simply walked away.

The brothers made me welcome, treating me as if I were a queen indeed, and not a worn-out princess sold in marriage to a man half my age. They bowed me into the abbot's room, which had been cleared for me. The rushes on the floor were fresh and smelled sweetly of thyme and rosemary. The window opened over the cloister walk below, and there was a soft breeze from the river. I sighed, looking down over the shadowed arcade where jasmine grew.

The monks bowed themselves out of the room after I told them that I would not take my evening meal with the abbot, and that the table in my room need be set for two.

I waited for Jean Pierre after the meal was served. There was no venison, but some conies had been caught the day before, and they made a savory stew. The fruit was fresh and plentiful, pears just picked from the trees in the cloister garden.

Jean Pierre did not keep me waiting long, but he apologized as soon as he came in. I saw that he had bathed and wore fresh linen and a tunic of spun silk. The tunic was wrinkled from his saddlebag, but I knew it was the best he had with him and that he sought to do me honor.

I rose when he came in and took his hand when he bowed to me. I smiled, gesturing to a chair the monks had set on the other side of the small table. He would not sit, however, until I was in my chair again, a glass of wine poured and in my hand.

I thought for a moment that he had changed his mind, that seeing me again after so long in my brother's house had made him think of me as a princess indeed. I feared that he would not so much as touch the sleeve of my gown, but would serve me at table, as if he were a page in my brother's court. This fear soon left me, for he poured a glass of wine for himself and sat down across from me, though he kept to the edge of his chair.

I did not wait for him to eat, but sliced fruit

and crumbling cheese for him, sliding the food across the table. He did not touch his stew but took some fruit when I offered it. We did not speak for a long moment, as I set myself to my dinner. He ate a little of the pear and sat watching me. I hungered for his touch, but I hungered for my dinner more.

I remembered the time I had spent with Henry, and the affection I had felt for him in spite of his faults. I thought of my love for Richard, and how it had survived so many years and would survive my death.

As I ate, my thoughts slid from where I was and who I was sitting with, back to the day I had first seen Richard, surrounded by his mother's women, the sunlight from the eastern window catching the gold hidden in the red of his hair. I lay my spoon down on the wooden table, the taste of the cream-stewed rabbit peppering my tongue. I felt the old sorrow that always surrounded memories of Richard yet again, as if the wound had been delivered in that moment, fresh and bleeding.

I was sick of that old pain and angry that now, in this peaceful place, in this moment of stolen happiness, the memory of Richard had come to rob me of what little joy I had found without him.

Jean Pierre was watching me, and he saw me turn pale. He leaned across the table and took my hand in his. He drew me to my feet, away from the remains of our unfinished meal. "Lady, I would ease your burdens, if I could."

With effort, I drew my mind back from the abyss of the loss of my first love, the only true love of my life. I looked at the man standing beside me and felt his hand warm on mine. I felt his touch as if from a great distance. I tried to draw my mind back from the past, from the man I would never see again. Richard had married another woman and had loved who knew how many since first we met. Richard, it seemed, would haunt me for the rest of my life.

As I stood, overwhelmed by pain, the touch of the Holy Mother came to me. She seemed not to notice the sin that I hoped to embrace. She overlooked all the sin I had been steeped in since I had come into my husband's house. The Mother seemed only to have compassion for my pain. With the soft touch of Her Hand, she took my sorrow away, if only for that one night.

Her Hand withdrew from me as quickly as it had come, but I stood able to breathe without longing, free of the past that had dogged me all my life. I met Jean Pierre's eyes, and it seemed that I saw him truly for the first time. He was a man who loved me enough to hold my hand, even as I thought of another.

His clear blue eyes shone in the firelight with more love than I deserved. But deserving has little to do with what we are given in this life. With the Hand of the Virgin lingering on me still, I leaned forward and touched his lips with mine.

He was gentle, as if I were made of spun glass, as if I might break apart at the touch of his hand. It was I who pressed against him, until a fire quickened in both of us. We moved to the bed, leaving the rest of our dinner untouched.

The monks must have known what we were about, for no one came in to clear the table or to wipe the dishes clean. We ate a little of the fruit and cheese in the abbot's bed, I wrapped in a sheet, and Jean Pierre wearing nothing at all.

I watched the play of the firelight across his body and could not stop myself from leaning over to run my hand across his chest and along his narrow, tapered waist. Our food was forgotten for a time and I wound up with soft cheese in my hair.

On toward morning, before we slept, we lay together, the last of the food put by, wrapped in cloth to keep the mice away. My head rested on his chest, my long hair cast about us like a net we both were caught in. He caressed me, but he was no longer relaxed, as I was. It was then I remembered what I had discovered as I lay beneath his body as he made love to me. He loved me more than I loved him.

"Princess."

He spoke the one word and for a moment, I thought that he would not speak again. I was sated as I had not been in many months, if ever, and sleep dragged at my mind as the tide pulls a ship to sea. I forced myself awake, for I heard his need. There was little I could give him beyond the love I felt, but I could listen when he spoke.

"I must take you back to your husband."

I heard the sorrow in his voice. I raised myself, leaning down to kiss his cheek. "You will bring me to my husband's house, Jean Pierre. I would have you stay with me there, if you are willing."

I saw that he did not understand my meaning. His eyes were still shadowed by the grief he had borne since he first met me. Knowledge of my body made this grief even keener – to know me and not be able to possess me honorably. I had become a poison in his blood, as Richard was a poison in mine. There was no cure for that poison, now that he had touched me.

"Stay with you?"

"If you are willing." I met the blue of his gaze and watched as comprehension dawned in him, and tears came into his eyes.

He knew how little I had to offer him, yet his love was so great that he accepted it with grace, as if it were a gift indeed.

I kissed him.

"You unman me, lady."

I smiled gently, so that he could see that I was not mocking him. "That is impossible."

He drew me close, and I rested against his chest, my cheek over his heart. This man would guard me with his life. He loved me, not for my relationship to my brother, nor for any gains I might bring him. He loved me simply, purely, and I could feel the purity and peace of his love surround me with every breath I took. I slept then, wrapped in the warmth of his arms, feeling safer than I had in many years, since my father had sent me away.

In order to keep my reputation intact, Jean Pierre left me before the sun rose. Very likely, some of the servants saw him walking to his own room, but if asked, no doubt he would have told them that he had risen early for prayer.

When he was gone, I prayed, kneeling on the *prie dieu*. I said part of a rosary for my daughter and for my husband, and then for Marie, who was always an afterthought with me during that time.

I turned my mind then to my sin, but I found that I could not repent. I knew that would come with time, so I left it and stood to wash my face and hands in the water left from the night before. I felt the Hand of the Holy Mother on me as I washed myself in the cold light of early morning. I saw that She was with me, even as I walked in sin. I wondered that I could still feel Her presence.

These thoughts left me as the servants came and cleared away my dinner from the night before. I had made certain that the bedclothes were clear of cheese, but the rest I left to God.

There was a certain coldness in his manner when the abbot bowed to me at the monastery gate. I nodded to him and raised my hand in parting. Jean Pierre had taken his leave already and stood far back, holding his horse by the bridle. I looked into the eyes of the abbot and was certain that a man on horseback was already riding to my husband with the news of my latest infidelity.

I could not find it in my soul to care, even for a moment. I felt free, for the first time in my life, both of sin and of sorrow. I faced my future with the calm certainty that while I would never have the best that life might once have given me, neither would I have the worst. I had seen the worst long ago when I had laid my daughter in the ground. I had seen the worst when I watched Richard walk away from me in the cloister garden at the convent of St. Agnes when I was sixteen years old.

Loss seemed to lose its hold on me, time loosening its grip. I came to see that all went the way of my daughter and of Richard. All the things of this world were not mine to keep, but only to enjoy if I was fortunate, and then only for a little while. I found myself musing thus as I took my leave of the abbot. I forgot him and his sour face almost as soon as we rode away.

The morning passed quickly on the road, with Jean Pierre never speaking to me. He was afraid even to glance in my direction and I wondered if the abbot had spoken harshly to him.

We did not stop along the road but crossed on horseback to my husband's lands. I was anxious to be home and to hold my daughter again. Her face came back to me as we rode, as did the look William wore when he gazed at her.

The thought of William brought me pain, the idea that he might be displeased that I had so openly chosen a lover for myself. It was a sharp quick jab which took my breath. I blinked and accepted it, looking across the pommel of my saddle to where Jean Pierre rode beside me. He flanked me, as if to keep himself between me and the rest of the world, but still he would not look at me.

I reached across the distance that separated us, for our horses walked close together, along a narrow path that had no turning. My brother's and my husband's men spread out before and behind us, so that we were almost alone among the shelter of the trees.

"The abbot has grieved you," I said.

Jean Pierre looked at me sharply, surprised that I would be the first to speak. I saw then that he thought to sacrifice himself to what he thought of as the greater good, the sanctity of my marriage vows, and the tattered remnants of my honor. I felt old suddenly as I looked at him, wondering at myself, that I was more worldly in this matter than this courtier who had been to Jerusalem and back.

Even then he would not speak. I saw that the path ahead widened before us, for we were nearing my husband's keep. If I did not speak now, I might lose the chance. I knew men and their pride, and how much it could cost me. Once there was room to maneuver, he might slip away.

"Jean Pierre, do not listen to a word the abbot said."

He thought to argue with me and only the

good manners he was raised to made him hold his tongue.

"I have no doubt he scolded you for abusing my brother's trust, his hospitality, and my husband's honor."

His color darkened beneath his tan and his jaw tightened.

"Let me tell you, as one who lived in a nunnery almost all my life, there are abuses in the Church that we have never even heard of. Our indiscretion was quite small and easily overlooked. Believe me when I tell you, if my husband does not object, the abbot cannot."

Jean Pierre looked at me for the first time since I had started speaking. "Lady, I have no doubt that he will object. What man would not?"

I was tempted to laugh, but I knew my laugh would sound bitter. I had come too far in a difficult life to embrace bitterness. I breathed deep, said a prayer to the Virgin, and let my bitterness go.

Jean Pierre had lapsed back into his own thoughts. He looked at me, startled, when I spoke again.

"William will not object, Jean Pierre. You will see."

We said nothing else. He was so far gone in love for me that he clung even to this small hope. As we rode into my husband's bailey, I wondered why the men who loved me were those I could not keep.

I looked at Jean Pierre as he got down from his horse. He bowed low to my husband, allowing William to come to me and help me down from my mount. As I looked past William, down on Jean Pierre's fair hair, I knew that I would try to keep this one for as long as I could.

"Welcome home, wife." William smiled up at me, and I was caught once again in the clear blue of his eyes.

The rest of the bailey receded in that moment, and there was only him. "Hello, husband."

He took my waist and swung me down from my horse. I thought that he would withdraw from me then, but he did not. We stood close, one of his hands still on my waist. He reached up and brushed back a curl from my forehead. "You are welcome, wife."

I smiled, beginning to come out of my reverie a little. "So you tell me, husband. I am glad to be home."

"You did not want to stay at court? I am sure your brother would have made you welcome."

"I am not made for court life. I prefer to be away and at peace."

"One can never be at peace at court." William's eyes darkened with memory, and I felt him withdraw, though his hand still rested on my waist.

"That is so."

The connection between us was gone as if it had never been. I felt my heart bruised yet again as he stepped away from me. Once the pain passed, I turned to my lover and held out my hand.

"William, you remember Jean Pierre, Count of Valois."

Jean Pierre blinked once at my boldness. He bowed to my husband again, then stood his ground at my side. I felt my heart warm at his romantic sweetness. I saw by his stance and by the set of his shoulders that he expected my husband to call him out for being my lover.

I watched as William took the measure of my lover with his eyes. To my surprise, I saw a hint of darkness in my husband's gaze as he looked at us, but it was quickly masked and fell away as if it had never been. I wondered after if I had seen it at all.

"You are welcome, count. My house is your house, for as long as you wish to reside here."

Jean Pierre said nothing but bowed again.

William met my eyes and quirked a brow at me, so that I smiled at him. "There is a feast prepared for you, my lady, if you would come and eat it."

"Yes, William, I thank you."

I thought my husband would walk ahead of us, but he reached out and took my hand in his. I stepped toward him and let him place my hand on his arm. He smiled down at me, the light from the setting sun striking the gold of his hair. He leaned down and kissed me then, in front of his men-at-arms. It was a chaste peck, the kiss of peace, to let all who watched know that whatever I did, whomever I took as my lover, my husband stood beside me.

Tears rose in my eyes, and I had to blink to

clear my sight. William led me into our home, and Jean Pierre came trailing after.

I could hear the rest of the baggage being taken off the pack mules, for my brother had gifted me with silks and spices. Later that night, when I returned to my rooms, I found all as I had left it, my new dresses the only sign that I had been away.

16

AN IDYLL

JEAN PIERRE WAS PUT IN THE ROOM NEXT TO mine. I thought at first that my husband was not going to publicly acknowledge that I had taken a lover, but one of the serving women drew back the unicorn tapestry along one wall and showed me the hidden door that lay in the stone beneath. The door was well oiled and opened without a sound to reveal Jean Pierre's room beyond.

I thanked her. She did not wink or nudge me, for I was far above her station, but neither did she seem embarrassed. I thought of my mother-in-law, the woman who had died years before I took her rooms for my own. I tested the door again when I was alone. Perhaps she had once taken a lover, as I had done.

My thoughts turned from this path almost immediately, for dinner was long over, and the serving women had brought my bath water. I sent them all away and bathed unattended, for

Marie Helene was in the nursery, watching over my daughter.

I warmed the water myself over a brazier, for it had gotten cold on the way up the stairs from the kitchen building. I would have to take a firm hand and get my household in order; I had been too long idle.

I stripped to my shift and bathed my hands and face. The soft scent of thyme and dried rosemary rose from the brazier at my elbow. I did not take off my shift, but washed myself beneath it, by the soft light of the fire.

Jean Pierre came in through the hidden door. I dropped my sponge, letting my hand rest on the edge of the silver basin. He stared at my body, revealed beneath the linen by the firelight. I stood still and let him look.

He showed nothing of the vulgarity of a young lover, there was no lasciviousness in his gaze, nor hunger, nor lust. I saw the purity of his soul as he looked at me, and his courage. He had braved my husband's house and had set aside his own honor for love of me. In that moment, as the firelight caught the shadowed blue of his eyes and the planes of his face hidden in the half light, I began to understand the depths of my love for him.

I did not move or speak but stood staring back at him. Something of my renewed love for him must have showed on my face, for his gaze softened.

He stepped forward of his own accord and took my hand. "I did not expect such a welcome, lady."

"In my husband's house?" My voice was breathless and did not sound like my own. I was an old woman by this time, a woman who had borne two children and who was now approaching forty, a woman who – though still beautiful –would never see her youth again. I had not thought that I could ever feel this way again, as if a bird had nested within me, fluttering against the cage of my ribs, just under my heart. I had not felt this way with anyone, not even with Richard.

When I raised my hand to draw it away from him, I found that it was shaking.

Jean Pierre saw it, too. He caught my hand and held it against his heart so that I could feel it beating. He pressed my palm against his chest and bent down to kiss me.

We did not sleep, but lay in my marriage bed, the fire dying in the brazier across the room. My bathing things lay forgotten on the table, and I smiled as I looked at them. "You make me forget myself."

Jean Pierre was not relaxed with me yet, as he would be in days to come. I could see that the cost of his honor was high, for he had never allowed himself to love a married woman before.

I had no doubt that he had heard the rumors about my husband and myself, the rumors of how our marriage was an empty one, as so many marriages were. I never knew for certain, for we never spoke of it.

Jean Pierre kissed me, not on my lips, a signal to begin the love play between us. He kissed me on my temple, where my hair hung down, trailing against my cheek. His lips were soft and warm, and I had begun to love the strength beneath them.

"I have not known myself since the day I saw you in that cloister garden, planting flowers."

"I rarely plant flowers anymore," I said, my voice wistful. "I work in my garden, but only from time to time. My husband has people even for that."

Jean Pierre smiled despite my mention of my husband. I saw that he used the strength of his will to put his dishonor behind him. My own dishonor did not concern him; he overlooked it from the start, for he loved me simply, as no other man ever did.

"You are no longer in the nunnery, love. Great ladies do not muddy their hands in the dirt."

"I am not great anymore, if I ever was."

He kissed my lips then, the warmth of his breath touching me like a blessing as he drew away. "I did not see you when you were younger, my lady, but I do not know how you could ever be more beautiful than you are now."

I felt a little of the wall around my heart cave as I lay with him, his strength beneath me, and the steady beat of his heart. I kissed him back, and we left off talking. I have never felt as safe as I did with him.

Of all the men I knew over the course of my long life, he loved me the most.

The next morning, I stood in the garden, watching my husband's people tend the neat rows of plants. The rows fanned out in circles around quince and pear trees. Some plants, the ones that needed it, had shade, and the others stood against the walls of the garden, drinking in sunlight. It was early, and there was not much light. I stood and let the sun warm my uncovered hair.

William found me that way, watching his people as they did what I had been raised to do during my years in the nunnery – work I no longer did.

"You might take it up again," he said.

It was often so with us, that we would begin a conversation in the middle, as one already in progress, with no need for explanation or clarity. It was as if he knew my thoughts, in a way in which I would never know his.

His eyes looked red from sleeplessness, and I wondered if he, too, had been up late entertaining, as I had been. The thought caused me a little pain, and I pushed it away.

"I have thought of it," I said. "I have also wondered if I might have been better suited to a religious life, tending the plants among the sisters, instead of being out in the world among men."

I said this by way of apology for publicly taking a lover and dragging his name as well as my father's through the midden. I did not regret taking Jean Pierre as my lover, for he was good to me, and I loved him in a way I had loved no other. I could not repent of the sin of loving him, but as I faced my husband, for the first time, I was ashamed.

William seemed to sense this, for he knew me better than I ever knew him. He reached out and took my hand and raised it to his lips. "I, for one, am glad that you are here, and among us."

That was all we said of my shame. As I stood there, I felt it fall away from me as a cloak onto a tiled floor. William kept my hand in his as he smiled down at me. "Lady, I have a house along the seacoast. It is built for watching for raiders, though none ever come."

"No Vikings, husband?"

He smiled, drawing my hand to his arm where I let it rest as he led me along the paths of the kitchen garden. "Few, lady, and none in my lifetime."

My lips quirked, and I thought to say that he had not been alive long. His eyes sparkled. He seemed to be thinking the same thing himself.

We walked under the shade of a pear tree. The fruit was hanging heavy, for it was midsummer, but it had not yet begun to ripen. William looked toward the kitchen building and saw that we were alone. The gardeners had gone back inside, and there was no one in the yard but the two of us.

"I have a house on the sea, my lady …"

"And you want me to go there?"

We stopped walking, and he looked down at

me. I had forgotten how tall he was, and how broad his shoulders. He was growing into his stature. He had been a beautiful boy when I met him, but it seemed now, two years later, that my husband was becoming a man. His blue eyes were clear, like the water in a fathomless lake, but I could not see into their depths. They were closed to me. I thought of Jean Pierre, and how his eyes showed all he felt, how his love for me was a thing he was proud of.

I took my hand from his. A bird came from across the yard and landed in the tree above us. As we stood and faced each other, it started singing.

"Yes," he said.

We stood alone, the songbird our only witness. I wanted in that moment to beg him to love me, to turn from my brother who would never love him back and to reach for me, the woman who would love him all his life.

But I saw enough in his eyes to know that such words could not be spoken between us, then or ever. He was young, no matter how tall he grew. With the constancy and certainty that only the young possess, he still believed that he would love my brother and my brother alone until the day he died.

I sighed and put the loss of my husband away in the mass of sorrows I kept over my heart. I turned my mind from it. Joy was to be found in the present moment. My sorrows were all in the past. Across the garden, I saw Jean Pierre emerge from the house, dressed in leather for the hunt. He had come to see me before he went riding out.

I stepped away from my husband. "As you say, William. I will go to the sea. The salt air will do me good, as long as I don't have to go out in a boat."

William smiled. It seemed I saw something, annoyance perhaps or a touch of jealousy, flash behind his eyes before he masked it. "A ship, lady. Boats large enough to go out on the Channel are called ships."

I laughed in spite of myself, the pain at being sent away from him dulled in the answering light in his eyes. I reminded myself that whatever else was true, this man was my friend, and was offering me a way to have my lover and leave his court in peace.

"You will return before the snows come," he said. "I can only spare you a month or two. After that, Marie will begin to pine."

It was kind of him to say so. Though my daughter loved me, Marie Helene was her real mother now. I had only borne her and then given her up to the care of others.

William bent down from his great height and kissed me. His lips were like a feather on my skin. I did not move, and then the slight pressure of his lips was gone. He left me standing among the flowers, and my lover came to meet me and take my hand. They were to go out riding together, hunting deer for supper.

Jean Pierre said nothing but looked down on me with love in his eyes. He kissed me, and I felt the pressure of his lips like a lifeline, tying me to the earth, and to what I could have, all my longing for what could not belong to me fading like a ghost.

"I love you," I said when he drew away.

He searched my eyes and saw that I was not lying. "And I love you."

He answered only after consideration, after seeing clearly that I did not offer him pap to soothe him but spoke only the truth from my heart. There were many kinds of love. I discovered that just as I had loved Henry and Richard, so I loved Jean Pierre and William. They were such different men, and with each, I was a different woman.

"We are going away," I said. "We are to stay in a house by the sea, far from my husband's court."

"If you wish it, I will follow you to the end of the earth." His voice was low and even.

I kissed him again, before drawing away to lead him out of the garden. "That won't be necessary. Just to the sea, where we can eat fish everyday."

"So, it will be like Lent," he said, his eyes smiling.

I laughed and drew him close for one more kiss. "No, my lord. Nothing like Lent."

The house was less than a day's travel on horseback. After kissing my daughter and Marie Helene good-bye, we left the next day for my husband's house by the sea. The place was old and rarely used.

The villagers were fishermen and watch-keepers only. They bowed to me and took off their hats, but I saw suspicion in their eyes. At first, I thought they judged me as an adulteress, but then I saw that it was the suspicion of country people for those not their own. I put them from my thoughts, for my husband had sent servants with us to keep me in state, a gardener to reclaim the grounds, a cook to make our dinner, and a gamekeeper in case Jean Pierre chose to go hunting.

William did not see me off when I left. Only Marie Helene came to say good-bye, my daughter in her arms, wriggling to climb down and run to me as I sat on my tall horse. My eyes filled with tears to see my only living child fight to come to me, and Jean Pierre took my hand in his. I felt the warmth of his skin through my glove, and my tears receded.

"We do not have to go, my lady," he said.

I looked up at my husband's house, to the windows of his rooms. He had not come down to see me off.

"Yes, we do," was all I said before we rode away.

The ride cheered me, for I had become, if not an accomplished horsewoman, at least a competent one. High summer had the land in its grip, so we rode past fields of grain that were turning from green to gold. In another month they would be harvested and milled for bread.

We rode slowly, sometimes holding hands. Jean Pierre never worried that others would think him less of a man for loving me. I felt as if

I had been given a little of my youth back when I was with Jean Pierre, a little of the time of simple pleasures that had been stolen from me to shore up the political power of others.

The house was barely three rooms wide. The servants lived in a separate building. William had sent word the day before that we were coming, so the few rooms were clean.

The entire top floor was the bed chamber, warmed by the fireplace that blazed in the room below. The warmth was welcome at night, when the wind came up from the sea.

There was a cliff near the house that looked down on the Channel itself. We went walking there almost every day, the wind blowing our cloaks tight around us. Sometimes I would leave mine behind at the house on purpose, so that I would have to share his.

For a man of action, Jean Pierre was very patient during our time together. I thought he might be restless and long for the excitement of the hunt, if not the court itself. But he seemed content to sit with me in the evenings by the fire after the servants had left, and to walk with me for miles during the day, eating the bread and cheese and fruit the cook had packed for us. The wine we brought from my husband's house and drank along that rocky shore was the sweetest of my life, and the nights I slept there were the most contented and dreamless.

One night, after our first month there, we lay together on the sagging bed. Though the feather mattress was fresh from my husband's house, the ropes of the bed were loose. I meant to have the servants replace them, but I never did. The creaking of those old ropes sounded like the sea outside our windows, and the wind that never stopped blowing from the cliffs.

The creaking of those ropes wakes me sometimes even now when I dream of them. I think myself safe in Jean Pierre's arms again, the fire of the brazier close beside us, the curtains of the bed drawn to keep out the chill. In those dreams, I feel his arms around me, and I wake with tears on the bolster under my head.

But this was long before he visited me in dreams, when I was still blessed to feel his arms around me in truth. That night as we lay together, sleep was far from us. We listened to the wind as it blew against the stone of the house, working its way around the shutters that were locked fast.

His hair was golden in the firelight, for we had not yet drawn the bed curtains. I ran my hand over the gold of his hair, which smelled of the salt of the sea. For we had walked that day along the cliff, as we did every day, unless it was raining. On rainy days we often did not get out of bed, much to the disapproval of the local gossips. In such a small place, as at court, everyone knew everything.

Our own people kept us comfortable, though, and our little house was snug and safe as no place else has ever been for me. Jean Pierre seemed to feel it, too, for he never went hunting, nor did he seem to long for the excitement of Paris, with the fine meals in the royal hall and the constant amusements of the court. We were content in each other's company. That night we savored our time alone for what it was, a stolen season.

"I wish your brother had married you to me." Jean Pierre did not look at me when he said this but stared into the fire.

I saw that a brooding mood had taken him, as it sometimes did. I pressed myself against him and drew his eyes back to me. "My lord, my marriage is a political one. The king had need of my husband, and when he no longer did, he gave him to me."

It was the closest I ever came to speaking of the lack of love between my husband and myself, the broken places in my marriage that I thought would never heal. Jean Pierre did not press me with questions as another man might have, but drew me close, and kissed my hair where it curled against my cheek.

"We are safe from politics here," he said.

I opened my mouth to agree with him, but his lips were on mine then, and we lost ourselves in love play. That was our last unfettered night, for the next morning, I woke with the first of my sickness, and could not eat until well after noon. Though we stayed a few more weeks, trying to cling to the idyll, to the stolen time we could not keep, it was never the same again after that night.

I was pregnant, and the weight of our child lay between us, the knowledge that another man would raise his son as his own. Jean Pierre would someday have to go about the business of arranging a marriage for himself, so that his father's line might not die out. We knew from the next morning on that the child of his heart would belong to another man. The son he longed to have for his heir would have to be left with me.

17

A SON

My husband heard the news that I was to bear yet another man's child. As Jean Pierre and I stood before him, I watched William for some sign of pain or anger and. I saw none. Only a tightening along his jaw, before he took me in his arms to give me the kiss of peace.

Jean Pierre refused to let me speak to my husband alone, for fear William might strike me to avenge his honor. Jean Pierre did not understand our relationship, as indeed I did not. Perhaps he thought that William would challenge him to a duel. Of course, my husband did not. After letting me go, William announced again that Jean Pierre was welcome in his house for as long as he wished to stay.

Later that evening, as William led me into dinner, he and I were able to speak. "Your man has a care for your honor," he said.

"Yes. It is a shame that I do not."

William laughed. "Your brother is cursing my name."

"All the kingdom knows that you let your wife run wild."

For all the love that lay between Jean Pierre and me, he was not a great one for laughter. William and I had found a comfortable place with each other where, if my wishful longing did not intrude, laughter always found us.

"It is my concern if I like a wild wife. They need not trouble themselves on our account."

I was still laughing when William handed me into my chair, where Jean Pierre waited, seated beside me.

I saw the light of jealousy in his eyes. I leaned over and kissed him. "I love you," I whispered so that only he would hear me, so that he would not forget. I knew a little of what it cost him to live in my husband's house.

Jean Pierre never allowed our situation to unman him, as a lesser man might have done. He accepted the limits of our life together and never reproached me for things I could not change.

He kissed me back, his lips lingering on mine, until my husband's court sent up a cheer, breaking into our reverie. I looked up, startled, but I did not pull away.

My husband raised his glass to us, and his smile wished us well. I saw something in his eyes, a shadow that he quickly hid from me, one that I never saw again all through that pregnancy.

It was evening, and my stomach had long since settled from the morning's queasiness. Jean Pierre drew our trencher close to us and cut a piece of roasted venison for me. He fed it to me with his fingertips, since all the rest of my husband's people had gone back to their own meals and their own lovers and friends. Even my husband had turned from us to his own current favorite, the young man named Gregory. We were alone in the midst of all those people.

"I killed this buck for you, lady."

I took the meat from his fingers with my lips, longing for the time when the meal would end, and we would be alone once more.

I drew back to take up my glass of wine and caught my husband's eye. He had been watching me, his face unreadable. When I discovered him staring, he only smiled at me.

I turned my thoughts from my husband, who sat with his own lover beside him. I turned from William once more and met my own lover's kiss. Jean Pierre tasted sweet, like the wine he had been drinking. Even as we sat there, the moment had the soft, gentle quality of a memory.

As the sickness of early pregnancy receded, I felt again the great calm that came over me every time I was bearing. My son began to move inside me. I would take Jean Pierre's hand and place it under my heart, so that he too could feel our child move.

My husband had already acknowledged the child, even as the baby lay still in my womb. This cost Jean Pierre more than his honor, and still, he never reproached me.

I found myself most contented away from my husband's house, sitting in the high grass near the river where the irises and daisies grew. Marie Helene would bring Marie, along with all my daughter's retainers, and we would sit in state in the sunlight, my daughter's people fanning out around her, ready to serve her every whim.

In spite of this, or perhaps because of it, Marie would often leave them to come and sit by me. I had my own blanket in the grass, until I grew too big to sit on the ground. After that, Jean Pierre would have them bring a folding chair. This leather chair was something he had found on Crusade, and he told me that the Saracens used them when on campaign. I laughed when he told me that, wondering aloud if it was sacrilegious to sit on one. He frowned until he caught me smiling, and then he laughed with me.

My daughter would come to me and sit on this chair, her slender hips taking up room next to mine. When I grew too wide for this, I would place her on my lap, and we would make daisy chains. Mine always held irises and daisies, too. We would wear them like crowns back to the keep before sunset, and my husband would greet us with smiles, saying we were the princesses of his heart.

This would make Jean Pierre frown, and I would have to kiss him when we were alone to make up for my husband's words. In spite of the painful position I put him in, my lover never reproved me, neither in word nor in deed, all the time that I knew him.

We spent many afternoons basking in the

sunlight that autumn, listening as the river wound past on its slow way to the sea. We took in the scent of the fresh mown grass and barley, for it was harvest time, and the farmers were in the fields, bringing in the grain.

Those afternoons by the river were engraved on my heart, so that, even now that I am an old woman, I can remember every detail of that time, the sunlight on the water, the deep green of the grass where it met the blue of the sky, the purple irises trailing in my daughter's hair.

Sometimes at night when I cannot sleep, and prayer is far from me, I think back on that time, and of those I loved seated around me. My heart opens up, and I find that I can pray again. For the Hand of the Holy Mother is always near, beckoning me. But I must bring my mind to trust in God's goodness, back to the certainty of my childhood. From that place in my heart, I can reach for Her Hand.

My unconventional family stayed together all through that winter, taking in the Yule log and Christ's Mass, standing under the stars as we walked to church at midnight. Both my husband and my lover watched my belly grow, and, in late spring, they both came into my rooms when I was delivered of my son.

"We will name him Jean," my husband said.

I watched as Jean Pierre swallowed this. I thought perhaps it rankled for another man to name his first child. But then I saw that he fought the urge to weep. By naming my son for him, my husband had touched him, as even my love for him could not.

I did not speak but took my husband's hand. Only later, when Jean Pierre had gone to order a mass said in my son's honor, did I turn to William and kiss his cheek. "Thank you, husband."

His hand was soft on my hair. I could almost not feel the warmth of his palm, so lightly did he touch me. His eyes were as blue as the eyes of my child. "You are welcome, wife."

Jean Pierre came back then, with Marie Helene and the wet nurse in tow. William stepped away from me, giving up his place to another.

My son thrived. Marie was suspicious of him at first, but when Marie Helene and I redoubled our efforts to shower love on her, she decided that she would take her little brother under her wing. It was sweet to watch them sit together before the fire in the nursery and then play in the tall grasses by the river as spring came on.

Jean was a favorite with my husband as well, who, when Jean Pierre was away in Paris, would take the boy up before him on his horse, riding with him everywhere, whether hunting or simply riding through the fields. Marie Helene hated this, for she feared for his safety, but I knew my husband would care for Jean as if he were his own.

I also knew that the men of my family were raised to danger and warfare. The sooner my son took up this mantel, the longer he might live. I prayed that he would make a good lord one day, combining the goodness of my father with the strength of my brother.

Phillipe came to us in the country when my son was christened. He stood as godfather to this child too, not wanting to leave a daughter to outdo a son in honor. He stood in the front of the church with my husband and myself, and for the first time Jean Pierre seemed grateful to give place to William. He had no affection for my brother, even if he was king.

Phillipe stayed only for the day, bringing a great entourage with him, all of whom looked down their noses at us, especially at me, laughing behind their hands at my disgrace, and at how far pious Louis' daughter had fallen.

None of these people were foolish enough to say anything openly in front of my husband or my lover, but their amused pleasure followed me everywhere that day. Though I was not ashamed of my life or my choices, I was happy when they left.

So, my strange family went on its way, with everyone getting along well, Jean Pierre and I being as discreet as we could. My husband became so discreet with his own lovers after the birth of my son, that I was never sure when he took one at all. The children were happy, surrounded by so much love, and I began to hope that we might live on like this always.

And perhaps we would have, if the rest of the world had left us in peace. If we had been a country family in truth with no ties to the court, if I had not been born a princess, if my lover had not been born a count, and my husband had not been the last survivor of one of the oldest families of France. Perhaps things would have been different. But I learned as a child that fate is not something that can be run from. It must be faced, like loss, and sorrow, and the inevitability of death.

PART III
COUNTESS OF PONTHIEU

18

PARIS

More than a year passed as I lived with both my lover and my husband and watched my children thrive. The day I learned that I would return to Paris was a brilliant day in high summer. I was sitting in the garden with my son. It was one of those rare times when both his nurse and Marie Helene were busy elsewhere, and I could sit with my son alone.

Jean had learned to walk, and now was toddling between a bench and the nearest tree, trampling whatever plants came under his felt-clad feet. At first, I scolded him, before I realized that he was too young to understand me, and that whatever authority I might have had was long since replaced by Marie Helene and her gentle voice and smile.

Jean laughed, his childish giggles piercing the air. I caught him up in my arms to save a clutch of lavender that had not yet come to bloom. I pressed my lips to his neck, and he shrieked, wriggling not to get away, but to come closer to me.

Jean Pierre found us like that, both his love and his son laughing. He had been called away on his own family's business and had just returned from Paris that day. He never stopped in the monastery since we first had been there, though William had smoothed things over with the abbot and told him often that Jean was welcome.

He could not look the old abbot in the face and chose instead to take his chances at inns along the roadside, where there were always lice and fleas. I always had to comb him clean after he had been to one of those places, something he seemed to enjoy. Once, I assured him that I would give him all the attention he could desire if he would only stay away from those inns. After that, he found a hayloft to sleep in, or else he slept on the ground.

That day he came to me straight from the stable. He was always one to put his horse away, brushing the stallion down himself, never resting until the currying and the oats were seen to. So, he came to me covered in the dirt of the road, a little wisp of hay still stuck in his hair.

He took our son from me and kissed him while I reached up and drew the strand of hay from his golden hair. I smoothed his hair into place, so that it fell in a curtain to his shoulders. He smiled and kissed me, with our son between us.

We were rarely all three alone, and I drank in the moment as I did the sunshine and the birdsong. The scent of crushed thyme reached us from beneath the tree where Jean had stepped on it. Jean Pierre and I stood close, taking in its fragrance, one more stolen moment.

"My love, there is news from court."

I leaned against him, letting my forehead rest against his heart. He shifted our son to his other arm and held me close. I took in his scent, leather, and horse, and the grass he had slept in. I sighed before I spoke. "What news, love?"

Little Jean looked between us, his laughter forgotten. I smiled at him so that he would not be afraid, and his father kissed his hair. My son's hair was as fair as his father's, but it was light blond and downy, and stood out from his head like a halo.

Jean settled into his father's arms, happy to be there, quiet for the first time since he had been left with me that morning.

"Your brother the king has a son."

I felt a lump rise in my throat, the memory of my childhood coming back to me. All the years my father and I spent on our knees, praying for a son to preserve the safety of France. The years we waited for my brother to be born, and then, once Phillippe Auguste came to us, the years we prayed for his safety and his health. The memory of those years came upon me like a flood tide, and I stood in their wake, not moving, leaning against my lover's breast.

"God be praised," I said.

Though I was no longer worthy, though I had left my honor and my father's honor in the dust long ago, I stepped away from my lover in that sunlit garden and knelt before God, giving thanks I no longer had any right to offer.

In that moment, all the years I had spent in the service of France came back to me. I put aside my state of sin and pushed from my mind my fall from grace. I knelt among the trampled flowers and gave thanks to God that He had seen fit to preserve the kingdom for one more generation.

I was still praying when my husband found us standing in his kitchen garden, flowers and thyme lying where they had been crushed under my son's feet.

William came and stood beside me. He offered his hand to help me rise. "I told you, wife, you kneel to no one."

"I kneel to God," I said, but I stood as he bid me.

"Well, I suppose that is all right." William's sensual lips quirked in a smile, and I found myself caught by the blue of his eyes.

Jean Pierre came to my side, and I drew my eyes back to the man I loved and kissed my son's cheek.

"So, we are for Paris, and a royal christening," William said.

I turned my eyes to Jean Pierre, still holding our little boy. Jean saw William and crowed, holding out his arms so that my husband might take him.

Without a look at either of us, William swept my son into his arms, raining kisses on his face and neck until he squealed.

"I can only hope that the king's son is as well-loved as mine is," I said without thinking.

"Amen," William said. He was not a religious man, then or ever, but I saw that he did not mock me.

Jean Pierre said nothing but stood on my other side, listening in silence as our son called another man by the name of father.

Late that night, Jean Pierre and I were alone in my room. He did not move to touch me, and I knew that seeing our son with William had hurt him. I went to him and kissed him, my shift trailing like a cloud of white around me. The linen had been well bleached and the delicate embroidery at the hem, neck and cuffs was Marie Helene's work. I had long since given up the running of my household to her and to Maisie.

I found that I was more suited to sitting in a garden, thinking of God and my failings, than I was to anything else. I had been raised to sacrifice my life for the good of France, and that sacrifice had already been made. I would have been better suited to live out the years of my life in a convent, free from the temptation to sin, but as I looked at Jean Pierre in the firelight, I did not regret our time together. I knew that I would love him all my life, even when choosing a wife took him far from me.

I stood beside our bed, thinking these things, my hand in his soft hair, when a scratching at the door beyond the antechamber made me pause.

The wash water had come hours before and the fire had been stoked in the brazier, so I did not know who waited for me in the hallway.

Jean Pierre started at the sound but relaxed under my hand.

"I will go see who it is," I said. "Perhaps it is the maid coming to put out the fire."

For it was a warm night, even for late August. We would be on the road early the next morning. My brother wanted his son christened quickly, in case he might sicken and die, as so many children did. But I knew in my heart that this son would live for the good of France.

Jean Pierre looked up at me, his face half hidden in shadow by the light of the fire. We both knew that it was not the maid waiting behind the door.

I stepped into the antechamber, the tiny room that held nothing but trunks and an old chair. The room was never used, except as a small passage between my rooms and the hallway beyond. I did not draw the door closed behind me as I stepped into the anteroom, and I knew that Jean Pierre listened for every sound.

I opened the door to my husband.

"Is he asleep?" William asked me, closing the door behind him.

"No."

The anteroom was small, and we stood close, for I did not want to take him back into the bedroom with me. My husband had grown taller now that he had reached his twenty-second year. Not for the first time I felt caught between him and my lover, as grain is caught between the millstones.

My husband smelled of the wine he had drunk at dinner and of the night air. I could tell he had been out walking the ramparts, the place he went when he needed to be alone to think his thoughts in peace.

He kept his voice low when he spoke, and I felt the pain I always did when he was alone with me. I reminded myself not to be a fool, that I had a man who loved me just beyond the next door, that my husband loved me as well as he could, and that I must be content with that.

But as I met his eyes by candlelight, my breath came short as it had soon after I met him, when we stood for the first time beside our marriage bed. The blue of his eyes touched me as no one's ever had. I knew this was probably because, as with so many things in life, I could not have him.

"I fear to see your brother," he said.

I looked into his face, knowing there was no comfort to offer the pain of lost love. I too had borne it, and nothing came to cure it, not even time. "I am sorry, husband. I am sure it pains him as well."

"I doubt that, wife. I doubt if he even remembers my name."

He smiled at me, his quirky smile that seemed to take in the world with a wink, as if the world was not a serious place, the dark place of duty and loss that I had always known it to be. William's smile seemed to mock his own pain even as he stood there. I knew him well enough by then to see beyond it to the living pain beneath. I did not speak of what I saw but pretended along with him that his smile spoke all he had to say.

I took his hand in mine. It was strange to feel his naked skin next to mine, for we rarely touched without gloves between us. His calluses warmed me where my hand rested in his palm. I did not think of myself as small, except when he stood by me.

"Well, I am for bed, wife. I came only to tell you that we leave at first light."

I knew this already, for Jean Pierre had told me. I looked into my husband's eyes, but I could no longer see past the gleam of laughter that he often imposed between us. The window to his soul was shut, the shutters drawn tight, as against a heavy wind. I had no way of knowing if he had gotten the comfort he sought when he came to me.

"Good night then, husband."

He said nothing, but kissed me, his lips warm and dry on mine. His kiss was featherlight, as it often was in my dreams, too fleeting to be substantial.

He left me, and I closed the door behind him. I stood for a moment with the candle in my hand. I turned to go back to my lover and blew the candle out.

We entered Paris to a fanfare of trumpets. Phillipe had stationed musicians along the top of the walls so as we passed through the gates of the city, we were greeted with music. I waved from my barge and William stood behind me, also waving to the people. They threw flowers, some of which landed at my feet, others which fell into the river and floated in our wake, bits of color on the dark brown water.

Men-at-arms stood at the water gate of the palace, their lances lowered in salute. My brother waited for us on the steps, and the people cheered to see him walk into the sunshine.

The sun shone bright against his dark head and as I watched, my husband knelt. William's fair head bent in supplication, and Phillipe leaned down to help him to his feet, a show of favor rarely accorded anyone.

As I watched my brother and my husband meet for the first time since our wedding, I felt no pain. I could see clearly that they loved each other truly, even now, after so much time had passed. I thanked the Holy Mother that my husband found love in my brother's eyes, even though he could not keep him.

I felt the touch of Her Hand on me, as I had not in many months, and the warm breeze from the river felt like Her blessing. I bent my head in acceptance, in time to see Jean Pierre step beside me. In front of all the world, he reached out and took my hand. I looked up and saw the sunlight shining on his fair hair, his blue eyes resting on me, nothing but love in his gaze. He kissed me, and the people cheered. I think from that distance they believed he was my husband.

Standing there by the river Seine as it wound

its way to the sea, I felt as if my life was complete. My daughter stood behind us, held in check by Marie Helene. The wet nurse carried Jean, keeping him from running wild as he was wont to do, now that he was big enough. My husband stood before me, content only to look on my brother. And Jean Pierre stood beside me.

I took in the whole of my life in that instant. I looked down the corridor of time and saw the years following one upon another, my husband content with his life, my children growing in good health, and my love beside me.

It seems to me now that such seeming certainty comes only before the greatest loss. But that day, I was free of pain, standing in the sunlight with the man I loved, the cheers of the people behind us.

Phillipe's son was a beautiful baby despite the enmity between his mother and father. I saw no evidence of their well-known rivalry as I watched the king and queen from where I stood in the crowded church. They behaved as polite strangers. Many wondered when they had found the inclination to make the heir to the throne, for they had no interest in speaking or even looking at each other.

I knew better than anyone how politic royal marriages were. Richard and I would have been lucky. Very few were blessed as we might have been. I turned my thoughts from Richard and took my lover's hand.

With the christening over, a royal banquet

was held in the king's great hall. Hundreds of people filled the place, but we were honored to sit above them at my brother's high table.

Phillipe caught my eye and smiled down the table at me. I was seated above the salt, but barely. My husband sat across from me, as if Phillipe were forgotten, engrossed in conversation with an old lord from Lorraine.

Phillipe met my eyes and quirked a brow, allowing a little of his good humor to show. I saw that the birth of his son had lifted a great burden from him. I remembered the bells that had pealed when Phillipe had been born. Every Sunday for six months they had rung across the land in celebration that the royal house of France was safe for one more generation.

My brother was not as religious as that, or not as superstitious, as he himself would have said. Still the country rejoiced, and I knew that for the first time Phillipe would turn his mind to something other than war. He would build for his son's future.

He had already begun a new palace on the right bank of the river, so secure was he in his rule. It would have high walls around it, but his Louvre would not have the river to shield it as his current palace did, tucked safe away on the *Ile de la Cite*. Paris was changing even as I watched, and I knew that I would not come back often, if ever. Now that the succession was secure, I thought to retire to the country to enjoy my children, and the love God had seen fit to grant me, in all its flawed forms.

Phillipe saw something of this in my face, I

think, for his eyes softened as he looked at me. He spoke to a footman, and as I watched, he had a choice bit cut from the boar in front of him. The footman brought the meat to my chair and with a bow so low that it might have been offered to a queen, he laid it on my trencher.

I felt tears rise in my eyes at the tender gesture. My brother and I had never been close, and he had never been one to show tenderness publicly, as it was often taken as a sign of weakness.

I watched as the rest of the table saw the favor that he granted me and whispered about it behind their hands. A few raised their glasses to me, and I nodded to each, still steeped in the manners I had been raised with. I seemed to feel my father's presence, as if he stood behind me looking down the table at his son.

Jean Pierre's breath was warm on my cheek as he spoke. "Love, there is news from Germany. I have just heard that King Richard was released this spring."

I swallowed the tender venison I had been chewing and took a sip of my wine, reveling in the sweet flavor of the Anjou vintage. My brother's steward had remembered my favorite and had it ready in a chilled flagon beside my chair.

As I met my lover's eyes, no sign of my old love and pain showed in my face. I was careful, for he knew me well. Jean Pierre searched my face for some hint of the past, but I kept it from him, hidden away in my heart. My love for Richard was a matter between me and God.

When I spoke, my voice was even, warm with concern and good wishes, but nothing more. "That is welcome news indeed. Though I doubt my brother thinks so."

Jean Pierre smiled, glancing down the table to where my brother sat enthroned. "I think nothing can mar this day for him. And this is old news. We are buried in the country, or we would have heard it sooner."

"Happily buried." I offered my lips for him to kiss. And for the second time before my brother's court, I felt Jean Pierre's lips on mine, warm as a welcoming sun, and sweet as the wine I drank.

Though it was sin, I thanked God for him. Jean Pierre's love blessed me all my life, and I was most aware of this blessing as I sat beside him at my brother's table.

The rest of the court saw the favor I granted him, though no one cheered as the people by the river had done. They looked away, and laughed quietly among themselves, certain that our love was a passing thing, like any other affair at court, burning bright but brief. I looked into Jean Pierre's blue eyes, and my brother's court faded. Let them laugh.

It was then that the bard stood to tell tales and to sing songs of heroes. I waited to hear a newly composed song about the grace of our house and the strength of my brother now mirrored and perfected in his son. Jean Pierre thought the same, for he settled back with me, his hand over mine.

But when the minstrel strummed his lute, we heard a different tune.

It began prettily enough, a light air praising love and beauty. The words moved from generalities about the bliss of love onto specifics. At first, I doubted my hearing, that such a song would be sung in my presence. But as I looked around the hall, I saw that this bit of music was one everyone else had heard before, for it had been sung many times in my brother's hall. Only my husband, my lover and I were the first to hear it.

The minstrel sang of my beauty, hidden away in a nunnery until brought to light by old King Henry. He went on to sing of how the light of my eyes and the sweetness of my face had driven the king into a frenzy of courtly love that was only assuaged when he possessed me.

Though overly romantic, the song was mostly true. The song went on to mention how my beauty had overcome Prince Richard, bringing even that warrior to his knees. The song told flowery tales of wars that had been fought in my honor, between Richard and his father, tactfully leaving out my brother's involvement. The bard knew well which side his bread was buttered on.

There was even a verse about the lovers I had taken since my marriage, sighting both of my lovers by name, and naming many more men of whom I had never heard. When I looked across the table at my husband, William only seemed amused, not surprised.

I caught the gleam of laughter in his eye,

and I started laughing too, a deep well of amusement rising from my belly into my throat. I tried to swallow it, out of deference to the bard, but he saw my smile and bowed to me, his story finished.

Phillipe was not offended, for plainly he had heard the song many times. He raised his golden cup to the singer, drained it, then sent it over to the bard as a gift.

The singer bowed, overcome at such generosity, but the christening had put Phillipe in a giving mood.

The bard lifted his lute to sing again, but Jean Pierre rose beside me and crossed the hall so quickly that I could not clutch his arm in an effort to stop him. His glove was on the ground before the bard could draw his next breath, and all the court stared at my lover as at a mummery.

Only then did I feel myself color in shame. For songs are harmless and pass as quickly as the air that gives them breath, but a challenge before all the court was a story that would live on for years.

I looked to William, and though he tried to move through the crowd to stop what was happening, men-at-arms prevented him, blocking his path with their pikes, sending him back to the high table. He returned to stand at my side, his hand under my arm in case I should faint. I was not faint of heart, but angry as I have seldom been, then or ever.

Dark rage rose like bile to choke me. If anyone had been in doubt of the song's truth, my lover standing to defend my long-lost honor would illuminate them.

The minstrel looked stunned, for clearly no one had challenged him before. It simply was not done. Singers and bards were not warriors. The thought was absurd, as well as an unimaginable *faux pas*. The court sat in total silence, so that when my brother stood, the scraping of his chair on the stone floor sounded in the hall like a trumpet.

Phillipe did not cross to the combatants, for another man rose and came to stand before the bard. The man was large with dark hair and hard eyes. His arms when crossed in front of him resembled great hams, their strength evident in their massive muscles. I looked to William but saw that he could do nothing now that my brother the king had stood to listen to the challenge.

"I challenge this bard to trial by combat, in defense of the honor of my lady."

The huge man who dwarfed Jean Pierre was more politic. He looked across the hall and bowed to my brother. "I would accept this challenge, for the sake of Raymond, master of song, with my king's permission."

I turned to Phillipe then, hoping that he would turn this nonsense away with a laugh. But I saw from the tight lines around his mouth that he was angry that the peace of his hall had been violated on what had been such an auspicious day. His son was forgotten in this melee, and Phillipe's wrath would only be appeased by letting the trial go on, as Jean Pierre had asked.

"I grant my permission. The trial will happen on the morrow. For this is a holy day of peace, sanctified by the christening of my son."

I saw in Jean Pierre's face that he had truly forgotten the reason we were in Paris. His color darkened then, but his anger did not leave him, and he stood his ground. The matter touched his honor. At times like these, among the people of my brother's court, he sorely felt the loss of it. He had turned away from his honor for my sake.

He, too, bowed to the king, though he was late in remembering to do so. Phillipe returned to his throne, and Jean Pierre returned to my side. My husband met his eyes and some understanding seemed to pass between them that only men might grasp, for William squeezed my hand and left me.

I sank down, for my legs had given out. Jean Pierre sat once again beside me, but I did not look at him until we rose to go. I stayed in that hall and drank at every toast and forced smiles when other songs were sung.

I knew that I could not leave as I might have at home, for whatever my brother was to me, he was also king. It was not for me to leave the hall until the last toast had been drunk and the last song sung. Jean Pierre sat beside me, but we did not speak again until we were alone in the rooms that my brother's steward had set aside for us.

Phillipe's face did not soften, and I stayed in my chair, my shame my only companion.

19

THE TILTING YARD

The meal in the great hall did finally end, though I spent the rest of the time holding myself upright, trying to keep my face scrupulously pleasant, almost blank, as I had been trained as a child. My husband and I walked out together, and he escorted me as far of the door of my room without a word in case anyone should overhear.

At the door, he bowed to me formally, as if we had just met. His mouth quirked, and I could see that he had to work not to smile. As he bent low over my hand, he spoke low enough so that only I could hear. "Don't fret, Alais. All this will be over and forgotten this time tomorrow."

I knew that what he said was not true. People would be telling tales not only of my disgrace, but of my lover's futile defense of my lost honor long after.

William met my eyes as he stood, his hand still warm over mine. I kissed him, still without speaking, and stepped into my rooms. There were no servants waiting for me when I closed the door behind me.

Jean Pierre was there before me, sitting alone by the light of one candle. "Love, forgive me."

I faced him without speaking. It was he who came to me and drew me into his arms. I did not resist but stood like a wooden doll in his embrace, my joints stiff as if they needed oiling.

Jean Pierre's heart was loud in my ear. I leaned my head against him, and he relaxed, thinking that I had forgiven him. This was not true. I had not. I did not forgive him for many years to come and only then after long prayer.

That night I stood still, mired deep in the anger that consumed me. That anger made me forget how short life is, and how fleeting all love and pleasure in this world. As I stood there, I was consumed by the sins of pride and wrath, forgetting once again that all things fade, especially the beautiful ones.

I did not have the wisdom think of this then, however. All I thought of was the mocking faces of my brother's courtiers and their knowing laughter. The gleam in their hawk-like eyes as they watched my lover stand to defend honor that had long since drained away, humiliating me before all who wished me ill. All of Europe would hear the story within a few weeks, how the notorious princess of France had taken yet another lover, but that this one pitied her.

"Love, I know that you did not want me to speak, but I could not stand idly by and watch them mock you."

I drew back from him and paced our little

room. The tapestries were old but well mended, the brazier where the fire burned was polished, the plate in the room well burnished bronze. It was a room that showed my status at my brother's court. I was a woman who had failed in her duty, a woman destined for a royal marriage who had botched it, her life ultimately thrown away on a marriage that was beneath her.

I faced Jean Pierre with all the rage that I had ever felt at men and their foolishness, and all that their foolishness had cost me. He faced this anger without flinching.

"You shamed me," I said.

Jean Pierre blinked. Of all the words he thought to hear from my lips, these were the last three he would have considered. "Love, I defended you."

"You confirmed the rumors. All the world knows of my infidelity. The court thinks me a loose woman. This is nothing to us. But for you to stand up before the whole court, to risk your life defending an honor I have not had since I was fourteen, shamed me."

He flinched to hear me speak of the early loss of my virtue. I saw on his face that he had always thought my relationship with Henry to be blameless, that all the stories of our love had seemed to him nothing but air. I was almost sorry I had spoken of it when I saw the pain in his face, but I went on, carried along by the tide of my anger, a tide that would wash away all in its wake.

"And now you must fight a man we do not know, a man who all at court fear, so my brother's people were quick to tell me. You risk your life for nothing, for less than nothing, and whether you fall, or he falls, my honor is still gone."

He took me in his arms again, and this time he held me fast. He would not let me go. "You are afraid I will be hurt," he said, as if that explained away my anger. The pain was gone from his eyes.

I saw again how much he loved me. Even the accumulated rage of all my life could not turn him from me. "You could be killed. And for nothing. For less than nothing."

He pressed his lips to mine to silence me, and the old heat between us warmed me. But my anger was still sharp, like a knife in my ribs, cutting off my breath.

When he pulled away, I was calmer. The tide of fury had receded, leaving a dull ache that did not leave me for days. "Withdraw from this combat," I said. "It is not worth your life."

"It is my honor at stake now, Alais. I cannot turn from a challenge that I myself have issued." He said this kindly, lovingly, as if explaining to a child why it could not breathe in the night air, for fear of sickness.

I saw that he would not be turned from his course, and for the first time, I felt fear. "But you will die."

He smiled a little, then hid his smile as if I were a fool and he did not want to taunt me with my foolishness. "Love, I have fought men all my life. I will not die tomorrow."

I tried to pull away from him, but could not, for he still would not let me go. "If you fight that man, it is from pride only. It has nothing to do with me."

"I fight for love of you, Alais. No man may malign you in my hearing and live."

I heard this last statement, and it was like the sound of a coin falling down an empty well. His words echoed in my ears, so that I thought I was fainting, as if I had lost the strength I had been born with, the strength that had helped me to endure loss all my life. I knew as I looked at him that if he fought on the morrow, I would never see him again.

Our first and last fight ended just that way, with him carrying me to bed. I refused him my body that night, thinking as all women who do this, that it would have some effect, that he would change his mind and cling to me, as if my will had the power to change his fate. I knew in the morning that I should have let him touch me, that I should not have slept at all but seized a night of love with him, for I would never have another.

I woke alone, as I had not in over two years. The tapestry by the window flapped once from a burst of wind that came up from the river. Jean Pierre had left the window open, for love of me. He knew that I loved the smell of the morning, and the sound of birdsong in my ears when I woke.

. . .

When I saw him again, he was already in the tilting yard, dressed in armor, a stranger covered in steel and mail. I almost wept to see him, but my fear of the night had fled. I thought those fears an illusion, come from my own sin and sorrow. I thought myself impious, that I would try to predict anyone's fate.

As I stood under my brother's canopy, the gold *fleur de lys* on its field of blue shading me from the light of the sun, I felt Fate's heavy hand. I would have screamed and run to Jean Pierre, I would have begged for him to leave that place and to come away with me then and there, in front of all those courtiers, with no thought for my brother the king or for my husband. But I had been raised a princess of France. I stood my ground in silence, certainty of pain hidden behind the blank mask I had worn since childhood. It was he who came to me.

"Lady, I would take your favor into battle." He spoke low so that no one else could hear. He had drawn his mount close to the stand, so that I did not have to lean down far to hear him.

I did not answer him, but tied Eleanor's kerchief to his breastplate, the kerchief he had long since given back to me. It fluttered jauntily in the breeze, as if he rode to a festival, and not to his death.

"I love you." I did not lower my voice or try to conceal what I said.

A woman in the stand next to me laughed but had the decency to hide her smile beneath her hand. I kissed him before he lowered his halberd.

He smiled at me, his love for me in his eyes, the certainty of his good fortune clear in his face. Had he not traveled all the way to Jerusalem? Had he not fought the infidel and lived? Surely, he would live always, in the flower of his youth, with his love beside him.

And that is how he lives for me, when I see him in my dreams. He still comes to me, even now that I am an old woman, with almost all my loved ones dead. He sits at my bedside and holds my hand, looking on my face as if I have not aged a day, as if I am still the woman he met planting lavender, sunshine on her hair.

Jean Pierre saw the sorrow in my face. He rose in his saddle in full armor, his borrowed horse motionless beneath him. He kissed me, his lips warm and soft on mine. For a moment, I thought that he might turn from his folly and leave that place and his honor behind him.

But a cheer rose from the crowd when he touched me. This was better drama than they ever got to see at court. They were all so jaded that they could not have simulated love even if their lives depended on it.

As they watched us, my brother's courtiers drank in the sight of our love and pain as a drunkard takes in wine. I could feel their hunger as they looked at us, their thousand eyes pulling on me, though I would not raise my head. I kept my eyes down, on his face, so that I saw only him.

Jean Pierre sat his horse, his pride rolling off him as waves onto an empty shore. He smiled at me, and I saw that he would not turn from his path, as if there were no other. In that moment, my sorrow at the loss of him and my pain to come faded, and I could see him just as he was, the man who loved me, the sunlight on his hair, and the pride of his house clear from the way he held himself erect on his borrowed horse, as if he were a prince himself. Though I knew his folly, I was proud of him.

He raised his hand to me and lowered his halberd for his ride around the ring. The crowd called to him, casting down flowers, all thought of his foolish behavior in the great hall forgotten. For my brother's court would forgive anything, even bad manners, if a good show was offered in its place.

Jean Pierre offered them a show in earnest as he rode around the tiltyard, waving to the crowd who cheered him. Even my brother's eyes had softened, and he relaxed against his heavy gilt chair, ready to take in the sport of the day for what it was, a bit of foolishness that would not last, all thought of challenge and dishonor forgotten.

I alone did not forget as I watched my lover ride toward his death. I looked on as one who has already died, who has seen all the sins of the world, and sits idle as they pass, for she can do nothing. All possibility of action fled, and the river of death dividing her from all she once could touch.

It was from this distant place that I watched Jean Pierre ride against the hulking Roland, a man whose horse alone was large enough to defeat an army. I watched as they made several courteous passes, no one scoring a point on the other, both enjoying the day and the warmth of the crowd.

So, it came suddenly, as a surprise to all but me when Roland's great lance broke off on his third pass, lodging in Jean Pierre's side. My lover fell from his borrowed horse, and the crowd was silent. The only sound was of a lone woman, screaming.

I heard this screaming, and I wondered, who would have the effrontery to behave so in my brother's presence? For he was king and such unseemly behavior was better left to peasants, and those who tend the fields.

It was then I felt my husband's hands on me, grasping my arms, drawing me from the sight of Jean Pierre bleeding in the dust. I found myself standing in the shade then, in the dark gloom of the castle keep. William and I stood by the door that led back out into the sunshine. I could see the dust of the tiltyard from where we stood. I could hear the people milling about, shouted orders, and whinnying horses, the sounds of the chaos that come after a battle.

The woman had stopped screaming, and still I felt as if I stood on the other side of the river Styx, as pagans had believed in the old myths, as if I was removed from the living and would always be so, that there was nothing that would ever take me back.

Then they brought him in, and my pain came back. My foreknowledge drained away, and there was only myself, and my bleeding lover, the long wooden stake still stuck through his heart.

I knelt beside him, pulling in vain at the wooden lance. I could feel then that it would not be moved, that to do so would kill him quickly, and that he did not yet want to die. His blood was all over his gauntlets and his cuirass. When he touched me, his gloves were caked in dust and blood. I could not remove them to touch his hands. I saw that my attempt pained him, so I stopped and instead bent over him, for he was trying to speak.

"Be happy, love."

I thought perhaps his mind was wandering, that he had already begun to cross beyond the veil. I said a quick Act of Contrition for him, for there was no priest nearby to give him the last rites, only courtiers with a sporting interest in my lover's death.

Jean Pierre heard me and squeezed my hand when the Act of Contrition was done. He smiled at me, blood caked in his teeth and in his hair, for they had drawn his halberd off when they had brought him to me.

I kissed him, blood and all. I could taste his blood on my lips when I pulled away. I held his hand, still warm in his leather glove. Only his blue eyes were the same as he looked up at me. I was reminded of the time we had stood together by the river near my husband's house, before he left for the Holy Land, the day when we had both thought that we would never see each other again.

Here we were again, beside another river. But this time, I clutched him as if the strength of my love might hold him, as if my tears might bring God to pity.

But I knew that God had nothing to do with the love I bore this man. This affair was adultery and an affront to God. I prayed as I sat there, my silk gown trailing in the dust, covered in my lover's blood, that God might spare him the burden of that sin, and place it all on me.

I was thinking these things, turning to the Holy Mother, that in Her infinite compassion, She might move God to hear my prayer. It was then that Jean Pierre's breath began to rattle, and I left off praying and clutched his hand.

Jean Pierre still smiled at me, though it was clear he was in pain and had made ready to cross into the next world. His hand felt strong on mine, as if he had never been wounded. "I love you. Do not grieve. Whatever we have between us, let it go, and be happy."

He was slow to speak. I could see that the light in his eyes was beginning to fade, that soon he would be on the other shore, and far from me. I wept and kissed him, telling him of my own love, of how I would always carry him with me, of how I would always pray for him.

I am not sure if he heard me. He drew his last breath and was gone. I sat in silence beside him a long while, my tears stopped. I held his hand in both of mine, able to draw his glove off now that it could no longer hurt him. His hand was blunt and wide, but tapered along the fingers, with square-cut nails and calluses along his palms.

I held his hand until the priest came to shrive him, but it was too late. His soul had flown already.

MY HUSBAND'S HOUSE

LITTLE ELSE WAS REQUIRED OF ME. I SAT WITH
his body and would not leave it, even as the
women washed him and bound him for burial. I
watched as they did all this, not raising a finger
myself, for it was not my place. Whatever else I
was, and whatever I had become, I was a
princess of France.

William kept others away, so that I sat alone
as the servants attended him, until even they
withdrew. I thought to kneel and pray for his
soul, but I knew the state of my own, and how
deep in sin I was steeped. No prayers of mine
could help him.

So, I simply sat beside him, my hand
touching his where it lay beneath the wrappings.
I sat with him until his sister came to take him
home and bury him, a married woman from the
country, a woman who had never seen me
before that day and looked as if she would be
pleased never to see me again.

She had no interest in greeting her brother's

lover, the notorious woman who had kept him from marrying, the princess who had simply added Jean Pierre to the long chain of immorality that she had forged since she was young, the harlot who had caused his death. This woman looked at me with scorn that she did little to conceal.

I rose when she came in and stepped aside to give her pride of place. She took in her brother's body wrapped in its linen shroud and knelt immediately on the *prie dieu* beside him. She did not hesitate to kneel in prayer, for she had no sin on her conscience as I did.

As she knelt in the silence of that room, her rosary between her hands, I knew that she blamed me for his death. As I took in my lover's face for the last time, I knew that she was right. I would have to live with that knowledge every day for the rest of my life and beyond, into Paradise.

I would not have been able to walk out of that room, I might be standing there still, if my husband had not come to take my hand and lead me like a child to bed. I did not sleep, and neither did he.

William sat beside me all that night, next to the cold bed where before I had refused to let my lover touch me. My husband's face seemed aged for the first time in sorrow, as he kept the rush light always lit, simply holding my hand.

We left the next day. I stayed in Paris just long enough to watch the cart bearing Jean Pierre's body sway out of the cobbled courtyard of the palace and down the road toward Valois. His sister was his last living relative and would bear his body to the family crypt. He was the last male of their line, and now the name of that house would fall to another.

I did not weep as I watched her drive away, nor did she. This Mathilde was of an old family, which had gone down into the dust. I saw in her that she had been raised in the precepts of my childhood, devotion to duty, silence in misery, eyes always front, face blank, all emotion and its expression subdued beneath the iron mask of obedience. I watched her ride away and saw as she passed that her face was inscrutable, and it seemed impious for me to weep when she did not.

So, I too stood in silence, until even the dust of the road had settled in the wake of their passing. I stayed there, the sun high and hot on my head, until William took my arm and drew me toward the barge. We would leave with the tide.

My brother did not come to see us off, but his current favorite came and presented me with Jean Pierre's sword. It was wrapped in layers of silk and lay in its scabbard, its handle worn from use. I saw that it had a jeweled hilt, and I wondered that Jean Pierre who loved all things simple and elegant, would have carried a jeweled sword. I realized later that he must have won it in the Levant. I, being his lover, had never seen it. There had never been any talk of war between us.

I stared at this sword, uncertain what I was to do with it. I did not want to touch it, for to do so would make it real. As it was, it seemed to have nothing to do with the Jean Pierre that I had known.

It was William who took it from the young man's hands. He smiled at the boy and thanked him, wrapping my lover's sword once more in the cloth. I think he made a pretty speech, for the boy seemed satisfied when he bowed and went back to the quayside.

I had turned my thoughts from the sword altogether, watching the brown water of the river sliding by, focusing on it instead of my pain. William leaned down and spoke low in my ear. "I will keep it for his son."

These words blindsided me, breaking through my numbness as if I had been stabbed through the heart. For a moment I could not catch my breath. The world darkened at the edges of my vision.

Marie Helene saw me falter, and she came to my side, helping me to sit, hiding me from prying eyes behind a hanging tapestry. My vision returned quickly, and my daughter's nurse brought me a glass of watered wine.

I sipped it slowly, grateful for their care, when I was the least deserving person on the face of God's earth. Marie Helene said nothing but left my son and daughter in the care of their nurses. The children stayed at the back of the barge, watching the rowers as they worked, casting long glances at me. They had never before seen me weep, and now they waited to see if I might do so again.

Marie Helene sat beside me all the way downriver, until we came in sight of Rouen. Something about the cathedral comforted me, as I watched its old towers rise against the sky in the distance. I had heard that they thought to build one in the new Gothic style, as the cathedral my father had begun to honor Our Lady in Paris. I would always love the old cathedral at Rouen, though. It was the last place I saw Richard, and Eleanor.

The memory of that old pain comforted me, for it was dull with time. I had gone beyond it and found joy. As I sat in that barge, Marie Helene beside me, I did not know if I would ever feel joy again, but I seemed to see the promise of a future in the heights of the old cathedral. It was a promise I would have to take on faith, after much prayer. I had a great many things to beg forgiveness for.

As we approached the city, the river drawing us ever closer to the distant sea, my children began to venture forward. They came first to sit near William, to listen to his stories of valiant knights who fought wars and slew dragons. I, of course, could not listen to this, so I did not hear when the stories ended. I felt it only when my little girl came to sit beside me, Marie Helene giving her place. Marie took my hand in both of her little ones and leaned against me, as if she might give me her strength.

Jean came then, and I almost could not look at him, so much of his father did I see in him, so much that it almost overwhelmed me. His eyes were the blue of some distant ocean, clear and far seeing, as his father's had been. Without displacing my daughter, I took my son into my arms, letting him sit on my lap, while Marie leaned into my side. I no longer had to look into Jean's eyes but could gaze down on the soft curls of his blond hair, where his father and I had blended together as nowhere else on earth. My children and I sat that way until we docked at the Abbey of St. Guillaume, the haven my husband's family had built, where the most pious of them were buried.

I sat with my children that night as they fell asleep. I had never done so before, and I could see from their faces that they did not know what to make of it. I think at first Marie believed that she might be dying too, but Marie Helene whispered only that I needed to be close to them that night. My daughter's face cleared of fear and filled with compassion. Her sympathy was almost my undoing, but I did not weep when she took my hand and told me very solemnly that I must not be sad, for I would see Uncle Jean again in Paradise.

I kissed her and thanked her and helped her climb into the bed that she and Marie Helene shared, a giant, gaping bed that was far too big for either of them.

I sat with Marie until she slept, taking Marie Helene's hand over my daughter's sleeping figure as I stood to go. I kissed Jean where he lay in his trundle, his nurse keeping watch beside him. She sat up all night in her great wooden chair, guarding him as if he were a prince in a German folk tale, a prince that someone might steal in the night, so valuable was he. I kissed him, and I kissed her, for guarding him so well when I could not.

When I left my children, I thought to go to the chapel to pray, but the old abbot knew me well and judged me harshly as he should. I could not make my confession to him. So, I returned to the abbot's rooms, the ones he had vacated for my husband.

William was waiting there, his face drawn as he gazed into the fire. We had not spoken much since Jean Pierre had died. As I stood in the doorway, I wondered at how little there was to say.

He did not speak but came to me where I stood under the lintel, neither in the room nor in the hall. He drew me inside and shut the door behind me to keep out the draft and the prying eyes of the abbey servants that were everywhere. He did not speak even then but drew me close to the brazier. He set me down by the fire, bringing a great wool blanket from the bed, for he knew that I would never sleep there again.

He sat beside me, his chair drawn up close, and he held my hand as I had held Marie's. We did not speak all that night.

I sat, gazing into the fire, wishing for the impossible, for one more day to show Jean Pierre my love for him, for one more hour to sit by the fire with him, to hear him speak, to hold his hand, as William was holding mine. I could not pray, for I had not yet confessed, so I sat in silence without even the comfort of God.

But William was there, standing between me and the dark. I did not sleep that night, and neither did he. He stayed awake with me and kept watch until dawn crept in at the windows, turning the darkness of the night to a cold, unrelieved gray.

My life was gray for many days, though I spent a great deal of time with my children, smiling for them to keep them from worrying, though Marie worried anyway. She was five years old by then, and a little lady as I had never been. She took pleasure at stabbing at her embroidery frame, patiently stitching, even though most of her stitches had to be drawn out just as patiently, so that she could begin again, always in the hope that she would make something recognizable with all of her labors.

We had been home some weeks when the flowers from Eleanor arrived. I was sitting in the kitchen garden with my children. Marie was embroidering under the watchful eye of Marie Helene, and William sat nearby, keeping Jean out of the herbs.

I sat on a bench, my face to the sun. The kitchen garden was the only walled garden on the grounds, and it was the only place I felt safe since Jean Pierre's death. I knew that my fear was based on nothing, and I knew also that it would pass with time, as all things do, even grief.

Spring had come again, and the scent of the warm summer to come rose from the river and drifted over my husband's lands like a blessing. It had been an easy winter, in spite of my personal pain. The harvest had been good, and no one had died on my husband's lands all that cold season.

Jean ran between the neat rows of plants, always careful not to step on them. He was afraid to upset me, as both my children were now. They had watched me all winter with wide eyes, waiting to see if I might cry. I never wept in front of them, and I often smiled, but they knew me better than they had any right to.

So, we were sitting as a family in the sun when Maisie brought the great basket out into the kitchen garden, a huge smile on her face. My first thought was that my roses down by the river had been raided, then I saw the brilliant colors, the deep red that I could not coax into growing in my own garden. I stood and crossed to Maisie before she could come any further, and I reached into her basket. It was filled with roses that had no thorns.

I took one and lifted it to my cheek, the softness and the scent of it taking me back to the moment Richard had first given one to me, so many years ago, when I was still young enough to think that God would give me a man to love, and let me keep him.

Tears came into my eyes, and I blinked them back so that the children would not see. Marie Helene knew what those flowers meant to me, and she called to the children and led them out of the garden by a side gate, telling them that it was time to leave work behind and to walk by the river. They both loved the river, so they left us without a backward glance, without even a kiss goodbye.

William took the basket from Maisie and bade the servants that followed her to leave the rose bush they brought by the garden gate, a bush still in bloom, its roots carefully wrapped for the journey.

There was a letter penned carefully in Latin on vellum, only one of the many languages that Eleanor wrote and spoke. It was the only language we both could read. William did not have my education, for he had clerks for whatever writing he needed done. But Eleanor had seen to it that all her daughters could read, including me. I opened the letter myself, breaking the seal that bore her crest, and read her letter out loud.

"My rose without a thorn. For speaking for him when no one else would. Aelinor."

She had signed her name in the *langue d'oc*, the language she had spoken as a girl, the language in which Richard wrote his love songs. I knew that she referred to Richard and his imprisonment, without actually naming him, for my brother's spies would have read her letter, and any blatant reference to Richard would not have been allowed to pass.

I sat once more on my bench beneath the pear tree. Its flowers had just reached their peak and had begun to fall.

William set the basket of roses at my feet and

came to sit beside me. "Now you can plant your rose bush and have those roses in your rooms until autumn comes."

"Yes," I said. "If they live."

We did not speak of Eleanor's letter again, the only thanks I ever received for trying to set Richard free. William took my hand in his, knowing as I did not how much those flowers would come to mean to me, how much they already meant, though I could barely feel it, so burdened was I with grief.

But the loss of Eleanor was an even older one, and those flowers assuaged that grief from that day to this. William was right, for like so much in my new life, the roses did flourish. They still grow down by the river, where their children have also taken root, their seeds caught on the wind and scattered, so that now they grow wild, even on the other shore.

21

MY SECOND JEAN

My grief withdrew from me a little every day, so that over time I came to know myself without it. I was a different woman now, for I had loved Jean Pierre as a woman, and not as a girl. All who read this who are past the age of thirty will know the difference of which I speak.

My children still came to me every day, as if without their vigilance I might fall into a decline. I was made of sterner stuff, but they did not know that. I came to love them more and more as each day passed, and no longer saw the shadow of my loss in my son.

Rose sat with me now, my lost daughter. I felt as if her soul came to me when I knelt in prayer in the evenings, after the rest of the family had gone to bed. I had long since been shriven of my sin, and now I prayed daily for the litany of my dead, and Rose prayed with me. She came to me now as the age she would have been if she had lived. She stood beside me as I prayed before

God, offering the names of my lost loves, her name always first.

It was a comfort to me, though for all I know it may have been a trick of the fading light, a deception of the softness of the candlelight in my husband's chapel, some form of illusion that I still do not understand. But it felt as if she were with me, as if she knew my soul with all its failings and forgave me, as even the Holy Mother could not, for Rose loved me as no one else did, living or dead.

These prayers brought me comfort, as did her presence, real or imagined. During that time, it was the love of my lost daughter that kept me certain of the unwavering mercy of God, as my own strength could not.

My son Jean was three by this time and was growing into a man of action like his father. William loved to see his fierce pride and encouraged him in it, as long as it did not infringe on the courtesy William diligently taught Jean to use when speaking to the rest of the family. William cultivated strength in my son, but he also cultivated honor, so that by the time Jean could reach the back of my chair, William was already showing him how to help me out of it.

Jean wanted a horse of his own so that he might go hunting, but even William stopped short of buying him a pony, deeming him too small. Instead, William would take him up before him on his own stallion, so that the little boy could see the hunt from his perch there, never knowing that the whole party slowed their pace whenever he was with them.

The end came on a day late in summer when autumn was beginning to threaten the green of the trees but did not yet hold sway. Maisie came to me in the kitchen garden, crying.

I could not get a word of sense from her, so I followed her instead. She led me into the bailey, Marie Helene and Marie trailing in my wake.

When I saw what waited for us there, I turned quickly and drew Marie hard against me so that her face was shielded from the sight. I could not do the same for Marie Helene, and she wailed, a horrible keening cry that had come from my own throat only once. I did not cry out myself but thought of Marie and of how to shield her, as no one had ever been able to shield me.

I called to Maisie, my voice low and commanding, so that she obeyed without thinking. Marie was already weeping, so I kissed her and looked into her eyes, leaning down so that she could not look away.

"Listen to me, Marie," I said. "All will be well. Go with Maisie now, and I will come to you soon."

She looked to me for guidance, for it was clear that Marie Helene could give none. She was as frightened by the sight of Marie Helene weeping and keening as much as anything else she had seen. I think she was glad to go when Maisie took her hand and led her away.

With my living child gone, I turned then to the dead.

Jean had fallen from my husband's tall horse onto the sharp stone floor of the bailey and lay with his back broken and his head cracked, his fair hair matted with so much blood that the golden strands now were red. Marie Helene had torn her gown in her grief, and clutched my son, weeping as if he were her own. I saw in her face the loss of her other children and remembered the loss of Rose, a distant pain, dimmed by time and prayer. I could not feel my new loss yet, which was a mercy from God, for there was much to be done.

I felt my father's strength in me as I took Marie Helene's hands in mine. I thought at first that she would not release him, but at my touch, she let me take him and arrange his body on the stones of the courtyard, so that it no longer looked as if he had fallen, but only that he was in sleep. Except for the blood in his hair. For that, there was no remedy.

She clutched me then, but she was no longer screaming, only weeping. I called a servant woman over who stood nearby weeping herself, for all had loved my son. He was bright like the noon sky, and just as warm. His sweetness kept his fire from burning those it touched. The serving woman took Marie Helene away, still weeping and calling on God, who did not answer.

The courtyard was quiet when she left, so quiet that I could even hear the sound of birdsong.

The groom stood nearby, still holding my husband's horse. He waited to see what my orders would be, for there was no one else there to give them.

"Take him to the stable and rub him down," I said, for I did not know if they had just come from a ride or had been about to go on one.

Grateful for something useful to do, the groom turned from me, leaving me alone with my son.

I knelt at his side, lifting his tiny hand in mine. I saw then that he had begun to grow calluses along his palm and thumb, for he had been working night and day with the wooden sword my husband had given him, waiting always for the day when he would be able to lift a real one.

I held his hand in mine while someone sensible fetched the priest. I watched over my son as he was given the last rights, though his soul had surely flown already. I made certain that all this was done there under the light of the setting sun, for the shadows had begun to grow long, coming down from the walls around us.

I washed my son's hair there in the courtyard, my gown already ruined with blood where Marie Helene had touched me. I knew that I would never wear that dress again, so I knelt beside my son and washed his hair in the water that someone brought from the well.

At first, I almost sent it away, for the water was in a bucket and was cold enough to drink. I opened my mouth to order the water warmed and brought in a decent bowl, as befit his rank and temperament. But then I realized that he would not be able to feel it. That was when I knew that he was truly dead.

I bathed him carefully, until the water in the bucket turned red. His brow was clean then, for the cut had stopped bleeding. I wrapped his head in a clean cloth and tied it carefully.

The women came to raise his body up and take it inside. It was time to dress him in spices and to lay him in the chapel, that we might pray for his immortal soul.

As I knelt beside him, standing between him and those who would take him from me, I knew that his soul had already flown to Paradise, for he was perfect in the image of God, unsullied and sweet as only young children can be, before they are corrupted by the evil of this world. As I knelt there on the cold stone, I wondered if Henry had ever been so sweet, before he grew into his power and became a man.

They took Jean from me then, and I let them. The weeping priest had loved him too and was ready to serve his office once the women had served theirs. I let them take him, so that they might serve him as I had done, and find comfort in their service, as I had.

I knelt alone in the courtyard then, the sun going down. It seemed I could still hear my daughter weeping. I knew that I must change my gown and go to her. As I knelt, my knees aching as they never did when I was at prayer, I saw my husband, alone in the shadows of the coming night.

William stood in silence, the tears on his

cheeks long since dried. I knew then that he had been there all along, watching my son's death and all that came after. No doubt the boy had fallen, slipping from the saddle before William could climb up behind him and keep him safe. I had seen them mount just that way many times and, every time, the child had been strong enough to hold the reins. But now my son was dead, his soul flown, and my husband was left behind in darkness as we all were, except now he blamed himself.

William stared without seeing me, his eyes still fixed beyond me to where our son had fallen. Jean's blood was still on the stones of the courtyard. It had begun to dry, darkening to the color of old wine.

I stood, my back aching. I saw from my husband's face that he needed comforting even more than my daughter did. I did not realize how deeply he hated and accused himself until he saw me moving toward him and looked at me as if I were the angel of God, come to earth to judge him. The expression of terror on his face was one I hope to never see again. He fled from me as from hell's furies.

I stood still for a long moment, wondering if I should let him go, let him grieve in peace as a man might wish. But I could not get his look of horror out of my thoughts, and I followed him. He was well ahead of me by that time, running full out, a young man in his prime, but I knew where to seek him.

He was on the ramparts, looking out over the valley where his lands lay, a view that moved in a gentle slope all the way to the river and beyond. William stood gazing out to the west, where the sun was going down.

The men-at-arms who stood watch there looked frightened, and I could tell that they were grateful I had come. I saw then that William stood too close to the edge, that the old stonework threatened to collapse under him, chipped away by time and weather.

I stood very still, wondering if I should not call the men-at-arms to take him in hand, and to bring him to his rooms by force. But I thought of the time just after Jean Pierre's death, when he had not left my side even at night, keeping the lamp always lit beside him, sitting with his hand in mine so that I might sleep.

I thought of the loving care he had showered on me all our married life, of how he had loved me as no other ever had. For he had let me live my life as I saw fit, within the ties that bound me to duty and family. He had given me more freedom and dignity in my own choices than I had any right to ask. And that was when I knew that I would throw myself from the ramparts myself rather than see him unmanned before his retainers.

I stepped forward. William did not turn to look at me, but he did not step closer to the edge either. I saw then that he was crying for our lost son, as I could not.

I gestured, and the men stepped away to give us privacy so that he and I were alone, staring at the horizon. The sun had set already, leaving the sky bathed in purple and orange fire.

I felt the first touch of my grief then, like a lover's hand, like a child's hand that could not be shook off. I stood there, my son's little hand on mine, and felt the first wave of loss, and the first hint of all the pain that was to come. I touched his hand with mine where I felt him pressing me, his phantom touch much stronger than it would have been if he were still alive. As he pressed me, I knew that his soul had not flown to Heaven yet, that he waited here to see that I would do right by his father.

For William had always claimed him. All had known that the child was his favorite and could not have been more loved if he was his son and heir in truth as well as in name.

I took William's hand in mine gently, the way I still felt Jean's touch. William turned to me, his face bathed in tears of remorse and horror, a remorse that would kill him if I did not intervene and set it right.

"You will not do as you mean to do," I said.

"And who will stop me?" His face was transformed by grief, the bitterness in his eyes almost more than I could bear.

But I did bear it, for I had seen worse.

Perhaps he saw something of this strength in my face, the strength born of years of loss. He seemed to consider that there was hope beyond his present despair, though he did not yet believe in it. The future was a path he could not tread, not even in his thoughts. Even his next breath was painful, and he could not turn his mind to it.

"I will stop you," I said. "I will not have you

bring about the ruin of your family from the sin of despair." My talk of sin almost turned him from me, but I gripped his hand. "It is a mortal sin, husband, and I will not let you go."

He saw my love for him in my face. He did not pull away from me, though he was strong enough to cast himself over the edge, and me with him. I felt his strength under my hand as he fought against himself to stay with me. He had always hidden his strength from me before, but I felt it then, the strength of a young man in his prime. Though my husband had never been to war, he had trained for it all his life. I felt his strength under my hand, but I was not afraid. I knew that no matter how strong his body was, his soul was stronger.

He fought himself there under my hand, until he turned from the edge of the precipice, from the illusion of freedom from pain, to me.

I took him in my arms as if he were my own son and held him against my breast. He lay there, his passion spent, his breath coming fast, as after the act of love. It was the first time I had held a man since Jean Pierre had died. It came to me that my husband was a man in truth, and not a boy, as I had always tried to see him.

I pushed this thought from me as soon as it came and turned my mind instead to my husband's pain, and to the loss of our child. I had set aside that death as I fought for my husband's life on that precipice. The pain of Jean's death came back to me then, like a shock of cold seawater closing over my head.

I remembered the sight of the blood matting

his fair hair, and the knowledge came to me that I must soon go to him, to sit with him until we could put him in the ground. I must go to my living daughter and offer her love and comfort, and Marie Helene.

William still clung to me, and I spoke low in his ear, his fair hair soft against my lips. "Husband. We must go to him."

"I cannot," he said. "I have killed him."

"It was an accident."

"He was in my care, and I failed him. I let him go."

"He is in God's hands now, William. It was God's will. He was too good for this world."

I said these things, wondering if they might be true. I wondered why God might have taken such a beautiful child, my husband's heir, and the light of his life. I had borne such a loss at the age of fifteen, so I knew how hard it was for William to draw his next breath. But I had had my faith to sustain me, the pure faith of my childhood that, at that age, had not yet been diluted by constant sin. I was older now, and though my faith was still strong, I did not feel the hand of the Holy Mother resting on me as I once had done.

Still, Her strength was with me, for I brought my grieving husband down from the ramparts. I thought that he would even come into the chapel with me to hold vigil by our son, but when we reached the door, he stopped, the scent of candle wax close about us.

"I cannot see him," he said.

"I must go in. Then I must go to Marie.

Promise me that you will go to your rooms and wait for me there."

He looked at me, his blue eyes red with weeping. He stared at me as if seeing me from a great distance, a distance so removed that he could not quite hear my voice.

I thought that I would have to go with him, when he finally spoke. "I promise you."

I knew that, like Richard, he did not give his word without keeping it. I pressed my lips to his, to give him my strength. I saw his man come behind him then and take his arm. I let his squire lead him away, to put him to bed as I could not. For I had others to comfort if I could.

I watched him walk away, and I wondered if the strength I had seen in him from the first day of our marriage until this dark day would hold. He was the strongest man I had ever known, but he also felt things deeply. I wondered if his feelings would be the undoing of his strength.

I felt my own pain then, come to take my hand, and I turned toward the chapel. My husband's strength was just one more thing I would pray for.

When I stepped into the chapel, I found my daughter and Marie Helene there before me. Maisie sat with Marie, their stools drawn close together. They sat surrounded by candles, both with rosaries in their hands.

I went to my daughter first and kissed her, telling her that I had been with her father, that he was sad but that he was well. It was the first and last time I ever lied to her. She met my eyes and drank in the lie like wine. Her need pierced my heart, but I kissed her and left her with Maisie, for Marie Helene needed me more.

Already she was clothed from head to toe in black, her beautiful blonde hair hidden beneath a black wimple and veil. Her rosary of pearls and diamonds was the only thing that was not black, except for her pale face and her wide blue eyes. She knelt by the body, ignoring the *prie dieu*, choosing instead to kneel on the hard, stone floor. I brought her a cushion, which she ignored. I knelt down beside her.

My son lay still, already wrapped for burial, only his face visible above the clean white linen. His face was drawn and gray, and in it I could see no sign of the little boy he had been. All laughter and light were gone, leaving only pale wax in its place.

I turned from Marie Helene and thought of my son's soul, lifting prayers to the Holy Mother in Heaven that She might see him safely into Paradise. I felt Her hand on me then, as I had not in many years, since long before I took Jean Pierre as my lover, and longer.

I breathed deeply in the warmth of Her presence, and I felt that She would guard him. I felt then the presence of Rose beside me and saw Rose taking her little brother up into her arms, her hair long now, unbound around her waist, and curly like mine, curly like his. In my thoughts, I saw Jean laugh and kiss her, until my eyes blurred with tears and I could see nothing more. But I had heard the Holy Mother speak. She held both of my children in Her hands.

I thanked God, repeating my rosary in

gratitude even as I wept. Tears fell from my eyes for the first time since I had lost him, for the first time since I had washed him, then sent him away to be tended by others.

I knelt by his body and knew that he was no longer there, that his soul was safe in Paradise. Marie Helene had no such comfort. Her lost children did not come to touch her hand, but haunted her, as I have never been haunted by any of my dead. Marie Helene did not believe the truth the Church tells, that life does not end with the last breath, but goes on, into a certain Paradise.

I had learned this simple truth at my father's knee, before I was strong enough to stand. This truth had sustained me through much loss, but it was not something I could hand to another.

So instead, I took her hand where it lay in her lap, her rosary forgotten. She clung to me, the diamonds of her rosary biting into my fingers. I took it from her as gently as I could, then brought her into my arms, and let her cry.

I thought to shield Marie from Marie Helene's grief, but grief comes to us all, even as children, and we must learn to bear it. Finally, Maisie rose and led Marie away, but not before my daughter came to kiss my cheek.

"Your brother is with God," I told her. "Fear nothing. For you will see him again."

Marie Helene wept harder at these words, but my daughter met my eyes unblinking, her tears already shed. I watched the workings of her mind as she took this in, as she examined my face for the flaws of a lie and came away only with truth.

She kissed me on the cheek then for the first time, as she always kissed me from that day on, gently, softly, with the certainty born from her own mind. She took the truth from me, as I had once taken it from my father. So, I had one more reason to thank God as I knelt on that cold, stone chapel floor beside my young son's body, watching my daughter walk away.

THE VALLEY OF THE SHADOW

We buried Jean the next day under the floor of that chapel, the vault under the altar opened to let him in. I heard the words of the priest, and I cast the first clot of dirt into the grave. I stayed long after the rest of the household went away: Marie Helene to her bed, Marie to the rose garden by the river with Maisie beside her.

I sat until the black dirt was smoothed over my son and the stones set over him. I watched as the servant women cleaned those stones until all hint of dirt had fled. I sat alone above his body, as if his life had never been.

I knelt then and thanked God for his life, and I thanked God for my own mind, that I would remember him. I ordered a sculpture made, not as he would have looked as a young man, but as he had been, a smiling child, his curls falling past his shoulders, his hand on his pet dog.

That sculpture lies over his grave still, and

the few that come to worship in that chapel marvel at it, for his image looks at them as if he knows a secret, that life is eternal, and that all is as the Church has said.

The day they buried my son, William did not come. He did not leave his rooms in all that terrible time, not to come to a meal, not to take his daughter's hand, not to see the sun as it set over the river. So, after two weeks of this, of the family waiting, after even Marie Helene had tried to smile again for Marie's sake, I decided that this would do no longer, and I went to him.

It was almost time for the meal in the great hall, a meal that had gone on without him, with me presiding over it in his stead. His men-at-arms had begun to look askance at me, and to wonder if their lord had lost his wits. They all knew my son to be another's, and they could not understand why my husband would take to his bed over someone else's child.

I heard the rumors, for Maisie brought them to me, grim and gray-faced, not wanting to hurt me but not wanting the tales to go unpunished. She was a simple woman, and sweet, not knowing that punishment for cruelty was impossible. Cruelty was more often rewarded, and even my husband's house could not keep such evil out.

So, I went to my husband's rooms on the second week after my son's death. Below, I could hear my husband's men carousing and drinking, for without my husband's presence to subdue them, they all but ran wild when I was not in the great hall. The serving girls were still safe, but only barely.

When I came to my husband's door, I found it locked against me. Thanks to Maisie, I had the key. I found the lock well-oiled, and it turned without a creak. I pushed the heavy wooden door open to find the room shrouded in darkness, as if it were a tomb itself. Only one lamp was lit, and that one smoked, so that I had to stand very still in the doorway and let my eyes adjust to the darkness before I stepped inside.

At first, I thought William was not there at all, that he had left rooms for parts unknown, locking the door behind him. But after I stood still for a long while, I saw a huddled figure bent low in a sway-backed chair. I would have thought that shadow a pile of cloth, the light was so dim, but then it moved, and I saw that the shadow was my husband.

I stepped into the room and closed the door behind me. William did not look toward me but bent double, his face in his hands.

I went to him but knew enough not to touch him. I drew a chair up to sit beside him. When he still did not look at me, I knelt at his feet. William himself had told me never to kneel to anyone but God. I broke our agreement and knelt before him.

His hair hung in lank strands, unwashed and uncombed. I saw beneath his tunic that he wore a hair shirt, and that his fair skin was scarred with red welts. I recoiled at this, for I knew that my husband did not believe in the solace of repentance. I knew that he wore the hair shirt, not as it was intended, as an impermanent penance to ask the forgiveness of God, but as a gesture of futility, of punishment merely – punishment for a sin that would not be redeemed.

He ignored my presence and did not turn to me, but I spoke to him as if he had. "You must come down to the great hall and sit among your men," I said. "I have kept order for as long as I am able. They grow more fractious every day."

He did not look at me, but something in his face changed. I could see that he was listening.

"Your daughter misses you," I said. "And I have need of you."

To mention Marie was perhaps a mistake, for his face clouded even darker, until I thought he might be lost to me completely in self-loathing, loss and guilt. But at the mention of my need, I watched him fight his pain to stay with me. William turned his head then, and met my eyes, though I saw what it cost him.

His blue eyes were shot through with red. He had slept little since Jean's death. Old bread turning with mold sat on his table with no bite taken from it, and the flagon of watered wine was full.

I touched his arm, and he flinched under my hand as if I had struck him. I wondered if he thought that I came to chastise him, if he thought I blamed him for the loss of my son.

It was God's will, the accident that had let Jean slip from William's grasp and fall to his death on the stones of the bailey. I knew better than to walk the road of blame, for I was far from blameless.

William must have seen something of this in my face, for he reached out to me of his own accord and touched me. He was careful, as if the skin of my face might burn his fingertips, but my cheek did not raise welts on his hand. After a long moment, I turned my head and laid my lips along his palm.

I did not kiss him, but the warmth of my lips seemed to soothe him. We sat like that for a long while, until I thought that we might stay that way an hour. But then the door opened behind me, and I turned from him to see who among his household had the courage to face him.

My little girl stood in that doorway, the only one of my three children still living. I rose to my feet to meet her. She did not look at me, but only at him.

I saw for the first time that my daughter was brave. She had slipped her leash, as I once had done, long ago, and had come to find me, even in the darkness of her father's room. I saw in her face that she was afraid, but her face held a hint of my father's stubbornness, the stubborn certainty that whatever fear took hold of us, duty always came first.

Marie was only six years old by this time, and small for her age, but I saw my father in her as she stood in the threshold of that darkness, her little face set in the determination that she was not going to leave us to it.

She stepped through that door and came first to me and took my hand. I squeezed her hand in mine, but she did not stay by me. Marie stepped deeper into the darkness, taking in the sight of her father's ruined face, ravaged with pain and weeping.

William could not hide his pain from her, his bitterness and sorrow had left no defenses. He could only sit and be as she saw him, a man who had seen the worst and had not yet turned from it.

It was in that moment that he turned back toward the light. William looked at the little girl who had crossed the hall alone to find him, the girl who had abandoned her nurse and Marie Helene, those who raised her and cared for her and coddled her without ceasing. She came and found him in the depths of his despair, and when she saw the pain in his face, she did not turn from him.

Marie went to her father and put her arm around his shoulders. She wiggled closer, so that he picked her up and placed her on his lap, as he had done so often before, in happier times, when our house had known no sorrow or death.

William seemed to come alive at this small gesture. He seemed more himself again with his child on his knee. He sat up straighter, and held her close, his only desire to keep her comfortable and safe, as it had always been.

Marie did not wince at the sour smell of his clothes and hair but looked into his eyes for a long time without speaking. She drew him close and placed her other hand along his cheek, where his light blond beard had begun to grow, for he had not shaved in many days.

"Papa," she said very solemnly, as if telling him a secret. "You know that Jean is in Heaven."

I saw William blink, his face a studied blank. I knew that he did not believe in God or the hereafter. I knew that religion was a fiction that held no hope or light for him. But as he looked at his little girl, he could not turn from her as he turned from God. "I know, Marie."

His voice was hoarse from weeping and from disuse. I poured him some water and wine from the jug on his table, and he drank it to please me, never taking his eyes from Marie's face.

"Then, Papa, you know you must not be sad. You will see him again." Marie spoke these words with the simple faith that only a child can know, a faith that even I barely remembered.

I knelt by her side, placing my palm on her knee. She did not look at me but drew her father closer with one arm around his shoulders as she took my hand. As we sat together, my daughter prayed that God would bless us and keep us safe from sorrow.

William's blue eyes were full of tears. I had to blink to see this through the tears in my own. He leaned down and kissed her, then me, his lips warm and dry, as if he had a fever. He stood then, still holding her, and I was glad to see that his strength had not deserted him, though he had not eaten in days.

Marie Helene was at the door then, and came through it, her face full of fear to find the only child left to her care braving the lion's den. I saw the relief on her face that not only was Marie well, but that we were all together, with William once more standing among the living.

Marie kissed her father once more before he set her on her feet. When she stood on her own, Marie Helene's hand in hers, she met her father's eyes unblinking. "Come down to supper, Papa." With that she left, leading Marie Helene out.

I watched her go, marveling that I had known my daughter all her life, but only that day had I seen the depths within her.

Marie Helene left the door open behind her, and I called for hot water and a razor before closing it again. I opened the shutters along one wall so that the late afternoon light could filter in from beyond the river.

William stood where my daughter had left him, watching me as I moved about his room. I picked up the old bread, and he took it from me just as quickly. "You do not serve here, lady. Leave it, and I will have it taken away."

I let him take it from me. I stood facing him, at a loss for words since my daughter had spoken.

William and I stared at each other and time seemed to stand still with us. I opened my mouth to speak, but he raised his hand and covered my lips. His fingertips were warm and dry. "Thank you for coming after me."

I took his hand in mine and kissed his palm without thinking, then froze, for such gestures of affection were not allowed between us. He stood staring at me. I did not move or blink until finally he stepped away from me.

When I spoke, my voice was rough, and I had to clear my throat to be understood. "Is there anyone I can send? Some friend that might come to you?"

I did not want to name a lover, for fear of offending him. In the last year, he had been so discreet as to appear a monk, and I would cut out my own tongue rather than to pry into his affairs.

William understood me, as he always did, with no explanation between us. "No, Alais. There is no one to send for."

I thought he would say more, but the door opened then, and Maisie came in clucking, with servants in her wake bringing hot bath water. His squire came in, with a grateful bow to me for braving the darkness behind the locked door. He went straight to the clothes press to find a decent gown and hose for my husband to wear to dinner. By now all the house had heard that the lord would sit in his own hall that night. Already the noise from the hall was calmer beyond the open bedroom door.

I turned to leave then, my work done, but William caught my hand and held me there, the blue of his eyes asking a question I could not understand. "Will you walk down into the hall with me, my lady?"

The formality of his address belied the desperation I felt in his touch. I smiled at him before I pulled my hand away. "It will be my pleasure, husband."

I left him then, for Maisie had begun to watch us from beneath her lashes, and I had never been one to make idle talk before servants, no matter how beloved. I moved to the door, but when I turned to draw it closed behind me, I saw him still standing where I had left him, his servants hovering around him, grateful that he was on his feet, if not fully himself again. He met my eyes across that room, and I could see him clearly, for Maisie had ordered trimmed lamps brought and the old smoking lamp taken away.

William met my eyes across his rooms, and it seemed to me that I was seeing him for the first time, that we were in a new land, with new thoughts between us. I did not ask myself what those thoughts were but went to change my gown into something suitable to wear when I sat in the high table at my husband's side.

23

FREEDOM

WILLIAM HAD LOST WEIGHT DURING HIS TIME OF grief. I felt his arm beneath his silk gown and found only muscle and sinew. Any cushion of fat was gone. He was still quite young, so he did not yet look gaunt. Two weeks without food could not do that to him, only his cheeks were hollowed out, showing the fine bones of his face.

I met him on the staircase that led down to the main hall. He met my eyes and smiled wryly, a little of his old light returned to his eyes. I knew that we would speak later, for the hall was full and waiting for our entrance. All his men had heard that he would dine that night at the high table, where all his vassals could see him.

They were all waiting for him as we came in, my hand placed formally on his arm. We walked in together as if stepping into my brother's court in Paris and some of his men rose to their feet in homage when he entered.

When William took his accustomed place at the high table, I stood beside him, in case he needed to lean on me. He had drunk a posset, but he was still weak, for he had still not taken any solid food. I would not have known this, if I had not found him myself, bowed down under the weight of his grief and cares so that he could barely lift his head an hour before. Now he stood before his people as if he were a king himself, and they watched him, always ready to take in high drama, especially when it cost them nothing.

He sat first, saying nothing, and everyone followed suit. I sat beside him and saw to it that his wine was well watered, for I knew he would be lightheaded. Even as I watched him, he ate little, but made sure to take something from every course, for appearance's sake. The court watched him as they would an invalid, or one who had taken leave of his wits.

I realized that was what they had thought of him, mourning for a child who was not his own. At last, they turned away, satisfied that he was well, or at least well enough to remain their liege lord. I watched the court turn from him and back to their own affairs, the drama over, at least for that day. There were some who kept their eyes on him, even as the minstrels came out and the dancing began. I thought that he would stay seated by me, as befitted a man in mourning. But he rose to his feet with the first stately dance and offered his hand to me.

I took it, though I felt for one horrible moment as if we were dancing on my son's grave. I looked into his eyes and saw my pain mirrored there as I laid my hand over his.

As he led me into the dance, the others parted before us, giving us pride of place. I felt as if we danced alone on a stage as we moved slowly through the steps. Marie Helene saw us begin, the music rising, and she turned her face away. Marie was not in the hall, and I was grateful that she was not there to see it.

I glanced at the courtiers who watched us dance and saw that they admired my husband's strength. They all knew what the death of my son had cost him, and to see him stand and dance before all reminded them that he was a man to be reckoned with.

It also reminded me.

The dance ended, and my husband sat down. He did not fall into his chair, but seated me first, as courtesy dictated, as if I were his wife in truth and not only in name. He sat and watched the rest of the dancing until the minstrels began to tire, and the music began to wind down.

He stood then, and the rest of the company stood as well, and bowed to him as he left the chamber. Marie Helene alone did not, and I saw the pain in her face that we had danced, my son in the grave only two weeks.

I could feel her pain as a slap even across that wide space, but I knew my place. My husband was in worse pain than she was, and it was with him that I left the hall, his hand still under mine.

I took him to his rooms and left him with his squire, putting him into the young man's good care. As I watched them together, I wondered if they had ever been lovers, but as the boy began to help my husband with his gown, I did not see evidence of a lingering touch or awkward hesitations. All seemed businesslike and calm, as if the boy only wanted to offer my husband quiet in his time of grief.

The meal in the hall had cost William something. Though he had eaten a little, he was still gaunt and pale, his eyes shining large in his face.

I went to him without thinking as he stood in his leggings and shirt, and I kissed him. "I will come back and sit with you as soon as I have seen to Marie."

He seemed surprised, but he did not draw back from my lips when they touched his cheek. He said nothing, which I took for assent. His squire bowed to me and closed the door behind me as I left.

Marie Helene was sitting by Marie's bed, as if without her vigilance, some menace might carry her off in the night.

I kissed my daughter, and she stirred but did not wake. She seemed to feel something of my presence, though, for she smiled in her sleep and touched my hand.

Marie Helene sat beside her in the old nurse's straight-back chair. She would not meet my eyes.

"You blame me," I said. "You blame me for Jean's death."

"No," she answered immediately, but her eyes were still dark as they met mine.

"Then you blame me for dancing."

Her gaze did not waver from mine when she spoke. "Yes."

I drew another chair close to hers. Our voices were pitched low, so as not to wake Marie, or Jean's old nurse who slept in the corner. The poor woman could not stand to be alone, and Marie Helene had graciously taken her into my daughter's household. The woman's own children were years dead, and she had nowhere else to go.

I sat close to Marie Helene but did not touch her. I could feel her anger and her pain from where I sat, as one might feel heat from a fire. She had turned her face away from me to watch over my child.

"I am sorry to pain you," I said. "We danced not for joy, but from necessity."

Marie Helene still did not meet my eyes, but I knew that she was listening.

"If William had not shown his men that he is still alive, and still strong, there would have been hell to pay, if not now, then soon. You were with me in Henry's court. You know what men are."

When I spoke of our shared past, so long ago, something seemed to call to her even in her grief. She met my eyes. Something of our old bond spoke to her, and the anger in her face faded to sorrow.

I took her hand then and held it. She did not speak, but I felt her relax in her chair. I knew that soon she would be weeping, for the loss of Jean had touched her deeply, reminding her of her own lost children. I loved my children, but Marie Helene had been their true mother. She had had the raising of them. Jean had been the smallest and had still needed her as Marie no longer did.

I knew that Marie Helene could feel my children slipping away from her, one into death and the other into adulthood. In a few years Marie would be old enough to marry, though I would see to it that she would not leave us until she was strong enough to stand for herself, if she left at all. For she was William's heir, now that Jean was dead. Perhaps a match could be made with a landless man who might come and live with us.

I turned my thoughts from these practicalities, for I still had to change my gown and go to my husband, to sit with him to stave off the darkness, as he had once sat with me. My own grief was standing by, waiting for a time when I might acknowledge it. I had seen my son buried and knew he was safe in the arms of the Holy Mother, as both of my lost children were. But this knowledge had begun to fade under the weight of my sorrow. I knew that my own grief would leave me in peace until my living loved ones were cared for, but my reprieve would not be long.

Marie Helene seemed to sense this pain in me. Her eyes had softened with the weight of our shared grief, and she leaned over and kissed me, as she had not done in many years, as she once would have done when I was young and alone in Henry's court, with only her to comfort me.

"I am sorry, Alais. I forget that your grief

must tear at you. I forget all in the face of my own pain."

I kissed her and set my cheek against hers, allowing myself to lean on someone for the first time since my son had died. "Thank you." I rose and left her, for I still had to take off my silk and don a gown of plain linen, so that I could sit with my husband and keep him from despair.

I turned at the door and looked back, only to see Marie Helene kneel at my daughter's bed as if it were a *prie dieu*, and my daughter the Holy Grail. I left her to her prayers, hoping that God and the Holy Mother might hear her, for there was no doubt in my mind that she prayed for all my children, both the living and the dead, that they might be kept safe and happy, whether here with us or with God beyond the shadowed valley we lived in.

I dressed in my own rooms quickly but with deliberate care. I knew that I would get no sleep that night, and I wanted to be comfortable. My long hair fell in curls around my shoulder. A few strands were shot with silver, but they blended well with the dark chestnut of my hair. So, I was dressed in a simple blue linen gown and shift tied with blue ribbons when I went to my husband's rooms. His servants had long since left, but the rush light was lit, and the door had been left ajar for me. I entered quietly, closing the door softly behind me.

William sat at his table, not slumped as I had

last found him, but leaning, his head thrown back, his face in shadow.

"Husband, I have come to sit with you, if you will have me."

"You are welcome, wife."

I could not see his face, but it seemed he watched me with careful scrutiny from where he sat, and it made me conscious of my body beneath the thin linen of my gown. I wondered at myself, that I could still feel this way in his presence, even after all these years, even when it was clear to me that he would never love me as I had once wanted him to, that we would never have the marriage I had once hoped to have.

I sighed and drew a chair up to his table, so that I might face him across its scarred surface. This was where he drew up plans for the outbuildings when they needed changing, and where he planned future hunts for the king to enjoy during visits that never came. Phillippe had never slept under my husband's roof since I had lived there. I wondered if William kept those plans, drawn on costly vellum, laid aside somewhere in a trunk, entertainments that he might draw out at a moment's notice if my brother were ever to come to him.

Once I was sitting, I could see my husband's face more clearly, and I knew that any hope he had of my brother coming back to him had long since fled. Something of the pain of Jean's death had burned away the last of his youth, so he sat beside me for the first time as a man in truth.

I mourned for the loss of the last of his innocence, but such loss was one we all must bear. I reached out and took my husband's hand where it lay on the table between us. I thought that it would lie limp in my own, but he grasped my hand tightly, as if I might otherwise turn away.

"Do you ever get over it?" he asked me.

As always, I knew what he meant without explanation. "No. I mourn her still."

He nodded, his hand still gripping mine. I thought that he would fall into silence then, and that we would sit and watch the fire in the brazier burn down. Though it was warm in his chambers for that late in the summer, he liked to keep a fire burning and the windows open. He, alone of all the people I knew, was not afraid of the supposed evils of the night air.

"And Richard," he said. "Do you still mourn him?"

I was surprised by this question, for the thought of Richard had been buried between us long ago. I searched my memory, almost afraid to open that long-closed chest with all my lost loved ones tucked away. I opened it carefully, afraid that, like Pandora's box, evils would rise to taunt me and destroy my peace.

But when I looked into that old, forgotten place in my heart where Richard lived, I found no pain. Only a little sorrow, like a faded rose that held no perfume. I met my husband's eyes unblinking. "No. I will always love him, but I do not mourn him anymore."

William nodded and sat still for a long time, his hand over mine, cradling it, as he had cradled it all those long nights when I was

mourning Jean Pierre in silence, unable even to
weep. He ran his fingertips lightly over the back
of my hand, until I became conscious of the
ridges of age that had begun to spring up there.
It was on my hands that my true age showed.

I moved to pull my hand away, to slip it onto
my lap so that I would not have to look at it, but
he would not let go. He met my eyes again, and
I found that I could not look away.

"And Jean Pierre?" he asked. "Do you still
mourn him?"

I blinked, for he had never uttered the name
of my lover to me since the day he died. I cast
my mind back to the horrible day by the tilting
yard, when Jean Pierre's life had bled out onto
the stone floor of my brother's keep. I thought
of his face as he smiled in death, of his sweet lips
whose last words had been of his love for me. I
thought of how fortune had given him to me,
how God had blessed me even in my sin.

I thought of all these things, and I found that
they no longer caused me pain. Perhaps it was
the death of Jean that had done it, but now it
was as if a great door had closed between me
and the next world, and Jean Pierre was locked
behind it.

The door had closed, and I was on this side
of it. He was lost to me, and there an end. I
could only pray for him, and that I might be
forgiven for the sin of loving him, that God
might let me see him again when I crossed into
Paradise.

I was silent a long time, thinking these
things, but William did not stir all that while. He

did not speak or pull away from me, but kept his eyes always on my face, watching me, waiting for my answer as if it held some secret for him, some secret that he must possess.

I wondered if his mind had become unsettled in his grief, that he could not leave off picking at old wounds. But as I looked at him in the dim light of that smoking lamp, I saw no evidence of madness in him. Even the horror of his grief had burned away. Jean's death had become the burden that William would bear in silence for the rest of his life.

For I had spoken truth: you never get over the death of a beloved child, be it one year or twenty since the child has gone from you. For him, it had only been two weeks since Jean was laid in the ground, but I saw already that his grief had taken on a weight and a solidity that it would keep. He shouldered the burden of it, as he shouldered everything else in his life, without flinching. He had long since learned, as I had done, to take what comes.

I thought of Jean Pierre and the loss of him. I made certain of my answer. When I spoke, my voice was even, as I had been trained to keep it when I was younger and sent away to live out my life in an enemy court – a smooth voice that conveys nothing but what the hearer wishes to learn.

"I love him," I said. "But I no longer mourn him. I bless his memory, but he is gone. I have come to accept that."

Something in my husband's face shifted when I spoke, like a current moving far down in the depths of the sea. Some strange heat seemed to cross behind his eyes, but I could not see it for what it was. I had no language for such a thing. There was no such thing as heat between us.

He knelt at my feet then, his hand still clutched over mine. His motion surprised me, and I made to push back my chair. He held me still, and I did not turn away. Something in his eyes stopped me even as it frightened me.

I wondered at first if this was a touch of madness inspired by grief, but I saw almost immediately that it was not. This was something new between us, something that was born even as he knelt before me, still clutching my hand.

"My lady," he said. "Alais."

I did not answer him but looked down into the blue of his eyes. His eyes were the color of the summer sky after a rain, pure and clear. It seemed for the first time that I could see beyond the closed doors of those eyes, that he had opened those doors to me, and let in the light.

"I love you," he said. "I thought that the time when we might have come together had passed away, cast off like refuse when I was too young and foolish to see what your love might mean. I thought to speak when Marie was born, but I did not, and when you turned to Jean Pierre of your own accord, I knew my time for speaking was lost. When he died, I thought to speak again, but your love for him was as strong as your grief, so I stayed silent, and taught myself to be content. But when Jean died …"

For the first time his voice faltered, and I could see the memory of Jean's death rise up in him again, the horror of the fall, the sudden slip of a leather glove, the desperate clutching to keep the child safe, the failure and the loss. I saw all this pass behind my husband's eyes, and I watched him battle it, as I watched him battle that same demon many times in the years to come. It was always hard, but he always won.

William came back to me when he had finished, his breath coming in great gasps, for he had fought against his horror and his grief as sinners fight for their souls at the gates of Hell. He looked to me and met my eyes, asking not for pity but for patience as he took his next breath. I had been raised to patience, so I sat silent, a hope I had never thought to cherish beginning to burn within my breast.

"When Jean died," he said, continuing as if the battle he had fought had never been. He asked for neither pity nor indulgence, only that I listen to his words. "When he died, I thought that I would die, too. And when I saw that I would not, I wondered why. The only reason left for my life is you."

He said this simply. He spoke with the quiet sincerity that was his very nature. "I have left your brother behind me. I mourned him, and now, it is over. I have accepted it. I hope that you will accept me."

I knew that my husband hungered after other men. I knew that he cared for them, as they loved and cared for him. Not for his position, but for the beauty of his soul, his kindness. It seemed that my husband was offering me his love. I supposed that some men loved both men and women, though I had never known my husband to take a woman as a lover. Perhaps I would be the first.

I did not know how to speak to him, so I leaned down and kissed him, hoping the touch of my lips would say more than my words could.

He kissed me back, and this time he kissed me as a lover might, fervently, desperately, as if I were water and he was drowning, as if he longed to die a long slow death in my arms.

His arms were around me then, and he lifted me from my chair as if I weighed nothing, as if I were a feather on the wind. He took me to his bed, the bed I had never slept in, and laid me down on it, still kissing me – first my eyelids, then my cheeks, my throat, and again my lips – all with the fervency that if he were to stop, he would most certainly die.

I wondered if this tide of emotion was but one more facet of his grief, if he would make love to me and hate me for it afterward. Even as I was thinking this, he drew back from me and looked into my eyes, as if he read my mind and heart and all their contents. I thought for one horrible moment that he might turn from me as he had turned from me on our wedding night and on every night since, but he did not. He looked into my eyes, and I saw that his eyes had tears in them.

"Alais, I swear to you by the God you worship, I will always love you, until the day I die. I took an oath before your brother and that oath I keep. But I add to it this oath: I am yours, now and always, as long as this body draws breath. And when I die, if there is any part of me that knows you, if there is any remnant of my soul on the wind as the Church teaches us, that part of me will still love you, until the winds stir it, and it vanishes into the vast nothingness of time. This I swear. May your God be my witness."

I wept then and clutched him, and he held me close until my sobs were spent. He kissed me gently and dried my eyes with his own tunic before he drew it off and cast it aside.

"I am yours," he said, "If you will have me."

I knew he was a young man, and I knew that men were not faithful. Henry and Richard had taught me that. But whatever this man would give me, I would take. I still could not answer him, for I could not find my voice. Instead I drew his shirt up over his head and cast it onto the rushes on the floor.

He reached down and unfastened the laces of my gown. He was clumsy and almost made a knot of them.

I caught his hand in mine. He looked at me, and I cleared my face of hope, so that he would know that he could believe me when I spoke. "William, you do not have to do this. I love you, and I will always love you, just as you love me. We can go on as we have been and be content."

"I do not want to go on as we have been. I am in love with you. You are the first woman I have taken, but you will be my last. This I swear before your God. May he bind me to it."

I thought this another dramatic oath born of grief and loss, but when he looked on me, I saw that he meant it. What surprised me more was the light of desire in his eyes. That light did not go out, even as he drew my gown off me, even as he touched me lightly, his hand riding smoothly over the linen of my shift.

We did not speak again, and I taught him the act of love as women do it, as Henry had once taught it to me. When he came to the finish of it, he looked at me with such wonder that I laughed in spite of myself.

"So, it is different," I said, trying to contain my laughter and failing.

His eyes lit with laughter, and with joy as he bent down to kiss me. "You are different." His lips silenced my laughter, their contours lingering over mine so sweetly that it might have been a dream that dawn would wake me from.

But when dawn came, we still had not slept, but lay together, a look of joy on his face that mirrored my own as if – in spite of our grief and our loss – we had been given a great gift. Our grief still waited for us. The enchantment we lay under would not last in the face of it, or so we thought that day. Still, we clutched each other as dawn lit the open windows with its first gray, pearly light, reveling in the love we felt and the aftermath of its expression.

As I looked at him, in the light of that dawn, I thought of all the loves of my life, those dead and those lost to me. I thought of Henry and of Richard, and I thought of Jean Pierre. I thought of those loves of my past, and then my eyes rested once more on William's face. In his eyes, I saw my future, the path of all my days to come.

.   .   .

Our love is with us still, in spite of our grief for Jean, in spite of all the years that have passed since that day.

He has taken other men to his bed, and now that I am older, we rarely share mine. But in all the years we have been together, our love has not faded. No other, man or woman, has dimmed my love for my husband, nor his for me. I have come to see it as a stream that will never run dry That is the enchantment in the end, one I hope I never to wake from: the love of my husband, running over my heart like a vast river in flood, buoying me even as it carries me to the great sea that lies beyond the shadows of this world.

24

THE ROSES OF SUMMER

I LEANED BACK INTO THE FITTED CHAIR THAT
William had ordered made for me, watching
Marie run down by the river, roses in her hair. It
was summer again, the first blush of summer
that came in from the sea, and my roses were in
bloom as they always were this time of year,
both in my garden and across the river, where
the seeds had long since blown and taken root
on their own.

Marie was older now, almost ten years old,
and I knew that we would have to think of a
marriage for her before much longer. I prayed to
the Holy Mother every day that we might make
her a good match to a man who would love her.
William promised me that he would look
carefully, and that I would have final approval
over the man he chose, no matter the
candidate's wealth or title.

It seemed that, despite my scandalous past,
there were many who wanted to be aligned with
our family. No doubt they wanted control

someday of Ponthieu for their son. Though a small county, it was close to Normandy, and important to the king. Perhaps they thought that such a marriage would bring them in closer contact with my brother, and to his son after him. We no longer maintained our ties with the court and had not been to Paris since our youngest daughter had been born.

Isabelle came to me then, led by Marie Helene who held her gently by the hand. She smiled at me, her three teeth gleaming in the front of her mouth, and I stood and scooped her up. I planted kisses along her cheeks until she squealed, and I set her down again. Marie Helene hugged me close, without formality, for it was three years now since she had remarried, and gone to live on her husband's land, on a demesne not five miles distant from us.

Marie saw her namesake in that moment and shrieked, all pretensions of being a lady forgotten. She ran to Marie Helene and cast her arms around her as if she was saving her from drowning. I felt a pang then, in spite of all our newfound closeness. For it was I, when she was small, who had turned from her.

Marie Helene whispered to her and kissed her, keeping her arms around her even as they sat on a blanket on the grass. Isabelle toddled to me then on her own and I lifted her up, grateful that God had given me a second chance with this, my youngest child. Isabelle knew who her mother was. I had made certain of it.

Her soft curly hair caressed my cheek as the wind blew it. I watched as Marie and Marie

Helene began a chain of daisies and of roses. We sat there in the sunshine until William came up with Marie Helene's husband Jean Michel, who bowed to me and kissed my hand, as if I were a princess in Paris and still beautiful. I laughed and shooed him away, and he went to sit by his wife.

Marie came to me then with her garland in her hands. I complimented her on her fine work and asked if it was for Marie Helene to wear against the soft golden strands of her hair.

"No, Maman," she said to me, for she had begun to adopt that name for me when Marie Helene went away. "I made this wreath for you."

I bent down so that she would not see the tears in my eyes, and she placed the crown on roses on my hair. I could have felt no more joy if I had been the Holy Mother Herself, crowned by Our Lord in Heaven on Her Celestial throne. I kissed Marie, and she went to sit beside Marie Helene again, taking Isabelle with her when she went.

I leaned against my husband where he stood beside me, though my chair easily would have supported my weight. The love in his eyes warmed me. I sighed, looking out over the river, for once blessedly content with where I was and what my life had brought me.

When it was time to return to the great hall for the evening meal, the sun began to slant over my husband's land from the west. We stood to walk the mile back to the house, and the servants cleared our chairs and blankets and picnic things, bringing them behind us as we walked.

Jean Michel carried Isabelle on his shoulders, a daisy chain threaded through her curls, and Marie walked close beside Marie Helene, whispering secrets. I walked with my husband, his hand in mine. We were silent, for no words could touch the contentment I felt. Or so I thought.

"There is word from the court, Alais."

I tried to read the look on William's face. As close as we had become, he could still hide his thoughts from me when he chose. "That does not bode well, husband. There is never good news from court."

"No," he agreed. "There is not." He handed me a letter then, and the servants passed us on their way back to the keep.

I opened the vellum, which was yellowed and old, much used and often scraped, so that the words it bore were hard to read.

It was Eleanor's script, drawn lightly and beautifully as always despite her age. Her letter sent word of Richard. He had taken an arrow at Chalus, fighting my brother's people. The wound had festered. He was dead.

I took this news in slowly, as if it were being told to another, and then I read the last lines of her letter above her elegant name.

"I have buried Richard in Fontevrault with his father, where I, too, will be laid to rest in my own time. His spleen I buried at Chalus, for it was his anger in the end that killed him. As for his heart, it lies buried beneath the stones of the new cathedral in Rouen, for reasons best left unsaid."

I felt tears rise in my eyes when I read this. For a moment, I stood again in that church by the riverside, in that old city that lay between Paris and my husband's lands. In that moment, I saw Richard's face as he had been that day, the last time I had ever seen him, tired and full of sorrow, loving me even then, but ready to go to the Levant, full of plans to free Jerusalem from the infidel. I thought of his face when I first met him, and of the way the sunlight from the leaded window outside his mother's solar had caught the deep red of his hair, setting it on fire.

I stood in silence a long time, until I heard the sound of Isabelle's high laughter, and the sweet tones of Marie's voice, asking me to come to her, calling me back to the living and to leave the dead behind.

I folded Eleanor's letter carefully and placed it beneath my shift, next to my heart. I took my husband's hand and led him toward our home, and our children, the light of the setting sun in my eyes.

William said nothing but stood by me as he always had. He said nothing even when he handed me a kerchief so that I might wipe away my tears before we went inside.

AFTERWORD

In honor of the tenth anniversary of the release of my first novel, *The Queen's Pawn*, I have chosen to publish this sequel as an alternate history. Though Princess Alais of France, first Countess of Berry and later Countess of the Vexin and Ponthieu, is an historical figure, like most women of the twelfth century, vast stretches of the details of her life are unknown. In history, as in this novel, Princess Alais was eventually sent from the protection of King Richard to her brother, Philippe-Auguste of France.

For the purposes of this novel, Alais was released to her brother's care after being held in England until the death of Henry II. In history, she was not released until Richard and Philippe Auguste both returned from the Levant and the war they waged as "brother kings" during the Third Crusade. History tells us that she was held not in England, but in Rouen.

The only other two facts that we know for certain about Alais, Princess of France, is that she married William, Count of Ponthieu, at her brother's bidding and that she bore at least one surviving child, Marie, who later inherited the County of Ponthieu, which went by the old ways and was not confined to the male line by Salic law. She may or may not have given birth to a son named Jean, but if she did, he died as many children did at that time, before he came of age.

By necessity, everything else in this book is a fantasy of mine. I have tried to give Alais, a woman I adore, a full and interesting life. Please forgive any inaccuracies and any oversights on my part. Alais has always held a place in my heart, and I hope you come to love her half as much as I do.

Dear reader,

We hope you enjoyed reading *Princess of France*. Please take a moment to leave a review, even if it's a short one. Your opinion is important to us.

Discover more books by Christy English at https://www.nextchapter.pub/authors/christy-english

Want to know when one of our books is free or discounted? Join the newsletter at http://eepurl.com/bqqB3H

Best regards,

Christy English and the Next Chapter Team

You might also like:
The Slow Rise of Clara Daniels by Christy
English

To read the first chapter for free, please head to:
https://www.nextchapter.pub/books/the-slow-
rise-of-clara-daniels

Made in the USA
Monee, IL
14 July 2020